YOU HAVE TO LET THEM BLEED

ANNIE NEUGEBAUER

You Have to Let Them Bleed

Page 279 constitutes an extension of this copyright page.

Print ISBN: 979-8-9881286-9-4

Cover & Interior Art by Roderick Brydon
Interior Design & Formatting by Todd Keisling | Dullington Design Co.

First Paperback Edition

Bad Hand Books
www.badhandbooks.com

ADVANCE PRAISE FOR

YOU HAVE TO LET THEM BLEED

"Truly scary, disturbing tales. Horror readers still unaware of Neugebauer's mastery are in for a revelation as story after story in *You Have to Let Them Bleed* leaves a deep impression. It's a collection I expect to revisit often." —Karl Richter, *Rue Morgue Magazine*

"I'm convinced Annie Neugebauer is an apothecary of dread, an archaic chemist capable of constructing disquieting tales that attack the very fabric of my being. The assortment of stories found within *You Have to Let Them Bleed* are agents of trepidation, fast-moving, panic-inducing narrative narcotics that only a master craftsman of horror could prescribe." —Clay McLeod Chapman, author of *Wake Up and Open Your Eyes*

"The voice of a poet, the heart of a killer, and the fury of a pugilist—this collection of stories and poems will work you over and leave you spent. Blending horror with magic, loss with hope, and fear with love, Annie Neugebauer is one of the most powerful authors writing today." —Richard Thomas, Bram Stoker, Shirley Jackson, and Thriller Award finalist

"The stories in this superb collection find the unnatural in nature, chaos in order, and the frightening in the commonplace. Annie Neugebauer is one of those rare authors who can summon terror from a kitchen drawer, a shift of colors, or a coin rolling across a countertop, and *You Have to Let Them Bleed* places her in the top ranks of horror writers working now." —Lisa Morton, six-time winner of the Bram Stoker Award®

"Annie Neugebauer stuns in this exquisite collection in which poetry and lyrical prose stand side by side. Dripped with decadent dread, *You Have to Let Them Bleed* showcases a stellar range of styles, from Gothic to psychological and beyond. This is one of the best collections I've read this year." —Cynthia Pelayo, Bram Stoker Award®-winning author of *Vanishing Daughters*

"From its opening notes, *You Have to Let Them Bleed* announces itself as a symphony of poetry and prose. A nightmarish treasury of shadowy gems, these tales will lurk in the back of the mind and haunt you in the cold hours. Neugebauer has woven a tapestry of darkness." —Angela "A.G." Slatter, award-winning author of *The Crimson Road*

"Annie Neugebauer's first collection *You Have to Let Them Bleed* is a great mix of the stories and poems she's acclaimed for, where something as simple as a kitchen drawer becomes ominous. Her deft prose and tone-perfect imagery make this a best collection of the year contender." —John F.D. Taff, Bram Stoker Award® and World Fantasy Award finalist

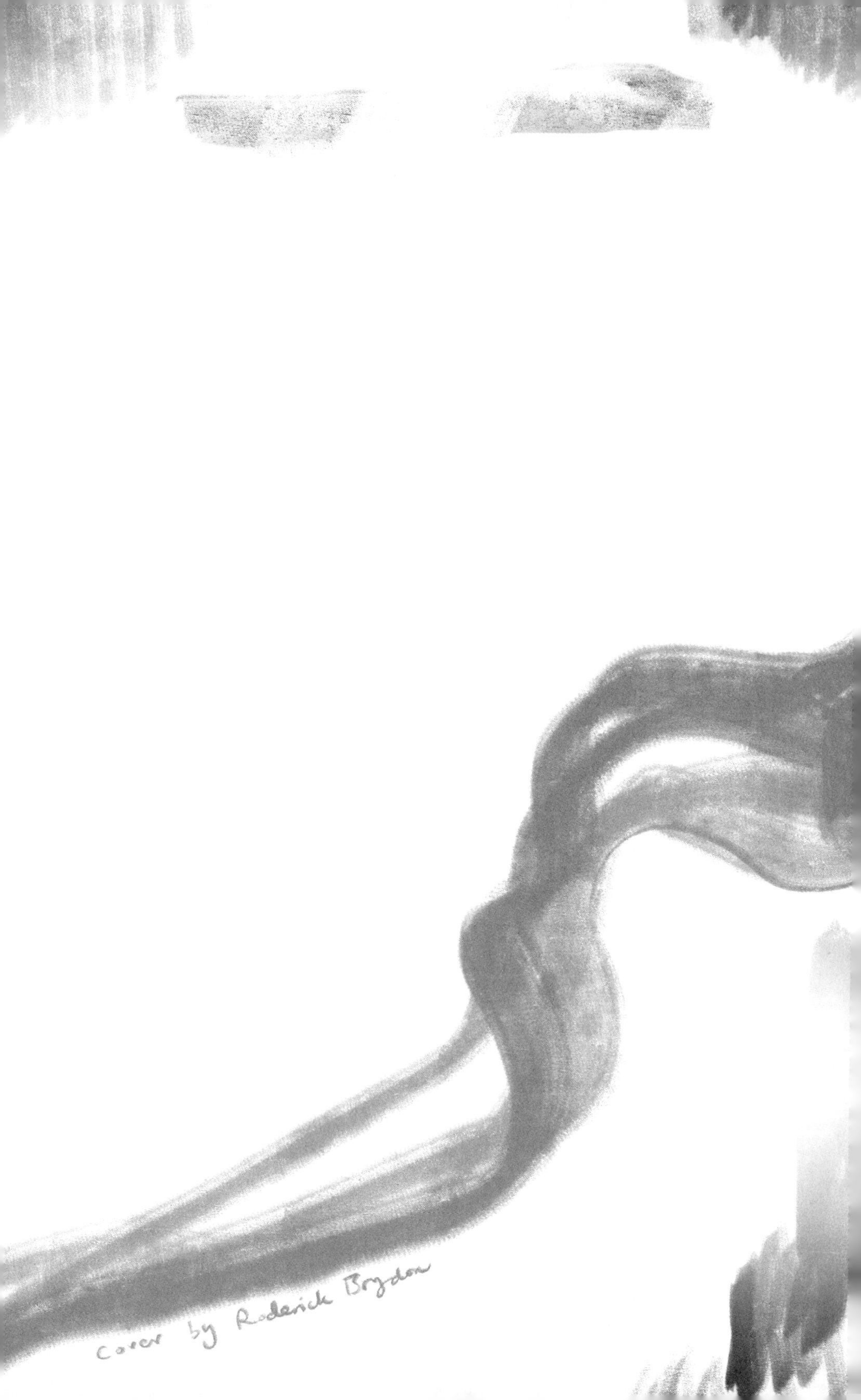
cover by Roderick Brydon

For my dad,
who saw my darkness
and loved me.

TABLE OF CONTENTS

FOREWORD

A "farm-crossed Romeo and Juliet" trade barbs while mixing a batch of picante sauce. It's a light-hearted scene I've witnessed in my son's home on many occasions. As with many of Annie Neugebauer's contemporary settings, it all feels warm and familiar…until the author slips in a slight wobble and then deftly stirs in another. Contentment under the fluorescent kitchen lighting still appears salvageable, but a pesky moth keeps bumping the plastic casing. Take one deeply charred heart, add an unrinsed herb, throw in a spicy jalapeno, then blend with a coffee spoon of Kafka. And there we have it—the recipe for a chilling, masterful Neugebauer story, *Cilantro.*

Horror twists its disturbing, aberrant, and fear-inducing path throughout this nineteen-story collection. Yet, horror is somewhat peripheral to the penetrating questions and themes explored by the author.

To what lengths will we go to be alive? How far will we go to protect what we hold dear? When the carefully negotiated life stories between couples begins to deconstruct, how do we handle the deep-seated feelings of betrayal and abandonment that follow? How well do we know the person on the other side of the bed? Our family? Our workmates? Ourselves?

Neugebauer creates stories like one of her exacting characters builds a momentous fire. She stacks twigs framing them in a triangle of meaty logs. Small sticks nimbly cross the twigs followed by longer sticks and topped finally by larger logs. When lit, the flame draws the eyes and you can't look away. Every twig, stick, and log are consumed, relished in the fire's growth and climactic burning, as every word, phrase, and sentence are essential to the escalation and denouement of these stories.

And what a variety of stories they are. Such that Neugebauer provides us with a poetic guide, The Shadowling Collector, who assembles these dark and beautiful stories into shadowboxes by color, eight short poems with distinct shades and hues that keep intermingling within a spectrum. Thus, the title of this collection, *You Have to Let Them Bleed.*

And what delightful, everyday items and activities the reader must now guard against after reading these powerful stories. The kitchen junk drawer, the blink of an eye, a lump in the bed, over-baking chocolate chip cookies, the bedroom closet, a misshelved library book, ticking off your sister, a babbling brook, parrots and other forms of mimicry. Oh, and melliferous honey.

One of the author's strengths is the ease in which her work bridges the past and present, the intertextuality that resonates with the reader leading to a deeper understanding of the narrative. In *The Cottage of Curiosities*, Neugebauer sends shivers through the tale with delicate, fine-drawn references from the Brothers Grimm and even Mother Goose.

In a present-day homage to *The Fall of the House of Usher*, Neugebauer refuses to allow the narrator an easy escape as did Poe. Throughout the story, Gothic echoes of Poe waft near the surface from which Neugebauer enriches and furthers the Usher legacy with a shocking horror of her own.

With *Churn the Unturning Tide*, the pregnant narrator and a group of women over fifty perform water aerobics. The entry of a small toad and a tarantula into the wave pool move the story into a different realm with a dark, deadpan humor and witch references aplenty. The women exhibit a collective behavioral disinhibition, described perfectly as voices "made of smoke and moonlight and a lifetime of corrosion."

Speaking of a lifetime of corrosion, allow me to introduce myself. I am Dan Hammond Jr, fiction writer, former DFW Newspapers book reviewer, and longtime critique partner with Annie Neugebauer. Through countless critique groups and dozens of workshops in the past thirty years, I've been exposed to thousands of stories from hundreds of writers. Some writers have made a name for themselves, and I'm always pleased to see their newest piece of work. But only once have I said—this writer is going to make it big. And I am honored to introduce her first collection of short stories to you, Dear Reader.

We need an Annie Neugebauer to write the obscure truths that we are often reluctant to face. This author embraces the deep chords within our nature and exposes them to us. That is what great writers do.

As readers, we can choose to keep the truth at arm's length. Or we can read on, hoping certain events will not occur but knowing they likely will. Because that must be the way this particular story proceeds from this particular writer. Reading truth can bring us great joy or great sadness, but it is always rewarding.

Take the brilliant juxtaposition of the final two stories of Neugebauer's collection—a story of fear and cowardice followed by a short story of sacrifice for the sake of art and beauty. In *That Which Never Comes*, Daniel spends a long lifetime afraid to face his fears and the truth about himself. With *So Sings the Siren*, the author offers a piercing examination of the lengths an artist must go to reveal their wings, their soul, and to create a unique truth.

Creating a unique truth is exactly what the author achieves in *You Have to Let Them Bleed.* This collection of stories details our culture in a chilling fashion. It creates a deeper understanding of inconvenient societal truths that are oft-neglected or consciously ignored, all within the framework of horror. The horror.

Allow The Shadowling Collector to now escort you through the perilous panorama of Annie Neugebauer's stories. Follow her lead. Do not stray down an empty hallway. And above all, refrain from drawing too near those enticingly dark and beautiful shadowboxes.

Dan Hammond Jr

THE SHADOWLING COLLECTOR

People underestimate
the depth of shadows—
the amount of colors
in black.

Upon the witching hour
I slip through the door
and venture out
to populate my shadowboxes.

Each pool of darkness
cloaks a color;
each puddle of black
homes a trinket,
a notion,
a story,
a creature
worth capturing—
worth putting on display.

So I slither them
into tin cans,

scrabble them
into wooden boxes,
flutter them
into wire nets,
and drag them
into canvas bags.

They are just so
dark and beautiful.

Once again, I go
stalking lovely,
collecting shadowlings—
saving them
for you.

PURPLE

Come here.
Look closer.
Don't be afraid;
I have secured them all
behind this glass.

True. They sometimes shift
from cubby to cubby
when I'm not looking—
which is maddening,
as I have placed them in order
from dark to light—
but they cannot get out.

Come, look at this one.

The purples are my favorite.

See the way it starts with
this little black shadowling,
so pure the light glints violet
off its shimmering shell?

Small but lethal.

And ah, true purple like iridescent
wings in the night.

This slick one, like
the bloody insides of a plum.
This treasure, crouched
fuchsia in the corner.
This panting one,
a dry, beached lavender.

Aren't they lovely?
Dear?
Aren't they just so lovely?

No!
Don't touch.
Don't ever,
    ever
  touch.

HIDE

When I met Cecilia I'd only been dead for twenty years and she'd only been alive for about as many. She was all golden-brown skin and mahogany eyes and legs that stretched longer than the last week of summer, and I was cold – so cold.

I stood several yards away in the shade watching her with her friends. We were at an outdoor concert where a local band did a shitty job of playing good songs. Cecilia sat on the grass with those legs sprawled easily in front of her, catching the sun, leaned back and propped on her elbows. She wore a big white floppy hat that should have seemed silly and out of place but instead looked perfect.

I brought my hand to the flesh over my sternum and rubbed the ridge there – always the first to give. I watched until her friends left, moving on to buy food or go the bathroom or perform some other human function, and then I walked up and sat beside her, crossing my own legs beneath me before I turned to look her in the eyes.

Beneath the brim of her hat little specks of sunlight patterned her face, tiny square dots crisscrossed over her straight Greek nose. She had full, deep pink lips but she didn't smile. I sat close enough to smell the citrus scent of her lip balm – to watch the barely perceptible gilling in and out of her nostrils.

"Do I know you?" she said, her lips working around the thickness of her consonants.

No, I said. I waited for her to look me over before I told her that I wanted to spread her open and plunge inside her until we went from two beings to one.

Her lips parted at my words, one rushed swallow, then she smiled slow and easy, like the melt of a popsicle in the thick heat of August. "That is a lot to ask of someone you don't know," she said.

I know, I said, putting a hand on her smooth thigh, just above the knee. Her skin radiated heat through my cool palm.

"Okay," she said. "You can buy me a drink."

I didn't want to buy her a drink.

"Okay," she said. "Let's go back to my place then."

We did.

Sometimes I feel guilty when it's that easy. Cecilia didn't even hesitate when I tossed the white hat across the room and peeled her shirt up. In fact, she raised her arms in the air to help me slip it over her head, although I left her wrists tangled in it for a moment when I caught sight of her navel. A small, dark dip in the smooth stretch of her tan stomach. Fascinating.

The navels are always the most difficult part, being deep and centered as they are.

Human skin makes such a strange sound when it's split down the middle. It's softer than the cracking of an egg, but it's harder than the tear of fabric. I guess the closest comparison would be the cleaving of a watermelon – sharp with a sweet soft center.

I don't know if it hurts.

I do know that it pains me to peel back the skin I'm in. It's agony to pull away the cold, hardening flesh that last belonged to me. But slipping into Cecilia's skin was warm – so warm.

I pulled it up over my shoulders and bound it over my chest bone.

I was once surprised by what I'm willing to do to survive. I can scarcely remember what that felt like.

I'd been dead for twenty-five years when I met Richard. I saw him at the beach, watching me: the length of my legs stretched out in the lounge chair, white hat pulling shade and tiny flecks of sun across my Greek nose. I did not smile at him, but he came over to me, and when his hand brushed mine I felt the difference.

His skin was warm, almost fiercely hot. I raised my eyes to his and they were honey brown, the color of the lightest part of tall flames. His hair glinted copper and his skin smelled faintly of the wood in a well-used sauna.

Through the thin fabric of my swimsuit cover-up, I rubbed the ridge of skin over my breastbone.

"Hi," he said. "You look familiar. Do I know you?"

He did not know me.

"Well, can I get you a drink? We have a cooler down the way."

I wasn't thirsty, I told him. I'd rather go somewhere private and get down to skin.

There wasn't a beat of hesitation. Too easy. "Skin it is, then," he said, helping me to my feet.

Skin it is.

WHAT THROAT

It was embarrassingly easy to get lost. Even for someone like Jo, who was familiar with hiking and knew better than to make the mistakes she made. She'd always heard it was easier than you think; now she finally believed it. A bit of distraction. Forging ahead when something niggled in the back of her head that maybe this wasn't the right way. Turning around instead of pushing forward. Dark creeping in. Paths blurring with natural breaks in the trees. And all of a sudden – not suddenly at all – she couldn't ignore the worry in the back of her head that whispered, *I don't know where I am anymore.*

Full dark was minutes away, and even if she found her original trail there was no way she'd make it back to her SUV before the light was completely gone. Darkness already filled in under the trees, and she didn't have any light but her cell phone – no signal – which would leave her battery drained if she actually did find an open spot. When it came to strange woods at night, Jo decided hunkering down was smarter and safer than wandering around, even if it did put her behind schedule on her road trip.

Panic scrabbled at the heels of her decision, taking swipes at her ankles with sharp claws, trying to trip her up, but Jo wouldn't let it. Panic got people killed in situations like this. Be smart tonight, then she could hike out in the morning. What she needed now was to level her head, get over the shame at the mistake she couldn't undo, and think.

She stopped walking to take stock. The air was warm now, which meant it probably wouldn't get much colder than cool. That was good because she only had a light sweatshirt with her. The sky had been clear earlier, so it probably wouldn't rain. This area did have big mammals, though how common sightings were she wasn't sure. Wolves, she thought, and mountain lions. Maybe bears too, but most big predators wouldn't mess with a human, so really her biggest concern was small critters. Snakes that were drawn to warm bodies and crawling things that would bite and sting while she slept. Were there poisonous insects around here? Jo figured there must be. She couldn't imagine actually sleeping no matter where she bedded down.

Readjusting her backpack, she chose the largest tree she could see in the quickly disappearing twilight and climbed it.

It was some kind of oak, with large, thick limbs she could rest on with relative comfort. She took off her pack and wedged it in the nearest fork, pulling out her water bottle. One was already empty – she'd drunk it casually before realizing she was lost – and the other was three quarters full. She took a small sip and put it back.

Leaning against the trunk of the oak, Jo scanned the forest below. It looked different in the dark. The tall grass that had looked so pretty from the path seemed almost flat from above, but she knew it hid pockets of life with motives of their own. The leafy patches blended and blurred with the grass, creating a vague patchwork her mind puzzled to make sense of. Motion suggested itself to her every few minutes, but she never tracked a target.

The trees were nothing more than silhouettes now, only their relative sizes indicating to her their nearness or distance. They all swayed in a breeze she couldn't feel, creaking and groaning like an old fence being climbed. Jo stilled, closed her eyes, and tried to feel the tree she was in moving, but couldn't detect anything but her own equilibrium messing with her. Her fingers tightened on the bark beneath her legs.

A sound popped from somewhere to the side. Her eyes jetted open. She held her breath, silent, straining. The crickets had stopped.

Jo counted to twenty, slowly examining each dark, open space between trees in every direction she could see. Still nothing made a sound. She had to take a new breath. She made it an excruciatingly slow drag so she could listen over it.

Nothing.

Even if there was something, it probably didn't know she was there. Maybe it could smell her, but what were the chances it could smell her, climb trees, and was a species aggressive enough to actually do so?

Yet the woods remained expectantly silent.

Was it listening too?

A snap – sharp and almost… intentional. Like a heavy, walking thing stepping on a stick it could have easily avoided.

Adrenaline dumped into Jo's system, her fight or flight instincts kicking in, but neither was a viable option. The only viable option was for her to sit perfectly, excruciatingly still and not make a sound. She fought the urge to pant and breathed in jerky trickles through her mouth. What was in her bag? Nothing useful. No gun, no mace, no blade larger than her pocket knife.

The next sound came from the other direction.

Her first thought wasn't, *Another one*. Her first thought was, *How did it move that fast?*

Her second thought was, *Why is it fucking with me?*

And then she heard the laughter.

That's the closest thing she could associate it with. Insane laughter. Her body crawled with goose bumps. Alien and wrong, a sort of indulgent, crazy giggle that bubbled up into a chitter. What was it? It wasn't the laugh of a hyena, and those didn't live here anyway. It was eerily human, but then so were the screams of goats and the imitations of crows. The word *mimicry* struck her, but she couldn't place it. Humans couldn't be that wild. Animals couldn't be that intelligent.

One long string of laughter, and then more silence. Even the hair on her head stood on end.

She sat there, breathing, listening, heart pounding, but no more sounds came.

Hours later, when her body was weak with stiffened tension, her heart calm because it couldn't sustain the panic, and her eyes dry from being held open so wide, the crickets finally returned.

Still, Jo didn't trust them.

Darcy had to admit, there was a morbid fascination in watching Chug go insane. She'd always associated insanity with intelligence. Only brilliant people went insane. They left the mundane mental issues to people with mundane intellects – Alzheimer's, dementia, PTSD – and took the real insanity for themselves. Chug had wrecked her theory. Chug was no genius, but he wasn't challenged, either. He'd been something of a meathead before this all started, yet here he was, slowly unraveling in a display of psychological fireworks.

Right now he was on all fours, moving around the inside

perimeter of the cabin, counting each tiny gap in the rough wooden planks of the walls, paying no mind to the wolves that prowled outside, snuffing and snarling for a way in. His dirty jeans made a soft scuffing sound against the tired, hard-packed floor.

Of the three of them, Chug was the worst choice to go insane. Maybe if she or Mario had flipped they'd be a more cunning brand – a greater mental threat to the others – but with Chug, it was brute strength Darcy worried about. If he decided to break for the door, would the two of them even be strong enough to stop him?

As he neared his original starting place on the front wall, he sat back on his heels. "Still fifty-six," he muttered, sighing in relief. Then he leaned forward and pressed his face against one of the slits he'd counted, peering out at the wolves. He barked, sharply, four times, and Darcy's shoulders ratcheted to her ears.

The counting made more sense, Darcy thought. It was like he was trying to ascertain his surroundings, focus on something unchanging. The barking was too bizarre. Besides, wolves don't bark.

Lately she'd taken to sitting calmly and watching Chug unravel. She found herself narrating so in her mind, explaining to her own psyche which behaviors made sense and which were beyond crazy – like she was setting boundaries. *Don't go past here*, she explained. *We can wake up to check everyone's positioning during the night, but we can't begin barking at the wolves.*

Then the use of "we" worried her.

Out of her head. She needed out of her head. But stuck inside the cabin, there wasn't much elsewhere to go.

Chug flipped onto his back, sprawling his arms and legs up and out, head rolled back to stare out the crack. Weak, late afternoon sun pierced through, shooting a single ray to land on the drool on his chin. A shadow crossed it, blocking the light for the space of a breath.

The wolves.

The kitchen and living room were open to each other and together they made up the entirety of the cabin. Darcy got up from the sofa and crossed the room, circling wide around Chug but still keeping an arm's length away from all the walls. She stopped at Mario's feet, waiting for him to look up at her from his fingernails, which he'd taken to chewing. When his black eyes met hers, she almost wept. Instead, she sank down to her knees right in front of his feet, his own knees drawn up in front of him, his back pressed against the cabin's only door.

He was keeping Chug in, yes. He was also keeping the wolves – and it – out.

Mario put out his hands, and Darcy laced her fingers in his. There weren't words. They had all been said: How long can we go on like this? Will the wolves be able to break in? Can they dig? What will we do when the last of the food is gone? What should we do with Chug? Who will be the one to go outside?

What is it?

The mornings were relatively safe. Nothing was truly safe, but mornings were the closest thing. The wolves didn't come around until afternoon. It didn't come until nightfall. If they were ever going to make a break for it, it would have to be in the morning.

Inches away, just beyond the old wood that made up the walls, two of the wolves got into a tussle, snarling and snapping. Something crashed into the door, bowing it. A wolf yelped. Darcy and Mario both jumped.

Darcy wondered now if it had let them hike in on purpose. It was more than a full day's hike to get here; why hadn't it gotten them then? They'd spent one night outside – not even in tents – before finding the old man's cabin. Had it intentionally stranded them?

Now they couldn't hike out without committing to another night in the open. Now it knew they were here, if it hadn't already. And now the wolves knew they were here, too, and their desperation was boiling.

Now tears did come, and Darcy didn't fight them. She bent forward to place her face on Mario's knees and cried. They hadn't let the old man back into his own cabin, God help them. They hadn't let the old man back in, too afraid of letting it in as well, and the wolves had gotten him. They'd even eaten the ribs and some of the bones, leaving only a skull and spine stretched out on the dirt.

Mario stroked her hair, despite it being unwashed for days.

The silence grew. The wolves stopped snuffling at the cracks. Their occasional howls tucked tail. Their steps in the dirt pittered softly, then scampered away with little whines of fear, until the only sound left at all was Chug's labored panting.

"Shut up, Chug," Mario whispered.

That only occasionally worked, but this time was one of them. Chug scrambled off his back and sat up, pulling his knees tightly to his chest, rocking, rocking, rocking.

It occurred to Darcy then, as her tears dried, that they were all sitting the same way now. Chug rocking, holding his knees. Mario blocking the door, knees drawn. Her sitting toe to toe with him, mirroring. They'd all gone fetal.

The crickets stopped. The silence outside grew large and expansive, sly.

Then, inches away, a kitten's small, content purr reverberated through the wooden door.

Jo's emotions flipped through an erratic rotation: furious anger, shame, determined calm, and panic. No matter: she was lost. She'd been hiking all day and she wasn't out of the woods. It had taken her less than a day to get in, so a full day would've been enough to get out if she'd chosen the right direction.

She'd climbed down at first light and headed out, hope guiding her like a desperate beacon, but she'd chosen the wrong direction. Despite calculating the angle of the sun and thinking about where she'd parked and her basic knowledge of the larger geographical area, she'd chosen wrong. It was as simple as that.

Now the sun was digging eagerly behind the trees, leaving her cool, thirsty, and exhausted. What was she going to do? Her road trip plans were too flexible; no one on the trip had a definite date to expect her by. No one would be wondering where she was. No one even knew she'd stopped for a hike. Seriously, what the fuck was she going to do?

Her self-berating halted abruptly. Ahead, in a small clearing, two wolves hunched over something, feasting. They were large and dangerously thin, their ribs prominent even through their shaggy gray fur. A bone cracked. Jo tightened her backpack straps, glancing to the sides, wondering if she should sneak, be loud, or simply walk away.

A low, wet growl rumbled behind her.

Jo gasped, turning. Two wolves stalked toward her, backs slunk low and heads forward, teeth exposed. Hungry. Eyes shining with desperation.

She turned to keep them in her line of sight while tracking the first two. They'd spotted her as well. No use in sneaking now. She raised her arms over head slowly and waved them, talking loudly, telling the wolves she was here and she knew they knew it, and don't attack; she'd be on her way. The first two stood, abandoning their meal, and pointed their red muzzles her direction.

They stalked closer. Jo bent, slowly, and picked up a large stick. She swung it in front of her like a golf club, warning them off. They showed more of their teeth and fanned out, working to surround her.

Sweat sprung to the surface of her skin. She couldn't run. If she ran, they'd chase. She could feel their energy crouched in ready potential. Hungry, hungry energy.

Swinging her stick and edging sideways, she headed to the nearest, largest tree. She got three yards before they seemed to collectively realize what she was doing. In a synchronized pounce, they lunged, bounding toward her.

Jo dropped the stick and turned, running at the tree. She hit it several feet up, gasping, grasping. The bark scraped deep grooves down her arms as she scrambled madly up it.

Her hand clasped the lowest branch. They reached the trunk moments later, snarling and snapping. She hauled herself up, one of them leaping into the air. She hung a yard above them. Her mouth was parched, her breath too fast. She climbed higher, as high as she could get and remain stable. It wasn't as big as the tree from the night before. That one had been almost comfortable. This one was just big enough.

Jo sunk to straddle the crook of the largest branch, staring down at the wolves. They paced around the trunk, silent in their temporary defeat. The largest of them went to retrieve the deer carcass they'd been eating and dragged it over. They all settled in beneath her and resumed their meal as the orange of the evening unraveled into blue.

When they began to howl, it made Jo thirstier. They tilted their muzzles up toward her so she could see the small black triangles of their mouths parted. The sound was low and melodious and slick, and she knew that they had water near, that their vocal chords were tight and smooth, that though they wanted for food they surely didn't want for drink.

She'd heard wolf song before, but from a distance. This was directly below her. This seemed almost *for* her. It was indescribably beautiful, trailing chills of doom down her spine. Could they outwait her? Would they stay all night?

But when the wolves did leave, how would Jo get out? Should she turn back the way she'd come, or would that just double her time until she was out of these terrible woods?

From farther away, just out of sight but still near, a new howl sounded.

It began low, almost a moan, and climbed to crescendo in a breaking peak that trailed on and on, wavering but never cutting off, until the final crystalline echoes of it thinned into silence.

Every nerve in Jo's fatigued body lit up. Her eyes stung with tears. Her fingers clutched bark. Her toes curled painfully within her boots.

All of the wolves went silent, their slim faces turned toward the howl.

That wasn't a wolf.

The thought made no sense, but it's what Jo believed. It was close enough to be called a wolf howl, but something else had made it. If not another wolf, then what? What thing could make a sound so close to perfect and yet so desperately wrong? What throat could bend the rightness of nature so?

In the silence, Jo peered into the sinking dark, and all of the wolves stood. The deer still had meat, but they turned their backs to it. They held their tails low against their hind legs and crept away, noses low to the ground, ears back.

All four of them slunk into the woods.

Jo continued to stare into the trees where that other howl had come from, but nothing moved.

Her chest heaved, quickly, though no fresh air drew into her lungs. Her dehydrated throat clenched around emptiness.

Minutes stretched and stretched, like a pine bough bending low under the weight of heavy winds. She sensed it moving but couldn't see it – felt it creeping but couldn't hear it. Every rodent nestled among the leaves held its breath. Every cricket sat frozen. Even the wind waited. The woods cowered in silence.

Behind her, below, at the base of the tree, it laughed a laugh that no lips should shape.

The laughter itself – close enough to be called laughter but somehow, deeply, *wrong* – gurgled and morphed and bubbled until the only sound coming from the base of the tree was the off-kilter babbling of a brook.

Darcy could hear each time Chug's eyelid slapped his eyeball. He stood, calm, facing the two of them, pulling out his eyelashes one at a time. Each time, the lid would lift in a strained tent until the hair he pulled it by worked loose from its root, and then the lid would smack back down. Pop. As he spoke, Darcy stared at his unlined left eye as he worked on the right.

"I'm telling you, we should've left last night. That was our chance. We might never get another chance like that."

It hadn't come last night. The wolves hadn't come either. The three of them had waited and paced and argued all night. Was it away, distracted somewhere else? Or was it a trick? Was it out there, finally silent, waiting for them to open the door?

Usually when it came the wolves ran and the crickets fell silent. So far tonight there'd been no wolves, and the crickets continued to chirp loud and clear.

In the nights since their confinement in the cabin, it had been a child crying, a kitten purring, a chit-chit-chit-chit-chit sound, a chainsaw, and a goat braying, but it had never been silence.

Chug had gotten worked up last night, when it hadn't come. He'd been the sanest he'd been since they locked out the old man – since he'd insisted they keep out the old man – and he'd been on the verge of forcing Mario out of the way of the door. It was their chance, damn it!

"It could be the crickets," Darcy had said softly.

That's when Chug had started pulling out his eyelashes.

If it had been the crickets, there was no way to tell. It always left before dawn and that's when the crickets stopped chirping, too, so how would they know?

They hadn't opened the door. They hadn't taken the chance. They hadn't run as fast as they could through the woods hoping they could make it to their car before it found them, before the wolves found them, before another dusk fell upon them when they were unprotected by wooden walls. They'd stayed inside and argued, terrified of the crickets' chirping, straining to listen and decipher. Had crickets always been so macabre? Had they always had that squeaky up-whistle at the end of their strokes? Had they always sounded *exactly* like… that?

Chug's eyelid snapped into place. He placed the new lash in his left palm, where he carefully cupped a feathery pile of them. "I'm telling you. I'm telling you we should run. If it doesn't come again tonight, we should run. We can't miss another chance."

None of them argued, but none of them agreed, either.

"The wolves still aren't here," Mario said. Darcy scooted closer to him, seeking his body heat. He put an arm around her waist. "They're usually here by now. The sun will be all the way down in a few minutes. They'd usually have come and gone, almost."

Darcy glanced to the diagonal slats of late evening sun that speared the gray dimness of the cabin. The whole place danced with dust. It occurred to her for the first time that they could easily starve here. They could stay trapped inside by that thing and their own fear and slowly shrivel up until they were just more furniture and dust. It suddenly seemed every bit as likely a way to die as going outside. The longer they waited to run, the harder it would be to build up the courage.

"Okay," she said, nearly whispering. "If it doesn't come in the next hour, let's break for it."

Chug's face lit up, his lashless eyes looking over-wide and shiny.

"Okay," Mario agreed, giving her a squeeze.

As they waited for the remains of the sun to slip away, Chug pulled the last lash from his lid and set about placing them all carefully around the perimeter of the cabin. Mario lit the candle on the tiny kitchen countertop. "It's dark," he announced, as if it wasn't all any of them could think about – that it was dark now and it hadn't come. That they knew of.

Darcy waited for him to urge them to go, but he said nothing. Even Chug said nothing. They stood side by side, staring at the door.

Leaves shuffled outside. Footsteps?

Darcy wanted Mario to go sit in front of it like he usually did, to give them all the illusion that he could keep it shut if something tried to break in, but he didn't move, and she didn't speak.

A knock came.

That's not the right sound, Darcy thought. That's not what a knock should sound like on that door. It was too hollow, too high for such thick, weathered wood. But how would she know? No one had knocked before.

It had never knocked before.

"Hello?" a shrill voice called. "Is anyone in here?"

Chills bloomed in circles over Darcy's skin.

It had never spoken before, either.

None of them moved. Darcy heard Chug's eyelids connect and part in a bald blink.

"Hello?" the voice called again. A woman's voice, strained. Strained with panic, or with impersonation? "Please, is anyone here?" The door handle rattled, but the latch was dropped on the inside. "I need in. Please!"

Darcy was shaking her head, back and forth, over and over. No. No, don't let her in. Don't talk to it.

"Who are you?" Mario asked. Darcy's head whipped to him, staring.

"My name's Jo," she said, relief clear in her tone. "God, please let me in. There's…" Her voice faded distant and back, like she'd looked over her shoulder. "There's something out here with me. Please."

"We have to let her in," Chug said, far too calm. "Can't leave her out there for the wolves. Have to let her in."

He said it as if it were obvious, as if he hadn't insisted they do just that to the old man. He blamed himself, but not one of them had tried to move his big body from the door that first night. Not one of them had argued to let the old man into his own cabin.

"Have to," he reiterated, walking to the door. "Have to. Have to. Have to."

"Chug, no," Darcy called reaching for his arm. "Don't. It could be… it. It might not be her." As if they knew her.

"Have to!"

"Please," the girl outside screeched. "Please, God! Hurry!"

Darcy's fingers connected with his big, beefy arms, and he froze as if she'd shocked him. "Chug, we should have let the man in. That was a mistake we *all* made. But this could be too." She looked over her shoulder where Mario stood, staring, his face drawn in indecision so tight it looked like pain.

"I don't know," Mario whispered. "I don't know."

"God, please let me in. You can't leave me out here." Jo's voice broke in half over the word *leave*. "It's going to get me. I can feel it coming. *Please*."

"HAVE TO!" Chug bellowed, charging the door.

Darcy didn't try to stop him.

He threw open the latch and pulled in the door.

A woman, maybe ten years younger than them, rushed in. Her hair was a nest of knots. She clutched her backpack straps as if they might hold her up. She darted all the way past the two of them lined up facing Chug, then turned. Together, all of them stared at the empty doorway for the span of several long seconds. Nothing was outside but descending dusk. The woods were still. Chug slammed the door and dropped the latch back down.

They all turned to stare at the new person, Jo, she'd said.

"How do you know it's out there?" Mario demanded, crossing his arms. "We were going to run."

Jo sunk to the floor, drawing her knees up, instinctively taking the position they'd all reverted to during the long, tortured nights inside the cabin. "It can be the frogs croaking," she said. "It can be the wind in the leaves." Then she started crying.

For the first time since they'd locked out the old man, Chug slept silently, no whimpering. Mario slept on the ground beside Darcy, and Jo slept stretched on the nappy old sofa.

Darcy stared up at her darkened form in the silence of the others' sleep. She couldn't close her eyes. She could hear Chug and Mario breathing, but the girl, Jo, didn't make a sound. Darcy watched her, scarcely blinking, trying to pick out the facial features and forms of a stranger through the shroud of dimness.

It turned out Chug had been right; last night was their chance. Jo told them the thing had been with her; it had treed her in the woods. She said it couldn't climb. They agreed to wait until sunrise, hike out, and spend the night in trees if they couldn't make it out in one day.

Darcy listened for something outside, for the wind or the crickets or the wolves themselves to sound, and sound wrong, but nothing came.

Hours passed.

Softly, sneakily, a tiny little click sounded. Darcy's eyes went wide, staring through the dark at Jo's silhouette on the sofa. She lay on her back, facing up, her profile silhouetted against the cushions. Had she clicked her teeth? Tapped her nail? Clucked her tongue?

Something creaked. Low and long, like hinges that hadn't been oiled in years. Like old wood being weighted. Like stiff leather stretching past its resting point. So faint Darcy could scarcely hear it. Had she been asleep, she wouldn't have.

She thought she saw Jo's throat move. A convulsive swallow, but then it kept going. Her larynx bobbed up and down, up and down, then out, bulging, squirming. Darcy's heart pounded in her temples, reflected into her ears by the bundled shirt she pillowed her head on. She held her breath to listen, eyes staring at the moving, writhing thing.

Minutes passed. Outside, the crickets remained silent.

Jo let out a rumble, and then a breath, and then another rumble, steady, rhythmic. The sound filled the cabin, but it wasn't right. It was close enough to be called a snore, but it was ever so slightly, indescribably *off*.

THE LITTLE DRAWER FULL OF CHAOS

I scooped the last perfect sphere of chocolate chip cookie dough onto the pan, pressing the little edges down with my finger and lining it up in its row and column, spaced evenly from the others. The oven preheat signal beeped behind me and I set the tray aside, sliding the first one in and setting the timer.

"Babe," June called from the living room, her voice muffled by the small nail she held between her lips, "will you bring me the hammer?" Her arms stretched up to hold a frame against the wall, a miniature level balanced across the top. I imagined the bubble was exactly centered.

And yes, our names are May and June. It's why our friends introduced us in the first place over five years ago; they thought it was funny. June had also turned it into the sexiest pun imaginable our first time together, so I called it a win.

I wiped my hands on my apron. "Yeah, where is it?"

"The drawer," she mumbled, a grumpy edge telling me her shoulders were starting to burn.

I opened the drawer at the edge of our kitchen island. If we didn't specify a drawer – the silverware drawer, the pen drawer, the sock drawer – it was always this one, because this was the only one in the whole house that didn't have a designated purpose. It was the anything and everything drawer. In my rush I pulled too hard and its wheels smacked against the end of their tracks with a pop, the contents shifting and sliding at the impact.

Loose rubber bands, a permanent marker, clothes pins, scissors, a bouncy ball, receipts, a ten-year-old film capsule, crumbs, a spatula…

"I don't see it," I called, shoving things around and setting a few larger items on the counter. Surely the hammer would be big enough to spot right away. I pulled out a box of matches and a spilled canister of toothpicks, then a koozie with a kitchen knife stuck through it.

"It's in there," she said with too much calm, probably trying not to aim her self-annoyance at me. She only ever spoke this serenely when she was on the brink of cursing.

I fumbled more, cringing at the dirt that collected under my fingernails when I touched the back corners. Loose screws, a red plastic piece that must've once gone to something, a sticky note pad, a hair scrunchie neither of us ever owned, much less wore. Cold metal. I yanked it out.

"This little thing?" I asked, holding up a floral-patterned hammer that looked almost like a toy.

"Yes!"

"You don't want a real one from the garage?"

"It's just a picture hanger. Come take this from me before I drop it."

I hurried past the two cats tucked neatly into their matching beds to trade June the hammer for the frame. She kept her thumb pressed to the wall where the nail would go, urgently placing the point and driving it home until the small metal hook sat flush with the wall. She set the hammer on the fireplace hearth and flicked the tenseness out of her hands. "Whew," she said, grinning at me. "I didn't plan ahead on that one."

I shook my head in mock disapproval as she hung the frame and re-leveled it before sticking small adhesive dots to the bottom two corners so it would never shift or move against the wall. It looked perfect there, clustered with our other wall hangings. That's how everything in our house was: thoughtful and tidy and beautiful.

Everything except the one drawer. I took the hammer and shoved it toward the back before scooping the rest of the things I'd removed back in, rummaging until everything shifted down low enough to shut it again. The junk needed to be sorted through, but even neat freaks like us need one place where things are out of order.

The timer on the first batch of cookies went off, and June skipped with unapologetic glee into the kitchen, waiting until I'd set the tray on the rack to cool before sliding her arms around my shoulders.

I was almost embarrassed by how much I enjoyed my job at the library. Whenever I told people I worked in circulations, the most common question was some variation on, "Oh, do you like that?" usually with their head cocked to the side like they were trying to figure me out. When I told them genuinely that I did, they always smiled, nodding like they were happy for me, but I could see them stamp BORING across my forehead in their mind.

Still, contentment filled me as I shelved books from the returns cart, rolling it through the rows with the quiet swish of wheels on carpet, stopping in front of the next section, plucking the corresponding books in a stack or handful, and sliding them one by one into the waiting empty spaces. It was soothing, useful. It calmed me like meditation. Dewey Decimal was a second language to me.

As I went, if any call numbers jumped out at me from the wrong spot, I pulled them from the shelf and added them to my cart to be returned to their rightful home. It didn't happen that often because we had "reshelf" carts spaced around the library, but some patrons still occasionally stuck a book into a random shelf. I never understood why, but it didn't bother me. I saw it almost as a challenge – an extra step in my quest for order.

I paused in front of the Js, searching for 818.54 JF's home. I only held the one book in my hand for this shelf. I could picture in my mind exactly where it went, my eyes scanning for the colors of the spines I knew stood on either side. I frowned. Where was it? I spotted a triangular shadow created by two books leaning in, holding another book's place. I almost stuck it there, but then I hesitated. That wasn't the right spot. But it was just where I was looking, and it was the right size. I checked the call number again, the tip of the book balanced on the metal shelf, ready to be slid into place. No, but—

"May?"

Li's voice surprised me so much that I twitched. Embarrassed to be caught searching for the right call number like some first-time customer, I shoved the book into the empty spot and whirled.

"Garry's dealing with an unhappy patron and there are ten people in line. I need you at the counter."

Heat crept up my face. It was ridiculously stupid, but I felt guilty for putting the book in the wrong slot. I stepped to the side to block Li's view, as if she would scan the call numbers and spot my mistake.

"Okay," I agreed. I stayed where I was, intending to fix the book after she turned away.

"Now," she clarified, looking at me expectantly.

I sighed, twisting my hands behind my back as I headed to check-out.

When I got home, I couldn't help slamming the door. It would be a takeout night, for sure. I stalked through the house, but all the lights were off. June wasn't home yet?

One of the cats, Pinky, sat on the sofa arm, staring at me. The other, Mibs, twined between my ankles as I walked, begging for dinner. June was half an hour late, which meant so was their dinner. I dropped my purse on the side table and fed the cats, not bothering to turn on more than the kitchen light. I grabbed a beer from the fridge and yanked open the junk drawer, fishing through it until I found the blue metal bottle opener. I popped off the top and tossed it and the opener both back in, my eyes absently grazing the mess as I thought about my day.

After the little rush, I'd gone back to fix the book, but the reshelf cart was gone. Li had finished the job for me while I worked the desk. When I looked for the book I'd misshelved, I couldn't find it. Instead all I could find was the empty spot where I should have put it in the first place. All afternoon, it had nagged at me. I'd checked different areas several times on my way around the library, casually testing out other theories. Had I been one row over? One letter over? In nonfiction?

The book was stuck somewhere random and I never did find it. I took a few deep swigs of my beer and sighed. Where was June?

I checked my phone; no texts. She must've gotten caught up at work. It wasn't like her not to check in if she'd be late. I messaged her to pick up some Chinese food on her way home. A painting hanging above the side table caught my eye. It was crooked.

Scowling at it, I set down my beer and stepped to adjust it, jabbing my hip on the open drawer.

"Fuck!" I hissed, startling Pinky where he hunched over his bowl. I slammed the drawer shut with a clatter.

Groaning, I hopped to the painting and lifted the bottom corner. Ah, the little sticky dots had lost their adhesion. I'd probably bumped it with my purse or knocked it loose when I slammed the door. I glanced at the new frame June had hung in the living room, but it was still level and perfect. I shuffled into the garage and dug out two new dots to replace the old ones. On second thought, I got a level, too, and straightened the old painting before pressing it firmly in place.

"There," I told Mibs, satisfied. She twitched her tail at me and narrowed her eyes. "Where's your momma?" I asked. She heaved a little sigh as if wondering the same thing.

My hip ached sharply; there would be a bruise. I went to the drawer, yanked it back open, and turned the whole thing upside down on the countertop. Junk and random crap rolled and scattered. I coughed at a little billow of dust. I was sick of that mess.

But as I began combing through things, I realized that there really weren't any other places for it all to go. Everything else in the house had a neatly settled home. These things wouldn't fit. I threw away a handful of the loose toothpicks, but my energy nosedived and I sighed in defeat. I worked the drawer back into place and scooped everything back into it.

I had to rattle and shake and shove for a few minutes to get things to fit again, as if the mass had grown since being released. Years of adding things to it had somehow inadvertently turned into the world's most random jigsaw puzzle. I let out a quiet stream of curse words while I crammed it all back in. It would've been easier to go ahead and throw things away, but at that point I took it personally. It had come out; it would go in.

Several minutes later, the drawer was closed – had there always been that little gap between the drawer front and the face of the cabinets, or had I slid it into the tracks wrong? – and the countertop was a dirty mess. I wiped it down and collapsed on the sofa.

When June finally came home an hour later with egg rolls and chicken fried rice, she chastised me for leaving all the lights off. I gave her the rest of my second beer and buried my face in her hair, no longer needing to tell her about my day, just glad she was home.

It started as me trying to convince myself that a misshelved book didn't matter. Really, who cares? Patrons do it all the time anyway, so what was one or two on my part? Telling myself that didn't ease my stupid harping, though, so I took the reshelf cart to the back corner of the building and intentionally placed a book in the entirely wrong section. It was a book people frequently checked out, too, and the section I put it in was one I'd never shelved in the past four years of working here.

See? I told myself. No one would ever find it, and even that wasn't the end of the world. Worst case scenario, it'd eventually be filed as stolen or lost and Li would order a new one. That's what the budget was for. It wasn't a big deal. Still, my fingertips felt hot on the spine of the little paperback as I drew my hand away, hurrying the cart to the opposite side of the building.

Despite my own humiliation at how absurd my feelings were, I told Li I was sick and went home early.

Pinky and Mibs yawned from their places sprawled across the living room rug, facing opposite directions, then slowly meandered into the kitchen. I guess they figured that since someone was home, it was dinnertime. With a shrug, I fed them two hours early, knowing June would be annoyed.

I pulled a cookie from the Tupperware on the counter and took a bite. My nose crinkled as I flipped it to look at the bottom. Overbrowned. Not burned, but definitely not perfect. I must have left the last sheet in the oven too long. I never did that.

The Tupperware lid had a crack in it. That was new, certainly. It was my best one. I pulled open the drawer and dug through for the masking tape. I tore off a strip and smoothed it over the crack, sighing. Now it wouldn't be air-tight.

Suddenly I felt flushed and buzzy. Maybe I really was getting sick.

As if prompted by the very thought of the word *sick*, nausea overwhelmed me. Heat boiled and condensed in my belly, tight and screaming, and fire surged up my throat and my legs went numb. With a choking retch, I bent over the open drawer and gagged. Tears stung my clenched eyes, my face burning. I had no time to do anything but clutch the edge of the countertop with both hands.

When the hacking that had seized me released its grip, I opened my eyes and sucked in a breath. Had I coughed something up, or just coughed? I looked down into the open drawer.

There was no vomit. All I saw that I didn't recognize from before was a strange, piecey mess. It looked like a pile of miniature pickup sticks, or metal shavings – the type of thing you could collect with a magnet.

It couldn't have come from me, could it? The stuff looked dark and silvery, sharp, fluid without being liquid, and already it was settling into the nooks and crannies of everything else in the drawer. I had *never* eaten anything like that. It must've been lead dust or some random debris in the drawer I hadn't noticed before.

My throat felt seared and raw from the coughing, though, my face tight, and my fingers tingled. Tears of exertion tracked down my cheeks as I shut the drawer. Sliding the overdone cookie into the trash, I shuffled to the bedroom and slid under the covers, shoes and all.

I woke suddenly, as if an alarm had gone off, but the house was silent. My eyes were wide, my brain stuttering. It was dark. Not just never-turned-the-lights-on dark, but dark-outside dark. I'd slept until nighttime? Where was June?

Sitting up in a rush, I grabbed my phone. The ringer was on, no messages.

My pulse began to flutter at the base of my throat. Maybe she'd come home, seen me sleeping, and just stayed out of the bedroom so I could rest.

"June?" I called out, pacing into the living room.

The lights were out here, too. All the blinds were still open, letting the dark in like a physical thing. Pinky stood silhouetted on top of the TV stand. Mibs was tucked somewhere in the shadows. I slapped the light switch and went to twist all the blinds closed. June hated when they stayed open at night; she said neighbors could see in and it creeped her out. By the time I'd shut all the blinds and turned on several lights, my heart was racing. I sat on the arm of the sofa and called June. Right before it went to voicemail, she picked up.

There was shuffling and some loud bass thumping in the background. Finally, she said, "Yello?"

"June? Where are you?"

"May! Oh my gosh, you guys, it's May!"

Distant voices.

"June, are you drunk?"

"I may be a wee tiddle drunk."

I dropped my forehead into my hands. "Where are you? Why didn't you come home? Or call?"

"Oh," she said, as if surprised by my question. "I quit my job."

"*What?*"

"Yep. Quit-er-roo and walked right out of there. No sir, no ma'am, no thank you. Done."

June had been talking about looking for another job for a few months now, but how could she just quit without telling me? "Babe, you didn't even give two weeks' notice? Or line up interviews first?"

"Nuh-uh. Fuck 'em."

Oh my god. "Okay, where are you? I'm going to come get you and bring you home."

"Oh! I should go home."

"Yeah. Don't drive. I'll come get you. Stay where you are." I grabbed my keys and purse and rushed to the door, noticing on my way that the picture frame was knocked askew. The new one. "Where are you?"

In the car on the way home, June was elatedly drunk, but when I asked her what happened, her laughter quickly dissolved into sobbing. They didn't appreciate her there. She'd been overlooked for the promotion she was perfect for. Instead of finding a new job, she'd walked out. Said she wouldn't waste one more day in a dead-end position.

As I walked her down the hall to the bedroom, she turned her head to look at the crooked frame. "Mother shitter," she said, staring at it.

I nodded my agreement.

She tumbled onto the bed on top of the covers. "You need to feed the cats," she slurred, eyes already closed.

The next day my hip ached and my head pounded. I hadn't been able to fall back asleep after I brought June home. Instead, I'd spent the night staring into the darkness of the ceiling.

The whole morning at work, I'd been prodding the edges of my well-being, checking for impending nausea, but other than the bruise and the headache, I felt fine.

About a third of the books I shelved, I put into the wrong places. It had become something of a game for me, or a dare. How many could I do? Part of the joy was in not misshelving all of them, only some. It was more exciting that way.

"May."

I turned to see Li watching me with a deep frown on her smooth face. She must be well over forty, but her skin looked twenty-two. "Yes ma'am?"

Her eyes scanned the shelf behind me. My pulse thudded. Was she checking the call numbers, or just arbitrarily looking? "I need you at the counter."

For one moment, I wanted to throttle her. I saw what my arms would look like reaching for her. I heard what we'd sound like crashing to the rough carpet. I felt what her neck would feel like under my hands, the smooth cordage of it, the warmth, the surprised wideness of her eyes as she looked up at me, her fingers scrambling to wedge under my own, but I wouldn't let up. I'd lift and drop her several times, knocking her skull against the ground, still squeezing, squeezing and squeezing until her face turned purple and she died.

"May?"

My mouth hung open in shock, staring at her. I blinked rapidly, clearing the images away. What the hell was wrong with me? I liked Li. She's a great boss. I certainly didn't want to kill her. I didn't want to kill anyone. It was just a random glitch of the brain. People do that. Think about driving into oncoming traffic, jumping from the top floor, stealing a policeman's gun. They don't actually do the things, just suddenly become aware of how easy it would be, that's all. It'd never happened to me before, though. I always thought people were fucking nuts when they confessed that.

"*May.*"

"Yes. Yeah. Sorry." I shook my head, returning the book I was holding to the cart. I wasn't in front of the right shelf.

"Are you okay?"

"Yeah, fine." When she gave me an *I don't believe you look*, I added, "June just quit her job."

"Oh, wow. I'm sorry to hear that. Are you going to be okay?"

I nodded.

"Do you need to take some time off?"

"No, no. I'm fine. Sorry."

"Alright then. Well, take your time, but I do need you at the counter."

The first thing I noticed when I walked in was that every frame hanging on the walls in our entryway was knocked askew, as if someone had run their hand along the wall and intentionally displaced them. Or maybe slammed the door really hard. Music I didn't recognize boomed from the bedroom.

Then I saw that the living room was a mess. I mean, not for other people, maybe, but for June and me, it was unheard of. There were clothes strewn about, a sweatshirt, a sweater, some socks, and a pair of pajama pants. Pinky sat on the coffee table licking a plate crusted with leftovers, his ears laid back either because he felt guilty or the music was too loud. A spilled glass of water hung over the edge, the rug beneath dark with damp. All of the lights were on, even though evening sunlight was still streaming through the windows.

I took the plate from Pinky and righted the water glass, carrying both into the kitchen. I rounded the island and jabbed my pelvis on the corner of the open drawer.

"Fuck," I hissed, slamming the dishes onto the counter. That was the second time! I looked down to shove the thing shut when I remembered the day before. That odd, dark, grainy mess I spotted right after my coughing fit. I looked into the drawer, searching for it.

I couldn't find any. I shifted some things aside, thinking maybe it had sifted down to the bottom, but the bottom was bare. I bent at the knees to peer into the back of the drawer, but its depths were cast in shadow. I tugged on the handle to try to draw it out further, but it was all the way forward on its tracks.

Suddenly, sickness hit me. A hot flush, a tingling wash, and the sharp, unnatural stuff rose up my throat in a turmoil of pain. Running to the bathroom wasn't an option; I didn't even have time to cross to the kitchen sink. I bent over and let it out with a silent cry, hands on either side of the drawer, careful not to touch anything inside it or what was coming out of me.

When it was done, the mess sat dry and glistening in a haphazard pile on top of the junk. I stood, wiping my face with the bottom of my shirt, and fought the urge to sit down in the middle of the kitchen and cry. My throat burned, scraped raw like before. There was no denying it this time: it had come out of me. I stumbled to the drawer we kept our Ziploc bags in and pulled one out, intending to bag some to take with me to the hospital.

I was interrupted by a warm breeze. The air conditioner churned and hummed heavily; it had been since I got home. Where'd the breeze come from?

My stomach flipped and I hurried toward the living room, catching my hip on the drawer corner again. "Fuck!" I hobbled through anyway, noticing the frame I'd fixed before already askew again. I ignored it and rushed into the living room, scanning.

The window by the sofa was wide open, the blinds raised, and the screen fallen onto the grass of our back yard.

"Oh my god," I whispered. We never left the windows open unless the blinds were down, because our screens were old and ill-fitted, and we worried the cats might push them out. Ours were indoor-only and would never make it on their own.

I whirled. Pinky puffed up at the sudden motion. Panic clawed at my raw throat. "Get," I snapped at him, waving my arms forward to startle him away. "Get away from here."

He turned and ran toward the entryway, but when he neared the closed bedroom door and its pounding music, he turned heel at the last minute, scratching and slipping to switch directions, and ran back toward me.

I leapt in front of him to keep him from the open window. He turned the corner to the side hall, slamming into the wall so hard he stopped, stunned. Then he shook his whole body and dove under the bathroom vanity, a space I'd thought much too narrow to hold him. Fine. Good. Better than him running outside. I shut the bathroom door to keep him in and give him time to calm down.

"Sorry Pinky," I muttered, searching for Mibs.

An hour and a half later, dark had fallen and mosquito bites swelled like measles on the surface of my sweat-slicked skin.

June and I each held flashlights, wordlessly sweeping them side to side as we walked back home. Without discussion, we'd both stopped calling for Mibs when we turned back. How many miles had we walked? We'd cased the whole neighborhood, but our sweet old cat was nowhere to be seen. I couldn't remember the last time my heart felt so heavy and tight and leaden in my chest. With every soft crunch of our footsteps on pavement, I fought the urge to lash out at June. How could she be so careless? I was too mad to tell her about my getting sick earlier, and with the nausea gone now, it didn't seem as pressing as Mibs missing.

"I've been thinking," she said. Her voice was so unexpected that I twitched. "Maybe we should have kids."

I stopped walking. She turned, shining her flashlight in my wide eyes, and I raised a hand, flinching away. "What?"

"I think it'd be good for us. We'd make good moms."

Five years of steadfastly agreeing that babies are great for other people but not so much for us, and now this? "What are you—where is this coming from?" Something about losing Mibs? Quitting her job?

"I've been thinking about it."

"Since when?"

"For a year or so."

"*What?*" I slapped a mosquito sucking at the bend of my elbow. How could she have not brought up something this big for a whole year?

She turned from me, adjusting her light, and resumed walking towards home. "Yeah. I think it'd be good. I feel like I finally see my life from a distance. That pointless job. Wasting time. I want to make something of myself. I want to make something. Mean something."

"But what about how we wanted real careers and how babies spit up everywhere and how kids are dirt machines?"

A few feet ahead of me, silhouetted by her own flashlight, her shoulders lifted and fell. I had never felt so distant from her. “I think it’d be good,” she said again.

While I crouched on the floor trying to coax Pinky out from under the vanity, June quietly went to bed. Pinky refused to come out, even when I offered him a fresh bowl of food. I could barely make out the white triangle on his nose, slightly off-center.

After replacing the screen, I shut the window and closed all the blinds. My stomach felt tight again, and I wasn’t sure if it was stress, hunger, or more of that ominous nausea. It didn’t feel as severe as before, though. Maybe I could avoid the hospital and make a doctor appointment first thing in the morning. I even ate some of the leftover Chinese food while hovering in front of the refrigerator. Then I went to the drawer, thinking I could bag some of that strange mess to show the doctor, but the drawer already stood open several inches.

I stopped, staring. Despite the bright kitchen lights, the inside was untouched, fully shrouded in darkness. My cooling sweat slid down my back, making me shudder.

Wiping my hands on my shorts, I went to it and yanked it open. A dead mosquito sat atop the pile. The shavings I’d vomited were gone, nowhere to be seen. “What the hell?” I murmured. Was I losing my mind? My head pounded, a deep achy echo reverberating at the base of my skull.

I slammed the drawer shut, and it bounced back open, gaping the same few inches as before, a black rectangle.

As I marched past it, not looking as if to spite it, my gaze landed instead on the picture frames above the side table. The one I straightened and the two beside it all tilted to the same side, toward the kitchen, as if the whole house had been lifted at the far end and was sliding forward. I'd fix them tomorrow.

When I slipped into bed beside June, I studied her face in the dim glow of my lamp. She was either already asleep or pretending to be. She hadn't apologized for leaving the window open, but I was sure she felt guilty enough without me demanding she talk about it. But where had the baby thing come from? Was she having some sort of early midlife crisis? She *had* just gone through an upheaval. This was my June. We always worked things out. She just needed time to process the change, then we could talk through it.

My heart softened at the sight of her as it always did, and I leaned over to give her a kiss. Something pricked between us, at the corners of our mouths. I sat up and pinched it away, twisting to hold it under my lamplight.

One of the dark grainy shards perched on the pad of my thumb, gleaming dully. My spine convulsed. I flicked it onto the carpet as if it'd stung me, turning off my lamp with an angry snap and diving under the covers, but as I lay there in the cave of my own breathing, eyes clenched, I wondered where it came from. Had it been on my lips, or hers? I had the bizarre mental image of June hunched over that drawer with a fork, scooping the stuff into her mouth when I wasn't looking, a little piece of it stuck to the corner like a single grain of rice. But that was ludicrous, of course. I'd thrown it up earlier. One piece had certainly clung behind, only to fall onto June when I bent to kiss her goodnight.

Softly, almost begrudgingly, as if listening to a bad joke in her sleep, June started laughing.

Something was biting my toe. I kicked, the top of my foot connecting with soft fur. "Mibs?" I muttered, clenching my eyes shut. But no, Mibs was gone. I squinted, but the bedroom was still dark when I cracked my eyes. Pinky's tail stuck out of the blankets, his teeth latching onto my toe again. "Shit!" I pushed him over the edge of the bed, sitting up, trying to find my bearings. Something somewhere was beeping incessantly. My head pounded.

"What the hell is going off?" I asked June, but she didn't answer. I turned, patting her shoulder, but the blankets compressed under my hand. She wasn't in bed. Groaning, I shuffled into the living room and turned on a lamp.

June stood in the dark kitchen, bending over the island. I realized now that two different things were beeping. "Babe?" I called.

She looked up, and I couldn't see her expression but something about her posture made me think she felt guilty. "Yeah?"

"What are you doing?"

"Just looking for the screwdriver."

"Don't you hear that?"

"It's why I came out here."

I stared. When it was clear she wasn't going to say anything else, I got the stepstool from the coat closet and walked to the smoke alarm in the hallway, yanking it off and ripping out the battery before I even stepped down. There was still another sound, though, equally persistent and grating.

With the smoke detector battery alert dead, I could make it out. It was my cell phone. Where had I left it? It sounded like it was going off over and over. The notifications guiding me, I finally found it under the sofa. It was ringing again as I pulled it out. What time was it?

It was June's mom. "Hello?"

"May, thank God. I've been calling for half an hour. Is June there?" I glanced at the coffee table, only now realizing that there had been a third beeping: June's phone.

"Yeah, what's going on?"

"Oh dear," she said, starting to cry. "Oh dear, Brandon was hit by a car."

June's little brother was twenty-five, but he was living at home with their parents. He was a sweet kid, but never quite got his life going the way he wanted to. Apparently he'd been out for a late-night walk, probably drunk, and been hit by a reckless driver, probably drunk. He was killed instantly.

I listened to June sob on the phone with her mom, trying to gather my thoughts, but I felt like the whole world was off-balance. The youngest family member isn't supposed to die first. I couldn't absorb it.

My phone rang. My mom. I answered on the second ring. "Hi Mom."

"Sweetie, did I wake you?"

"No, we're up. We just heard."

"Just heard what?"

I glanced at the clock. It was after three a.m., too late and too early for my mom to be up. Suddenly tense anew, I asked, "What did you call for?"

"I have something to tell you, baby girl. Are you sitting down?"

I recognized the tone of her voice, one laden with near-relished drama. Whatever she was about to tell me, it was something she'd been working herself up to. I nodded, breath held, and though she couldn't see me, she must have known I'd nod.

In a teary, flamboyant tone, she told me, "May, I'm leaving your father."

It was after lunch by the time we drove home from the hospital. Turning onto our street, I saw a little boy on a bicycle, and I imagined hitting him. For a moment, I thought about how very easy it would be to slam the accelerator and roll right over him – how the bike would sound against the pavement, his body under my wheels. Is this what the person who'd hit Brandon had felt? Curiosity like a dark compulsion?

"May," June gasped.

I swerved, overcorrecting. I had been veering softly toward him. I shook my head, dry eyes pricking with exhaustion. "Sorry," I whispered. The boy glared at me as he rode by.

She returned her temple to the passenger window, eyes glazed.

The funeral wasn't for three days. We'd stayed at the hospital as if guarding his body, hours, until a nurse had kicked us out so they could start the autopsy.

My mom and dad had been together for over twenty years.

Li called to ask why the hell I was late for work. She was sympathetic, but told me if I missed another shift without calling I'd be let go.

When we stumbled into the house, it seemed even messier than before. A small picture had fallen off the wall and shattered, the frame dented in the corner. We ignored it. Pinky didn't come begging for food.

June slid to a seat on the fireplace hearth, her head leaned back against the brick. I made it to the kitchen island and tossed my bag on it before collapsing over it, head in my arms, but the drawer was open all the way, right beneath me, and I silently, almost smoothly vomited into it again, that dark, piecey, impossible stuff. The inside of the drawer looked deep and shrouded, my mess disappearing into it instantly.

June never opened her eyes to check on me.

With a wretched sob, too exhausted to do more, I wiped my mouth and shuffled into the living room, collapsing on the sofa and falling immediately asleep, sucked under.

When I woke, my eyes landed on the lit screen of my phone. Everything else was dark. I reached for it, trying to work up enough spit in my dry mouth to swallow. Hail was pounding the roof, wind buffeting the house. The violence of the storm seemed impossibly loud in the darkness. It was a text from June's family's lawyer. *May, you have a sizeable bequest from Brandon. Call me when you're able to discuss collection.*

Me? I checked, but it was my phone. Shouldn't it be June? Or her parents? I began to type back that he had our numbers mixed up when I heard something else beyond the din of hail and thunder.

In the dining room, something crashed. It hadn't been the text that woke me, or the storm. It'd been that: the sounds of things falling. I had the vague impression that it had been going on for some time – that I'd heard it half-awake and chosen to stay asleep as long as I could.

I paused, listening. Was June knocking things over? Silence for several long moments, and then the sound of metal hitting the kitchen floor. A long scrape.

I hurried through the house, stubbing my toe on a dining room chair that was pulled out as if waiting for a nighttime visitor. Hopping and cursing, I shoved it back into the table, only to see silhouettes on the floor. I lurched to the light switch and slapped it, but it didn't come on. The power was out. I turned my phone screen down to illuminate instead. Things were scattered on the floor –

random things, not even things that could logically have fallen to land where they sat. A single tennis shoe was under the chair I'd pushed in. A spatula was perched upright inside it. Rubber bands dotted the table. A bottle opener hung from the cord pull on the blinds. A stray library book sat on a chair, spine cracked open. Dishes littered the floor like children's toys.

For a moment I thought the hail had escalated to a tornado, but our windows were closed, doors shut, walls intact. This mess couldn't have been caused by the storm.

I hurried into the kitchen.

I bashed my hip against the drawer, which was all the way open.

"FUCK!" I yelled, dropping my phone and sinking to the ground. Right in the center of my existing bruise. "Fuck, fuck, fuck." I pressed it.

As the sharpness dulled, I looked around. I'd never seen the kitchen so dark. The storm raging outside was thick and heavier than night, and with the power out, not even the green numbers on the microwave clock lit the space.

"June?" I called.

Hail pummeled the house like hundreds of angry fists.

I stretched out my hands, feeling around me for my phone. Instead, my fingertips connected with something cold and metal. I explored its vague shape in the dark: the small hammer. I could picture its useless floral pattern. I set it aside and felt more. The cookie container, open, crumbled pieces rough and dry. Something soft and full: a couch cushion. Something warm and furry. I shrieked, and Pinky hissed at me for touching his tail.

"June?" I called again.

Where was my phone? What the hell was going on?

That's when I felt a faint breeze, a stirring in my hair. It was coming from behind me, pushing toward the living room. No, that wasn't quite right. It was coming from in front of me, pulling.

Reaching my hands above to keep from slamming my head on the bottom of the drawer, I knelt, then stood, pulling myself up along the island cabinets. Now the breeze was below me.

It was coming from the drawer.

I felt around it, timidly confirming that it was open. The current sucked at my fingers like a vacuum. I tested the bottom, the edges, the front corners, but the drawer was empty. How had everything fallen out when this breeze was sucking inward?

The middle was empty, the sides. I stretched towards the back, feeling for that far backing and the deepest corners, but my hand kept going, and kept going. My arm was in past my elbow before the bottom of the drawer just sort of dropped off, and my hand caressed empty space, truly empty, as if the space beneath my countertop went on forever, infinite and aching. I thought not of the eyeless, glowing fish in the ancient seas, not even of the gelatinous, Proterozoic sludge of the time before seas, but of the fathomless, unfathomable nothingness which our tiny, tidy little world forced itself into, compelling itself into time.

The current pulled harder. I jerked back my hand so fast I scraped my forearm from wrist to elbow.

A loud, dull thud came from the living room.

"June?"

No answer, just another thud. Several, steady, like a drumbeat. I didn't know why, but my heartbeat sped, double-timing within the rhythm of that sound. What was it?

Thud, thud, thud.

I lurched for my phone, feeling frantically along the floor, tossing aside random shit until I touched its smooth weight. I ran wide around the open drawer and hit the flashlight feature as I went.

Thud, thud, thud.

The sound was wetter now, becoming more of a smack.

My light found June sitting on the fireplace hearth, her back to the brick wall, spine tall and upright. She was pulling her head forward and slamming it back.

"*June.*"

She didn't even look to me. Her eyes were open, wide and glazed, a small smile on her lips as she continued forcefully driving her head back.

Whack.

Blood splattered in a fine spray with each hit.

"No!" I ran.

Whack. Whack. *Whack.*

I dropped my phone on the hearth and shoved my hands between her head and the brick to cushion her next blow, but it didn't come. She slumped forward, onto me. The up-light of my fallen phone showed an indistinguishable mass of ruin. The back of her head was a crater, a melted chasm. It wasn't even recognizable as a head anymore. A high, keening cry leaked from my throat.

Sobs wracking my core made it hard to hold my breath as I felt for a pulse.

Nothing.

I called 911. The hail had stopped. So had the wind. The operator's voice came out faint and tinny. "911, what's your emergency?"

The pull through the house was growing. I felt my body being sucked toward it, like a fish caught in a current. I stuttered our address as I veered into the kitchen. I put the operator on speaker and lowered the phone, flipping it over for the light. The frames were off the wall, one lying face down on the floor, the other balanced on a corner atop the side table.

"I need an ambulance," I shouted. I thought I'd already said it. I repeated it again. The operator continued to ask over-calm questions as I rounded the island and stood in front of the empty drawer. Was it empty? I lowered my phone, reaching it partway in, shining the light toward the back.

My phone was sucked from my hand. "June," I whispered, lost.

Its light went spinning, tumbling, falling an impossible distance. I saw it tumult for miles before it disappeared, obscured by a jumbled disarray of vague shapes, dark upon more dark, and were they moving?

The opening was big, so big, big enough to reach in past my elbow, past my shoulder.

It yawned, waiting, and I balanced forward on my toes, feeling metallic, feeling magnetic, feeling like a thousand little pieces of unrelated detritus, leaning over as I stared into its gaping maw.

BLUE

Follow me,
deeper,
where shades of purple
give way to hues of blue.

What's that?

Ah, yes.
You are very astute.

The distinction between colors
is a spectrum, a merging.
One intermingles with the other,
blended so,
and try as you may
to control them, darling,
you have to let them bleed.

No no, love. You
need not worry.
The mesh will hold
them in all the same—

while letting
their multitude of stories
infest our brains
through our ears.

You might be afraid,
tremble,
feel wavery on your feet;
but steady,
take my hand.

I will hold you
while they tell their tales.

I will protect you
while they whisper.

Shh, now.
    They begin.

THE CALL OF THE HOUSE OF USHER

> "In this unnerved, in this pitiable, condition I feel that the period will sooner or later arrive when I must abandon life and reason together, in some struggle with the grim phantasm, FEAR."
>
> –Roderick Usher

Strange! Undeniably strange and unpredictable that I would be here, now, dragging myself into this clean, brightly-lit kitchen in an ancient, decrepit house that was surely, almost certainly – possibly – never mine. I could not have foreseen it, but I look back so clearly, as if each step led undeniably and irrevocably to the next. As if I might have known, if only... ah, well. There is no use in that. Let me tell you how it began.

I was leaving the library at night after several hours of fruitless attempts to finish my long-belabored novel and having the building closed against me. The unfaltering fluorescence of the place pushed me into darkness, and as I walked to my car in dejected spirits, wondering if the work was perhaps ill-fated and never meant to be, I blinked.

Now, you may wonder at my telling you such a mundanity, but the blink is important here, as this was the first time I saw *Her*.

She came to me in the space before I blinked.

When I opened my lids, she was gone.

I could not have told you more than this, at that point, because there was no more. Simply a blink and Her passing before it. A vague sense of confusion and unease crept into my limbs like the beginnings of catalepsy.

It was nothing, at first, but it continued to occur over the next few weeks, and the recurrence of it began to sink into me. I would almost reach the point of forgetting about Her appearance, and then it would happen again. A blink. Her passing. The vague smell of stale dust. Questions bombarded me with their elusiveness: *What is this, and why can't I see Her fully? Why does she appear so fleetingly? What does she want?* I had no answers – have no answers still – only the dark blur of Her passing with the downsweep of my eyes.

I began to feel crazed with it.

As I attempted to go about my daily life, I found myself expecting Her appearance, yet she never came when I was ready – when I thought to trick Her into revealing herself. At times when she was at the forefront of my mind, I would squint slowly, hoping to maintain Her image, but she eluded me. I developed an odd sort of dread in Her coming. I feared Her.

I became strange, keeping my eyes open for as long as possible between blinks, hoping to ward Her off with my constancy.

Even my friends could not understand my pervading sense of dread, or my desire never to be left alone. They would lean in too closely, sometimes, and tell me I was getting carried away. When they were inches from me, I would blink, thinking to face Her with a witness present. But of course, she did not appear then. I was ready then.

She only came when I was alone.

I did not have to be in the solitude of my city apartment, although she often swept by there, appearing in my periphery as my eyelashes came into view, but disappearing before I could look – leaving only the elusive scent of dust in her place.

She was slow-moving, but fleeting. She was pulling at my hairs one by one, making the dryness of my eyeballs prick in anticipation, but she never came then. Anticipation wracked me.

I was mad with it.

My loved ones began to avoid me just as I avoided long empty stairwells. Somehow, I knew that she would chase me then, nipping at my heels and slinking along the flights above me in a dark smear, gaining as I ran.

I avoided parking garages, too, along with alleyways, empty fields, and swimming pools at night. She became the obscured shape beyond the shower curtain. The skin on the back of my neck. The billow of air behind the drapes. She was everything that frightened me, but hidden. The more I avoided Her – my eyes spread open like two biopsied tumors – the more she pursued me in the corners of things.

And I could not avoid my home forever.

Safe havens became a bane for me. Solitude is Her bedfellow. I sought the bright lights of 24-hour diners, the curious glances of bystanders, the ever-beating pulse of humanity. But they stared at my overly wide eyes, just like my friends. They turned away from the dryness of my refusal to blink. They whispered behind their hands, and she was there, too. She was just beyond the space they looked away from, hollowing me.

About this time, when my irrational (for that is what I told myself the fear was, in the light of day when reason seemed a possible feat once more) fear had taken hold of my sanity and begun pushing me to believe and do things that I would never have thought myself capable of, I got a letter by post. This was singular, as very few people use paper mail in these modern times, so I opened it with haste and was more than a little surprised at its contents, which read something thus:

> *Brother,*
>
> *You are wanted at the site of our family estate. I fear it lies in utter disrepair, but I doubt not that you possess the facilities and wherewithal to make it a source of family pride once again.*
>
> *I can picture you as you read this – pale, smooth brow furrowed in confusion even as your dark, dry eyes widen in disbelief; but I assure you it is true. We are indeed the last of the line of the House of Usher. Do not deny your lineage.*
>
> *Enclosed you will find directions to the estate, which lies some distance from your current home. I will be waiting for you here. Until then.*

The letter was unsigned and undated, and at first I dismissed it as some type of hoax. For you see, I was and have always been an orphan. I have no parents, sisters, or brothers to call my own.

So how then, could I receive such a correspondence? And yet, the speaker of the letter described me so accurately and had alluded to my ability to rehabilitate an old building. I was currently doing exceedingly well in the field of historical housing reconstruction. I checked the envelope again, and indeed, it was addressed to me.

A strange sort of hush fell over my apartment at this time, and I felt as though I were not alone. I whirled, half expecting to see the speaker of the letter standing behind me, but there were only shadows and the soft shifting of the vertical blinds as the fan sent wind around the room.

I could still feel eyes on me. *Her* eyes. I could not allow myself to blink. She would be there. Oh! She would be there!

With all of the false bravado I could muster, I spoke into the empty room. "Who are you?"

The blinds rustled. I clenched the letter in my fist.

"What do you want from me?"

I thought… I thought I saw something move from behind the long white lines of the blinds in front of the sliding glass door. Her.

She didn't speak – she never speaks – but I heard Her still. Not in words, but in knowledge. *Go*, it seemed to say, *or I will show you.*

"No," I groaned, clutching the letter to my chest, my eyes beginning to water. I would have to blink soon. I thought I smelled dust.

The blinds bulged outward, as if a human form was pushing forth, and I screamed.

"Stop! Please. I will go. Just leave me. Leave me!"

There was soft, metallic clinking as the strips fell back into place. I blinked, once, and they were as they had been – flat – with only the slight breeze of the ceiling fan shifting them back and forth.

I wish I could adequately describe to you the sense of doom I felt at my decision to obey this mysterious letter from a sibling I never had. In that moment, I had no choice. I was compelled by my own dread. Compelled to seek a fate that could only condemn me. I was forlorn.

In the days that followed, She did not return. I began packing my things. My friends could not understand my reasoning. "A change of pace," I told them, and in my slightly less harrowed mind, I began to believe myself. I saw that I had become deeply disturbed, that I was giving in to fears and delusions no grown man should suffer, and that they seemed to be rooted in *place*. Never mind that She had followed me everywhere. I simply needed something to believe, and at this point, "a change of pace" seemed sufficient.

Besides, country air has long been believed to aid ailing minds.

And country it was – wild, abandoned countryside that had not seen the tread of man for some time. It was with great difficulty that I made my way across the desolate terrain. Thankfully, I had only myself and my meager possessions to attend to.

I finally came upon the site described in the letter, and I almost turned back without pause. The choice of the word "disrepair" seemed generous, given the state of shamble and decay below.

I stood at the edge of a deep hollow – a valley, of sorts – at the bottom of which lay the remains of what I could only assume had once been the House of Usher. Which meant that the mucky gorge in which it lay must have once been the tarn indicated in the directions. If it had ever been full of water – which I found difficult to picture, as it had a mansion in it now – the water must have been the darkest shade of brown. Or perhaps gray, or a combination of the two, mired together with a strange phosphorescent green pulsing from within…

I blinked. Where had that image come from? I glanced out of the corners of my eyes, almost expecting to see the dark flash of Her, but there was none. She had not come to me since my decision to travel here.

The day was oppressively hot for mid-autumn, and even the rapidly-overtaking evening didn't bring relief. A bead of sweat fled down my forehead as I studied the destitute structure.

It was large and looming in spite of its location below me, and in its damaged lines I saw a gracefulness that might once have been stately, if not beautiful. Now it sat hunched in upon itself, like an animal that was broken but still deadly. Its simple stone façade was overspread with flora of a dismal green color, and an odor of dank rot emanated from the whole in a wave of heat as if the thing were *living*.

On either side of a wide, jagged split running the whole length of the façade were two glassless windows that gave the appearance of eyes.

As I stared down at them, they seemed to stare up at me. Blank, vacant, dark. Never blinking – like my own.

In one of them, I saw a faint movement of light. At first I supposed it to be Her. She haunted my eyes, why not the eyes of this building? But that, I realized, was an irrational thought. Nor did I have feelings of unease as I invariably did when she was around. I thought there must be someone within the fallen house.

I glanced around the perimeter of the gorge in hopes of spotting signs of my so-called sibling who promised to be waiting for me. I could now see the moon rising in the pale sky, as if a sliver of fingernail balanced on the dead, pointed branch of a gnarled tree. Night was falling. I knew I must go further or retreat.

Having in mind that brief glimpse of life within the dead eye windows, I decided to see if the writer of my letter was indeed within the dwelling.

As I descended the steep walls of the old tarn, I was surprised by the dryness of the dirt. The smell and appearance of moisture seemed to be a false one. By the time I made it to the half-open doorway directly in the path of the large fissure splitting the house in two, my nostrils were coated in fine dust.

I walked inside.

I was at once struck by the enormity of the space. The house was even larger within than it appeared to be from without. In spite of the cracked ceilings, walls, and floor, the arrangement of the vast entryway seemed orderly – as if the house had split and the inhabitants had fled, leaving the room untouched. A thick layer of pale dust covered almost every surface, but some trick of physics had left one thing clean near to gleaming on the far wall: a family crest.

I walked across the floor, careful not to step in the crack which looked deep enough to wrench an ankle, and stared up at the magnificent crest displayed in the place of prominence. It was whole, placed directly over the crack that split the wall. I knew not what held it in place. The image was crowned with the helmet of a knight, and above that scrolled the words, "The Ancient Arms of Usher." So I was at the correct place. The family must have been very old indeed to use the word "ancient" on an object that itself seemed to be so.

"Hello?" I called out. "Is anybody here?" My voice echoed around the building with surprising clarity, making me wince. "I have come based on a letter…"

I took another careless step forward when something at my foot caught my eye. It was some bundled shape, seeming almost to hover over the two-foot crack in the floor. I shifted my position to lean over it, attempting to decipher its form. I squinted into the dimness of the room, and all at once the shape made itself clear to me.

It was a corpse – no, two corpses. Lying together toe to toe, head to head, wrapped in one another's arms.

I thought to scream, but my breath was suddenly a noose at my throat. I widened my eyes, staring down at the dead balanced so precariously over the fissure.

It was a man and a woman. Obviously young in life, ancient in death. Something about the state of the air here – perhaps the lack of moisture, although I am no chemist – had preserved the corpses surprisingly well. Both were pale-complected, although the skin had withered with time. Both had airy raven tresses, although death had drawn them unnaturally thin at the decaying scalps. They each had coins placed over their eyes, which I found singular, as it implied that someone had found them here and chosen not to bury them.

But it was the woman who caught my eye. Particularly, her cheeks, which somehow gave the illusion of a slight flush, even after all these years. And her lips seemed curved into the subtlest of smiles, as though content to be wrapped in her lover's arms for eternity.

I found myself entranced by this. By her strange sort of smirk. By her long, curling hair. By her preservation.

I knelt at her side, unthinking, and reached out one hand to brush the pale pink that coated her cheek. The very tip of my longest finger scarcely brushed what I must have only imagined to be warmth when the whole of both corpses collapsed in on each other, toppling over the edge and into the fissure below. The flesh and clothes on them turned instantly to powder.

I was left kneeling there, my hand still held in mid-air as if to caress her cheek, blinking at the little poof of dust that reached my face, and staring at a pile of so many indistinguishable bones.

All I could see was one skull – hers based on the dark curls I could just make out against the dirt below – looking up at me with dark, hollow eye sockets like empty windows. The coins had fallen off, winking at me from the depths. I shuddered and stood abruptly.

What had I done? I was preparing to leave immediately, ashamed of my desecration at this strange place, when I saw the white sheet of paper taped to the inside of the front door. I walked over and pulled it down. It read thus:

Brother,

If you are reading this, you have made it safely to the House of Usher. Welcome! I am sorry to say that I have been called away. But I have prepared a room for you on the second floor, and although (as you can see) the house is in shambles, this particular room is nice enough to inhabit while you begin your restoration of the family estate.

Enclosed you will find the deed to the property; sign it and all is yours. Do not wait for me. I will return as soon as I can. Until then.

Again, it was unsigned and undated. Unable to resist my curiosity, I went up the grandiose staircase to see the room in question.

It was indeed a nice room, overly spacious, gothic, and unnervingly clean. As it suddenly began to rain, I decided that I would stay the night before heading home.

One night turned into many. I slept better here, in this ancient home I'd never known, than I had anywhere else I'd ever stayed.

Over the next few months, I did begin reconstruction of the estate, which cost me hundreds of thousands of dollars, but I had that money to spare and I soon grew passionate in my attempts to put the old mansion to its former magnificence – with some modern additions for comfort. My supposed sibling never returned, but neither did *She*, and as the project neared completion, I grew to like it here. I began to feel more like myself than I ever had before.

When the final stained glass window was installed and polished, the ultimate chandelier electrified and gleaming, the new kitchen completely modernized and galvanized, and the last floorboard mended and re-stained – the bodies left between the joists and boarded over – I sold my apartment in the city and signed the papers my "sibling" had left me.

The House of Usher was officially mine.

I felt at home. I was not just the owner of the house, but the rightful master. I walked down the stairway and the walls seemed to stand straighter in salute. I opened doors and entire rooms seemed to sigh in relief. I drew drapes closed and the fabric seemed to billow out to caress me in loving embrace.

I began to write again. The words came fervently, feverishly – as if in a dream. Every evening, I sat at a large oak table that I had restored into a desk and wrote for hours in one of the upper chambers. I came within pages of finishing my novel, my life's work. I was ecstatic.

And then things begin to change.

The words slowed, began hiding. I found myself restless and discontent. After a few nights of this block, I started moving about the estate, trying to find desks, counters, or fainting couches that would bring back the spark of creativity inside me. The doors that had once welcomed me now banished me from their presence. The stairs thrust me downward. The very carpets seemed to crawl underfoot, leading me to one place. A new place. The only place I'd yet to try writing.

A seat directly over the bodies under the floor.

Here, sitting ramrod straight against the hard-backed chair, I was able to write once again. But this time my progress was not met with relief and joy, as before, but rather with a bitter sort of weariness that I could not talk myself out of. Begrudgingly, I abandoned my spacious writing desk and returned to this uncomfortable spot in the middle of the main entry every night.

Days blurred by in a greasy smear. One night, I noticed that there was a small crack making its way down the wall with the family crest on it. I blinked, surprised that the new plaster had weakened so quickly, and She was there. Just beyond my periphery. A feeling. A whiff of dust.

"It is just the shadows," I told myself, but I put my writing away and moved the chair against a far wall.

But the next night, I returned. I had to; I could not write anywhere else. The crack in the wall had begun to split the gleaming floorboards. And it was no illusion. This time, I blinked and saw the dark flash of Her hair as she turned away.

Fool! I could have known. I should have known! I never should have signed the papers to this house. I would have done better to sign my soul to the devil – and perhaps I have! I should have listened to my sinking gut and *seen* that *She* was luring me here, that She would return.

Now I am alone here, destitute and stranded, and my beloved mansion has become what my loathed apartment once was: Her domain!

She comes to me in the space before I blink. When I open my lids, she is gone.

I do not know why I call her "She." A fall of hair? A glimpse of skirt? A flash of feminine smile? It is beyond me. My vision cannot reach Her.

She is not a ghost.

Ghosts are cold, pale things that long to be seen. She is darkness. She is the shadow behind the door as I turn to lock it, receding when I put light upon it. She is ever-taunting.

I quit writing. I quit blinking. My eyes begin to ache with a familiar dryness, like when the corpse dust puffed into them.

But when I sleep, she reaches me, like two long hands of smoke running through my hair. She brings me nightmares – terror of inconceivable means – but when I wake up, warm and sweating and shaky, she is gone before I can pin Her down.

I have stopped sleeping.

Insomnia is a dark, unnatural thing. I seek it frantically, as I sought Her in the beginning, before I learned to loathe Her. Before she ripped away my sanity when I wasn't looking.

But even insomniacs eventually sleep between heartbeats. That space is like the space between blinks, and she finds me. I am unprepared for Her – as she likes – so she tugs organs around in my body while it sleeps against my will. I awake screaming, and still I cannot see Her face.

I see more of Her, though.

Every visit, brief and shadowy, further cements the impression of Her in my mind. She runs quickly even as she paces solemnly by, Her skirt floating behind Her like a cape. But Her head always turns away as I look at Her, a wash of dark hair flinging me the vestige of dust before she dissolves and I am left trembling.

I cannot go on like this. My body begs for rest – demands it – but my heart tremors and rebels at the thought. It is too dark here. I begin to see Her in every corner of my overly large chamber. She awaits me beyond the flickering of every period-accurate, candle-lit sconce.

With one hand I pry my left eye open, the right closing in relief, and crawl on hands and knees from my room down the long, winding staircase that I helped to rebuild, across the beautiful floorboards that the bodies rest under, and into my contemporary kitchen – the shadow of Her nipping at my heels like a wave of air.

I reach tile. It is bright here. No shadows. I installed fluorescents in this room alone. But as my left eye twitches for moisture, my right catches glimpses of Her.

She is growing bolder.

The lights in the kitchen flicker, once, and I scream.

She cannot have me.

With my last ounce of strength, I force my eyes open wide like a lunatic and grab for the sharp, gleaming kitchen knife. When the steel shifts, she flashes through it, running, Her hair flipping around to cover Her face.

I can feel my eyes closing against my will.

Without another thought, I plunge the blade into my chest.

The dull hilt protrudes as I collapse on my side, my eyes finally closing for good, and I seek peace.

But there is dimness. She is here, no longer running.

She has no need to chase me anymore. I am Hers.

She turns, finally standing in the vision of my inner eyes, still. Her long, dark hair flares once more, and she is facing me.

Except she has no face.

There is nothing there but shadows, a pit of unknown where the pale oval of skin and blushing cheeks should be.

I try to scream, but I no longer have a body.

She has no mouth, but I hear laughing. She is still laughing, still smiling in Her faceless face as she approaches me slowly.

And I no longer have eyes to open.

THE BABY

At 4a.m. the bedroom was darker than the blackened crust on the bottom of my heart, scorched from an extra five minutes because someone didn't know how to use the goddamn meat thermometer. Things keep cooking when you take them off the heat. How do people still not know that?

The baby's crying woke me, which was weird because I didn't have a baby. I'd rather not completely wreck my vagina, thanks. I mean evolution only got so far as to not kill *most* of the women who squeeze a human out of their bodies. It's not like we have a clocksmith perfecting these things from above. I don't want to play the "take my chances" game with my favorite body part.

So I sat up and almost had the urge to elbow Cody and say, "Dear, the baby's crying. It's your turn," just because sitcoms really ingrain themselves in our minds and that's kind of what you say when you hear a baby crying at 4a.m., but at the same time, a wire of fear had wrapped itself around my waking mind and finally the thought broke through: *Where is the baby?* If it was so close its cries woke me up, it was like, what? In our house.

I sat up in bed, but Cody kept snoring. I thought somehow that was right. I thought he wasn't meant to hear it cry, only me. I thought that if I hadn't been there, the baby wouldn't have cried at all. I slid my phone off the nightstand and pushed the button so I could use the small light of the screen, slipping out of our bedroom and closing the door behind me.

The crying was small and shrill but desperate, winding itself up and out of some distant hiding spot, with a faint gurgling sound behind it like the baby was so worked up it might actually scream itself to death. It must've been right outside the house. On the front porch, maybe? I pictured those old movies, half-expecting to see a basket with a bow on the handle sitting by our door, but the steps were empty and the crying as distant as ever.

Despite my vague anger at this nuisance and my small, thumping fear at the strangeness of it, concerned panic began to build in me. I followed my ears like a hunting hound, searching out this infant as if it were my prey. I didn't know what I wanted to do with it. I did want the crying to stop.

I ran around the house willing the sound closer, room to room opening doors and listening for a volume surge, but there was none. The baby remained distant as a night bird, muffled behind barriers, and Cody still didn't rouse. Finally, my leg veins thrumming with heat and my head pounding and tears working themselves up behind my eyes, I rushed into the kitchen and started flinging open cabinet doors. The top row over the stove. The two half ones over the fridge. The glass-front set where we displayed our wedding china. Then the bottoms. Under the sink. Beside the oven. And finally, under the peninsula.

The cry blasted me, echoing out and up, a shrieking peel of unhappiness so raw and ruddy and pure that something inside tweaked my spine and made me gasp. Despite my hands flinging themselves forward to help, I stepped back, peering into the shade inside the cabinets.

What the hell was in there? I mean fuck, there couldn't just be a baby inside my kitchen cabinets. It didn't make any sense. But the scream was distinctly coming from inside, right behind the shadow line. I clenched my fists at my waist and stepped back again, ducking my head slightly to see better. The crying grew to a near-breathless wail so violent the baby would surely choke. The baby would surely die. The baby, was it a baby?

I saw it then, propped awkwardly in the far back corner beside our toaster. I saw it bundled tight with a fat red face, eyes clenched, skin peeling, mouth open in that terrible, demanding cry. And then all at once I was invisible fire, heaving, wings and bosom and vinegar so crisp it'd make your eyes water, but you can't say shit like that in prose. Sorry.

I was out of my body or some crap. That's better. For just a second I thought this was a poem.

"Cody," I said, holding the infant tightly to my chest—it wouldn't shut up unless I held it tightly to me—and slipping back into bed. "Cody."

"Uh?" he grunted, shifting in the dark.

"I found a baby."

Silence.

"Cody, wake up. Did you hear me? I found a baby."

Finally, he rolled and pushed up onto his elbows. I couldn't see but could picture his face scowl-squinting at me. "What Jess?"

"I found a baby. In the kitchen. It was crying, but it's finally stopped."

He flipped on the lamp on his nightstand, illuminating his messy bed-hair and my blue nightshirt and the little bundle that clutched at me ferociously even in sleep. "You found a baby?"

I lifted my arms slightly, like I was offering up the thing, but it clung, breath hitching into a pre-wail hiccup, so I drew it tight again, nodding. "Do you think we should keep it?"

Cody scrubbed his face with his hands. "I thought you didn't want kids."

"I didn't want to *have* kids. This one is so small though. And it was crying. I think maybe it's ours now. We should keep it."

He sat all the way up and peered down, squinting at it. The lamplight was golden, highlighting the tiny feathery hairs on its head, making them glisten like gilded thread. Cody reached out a hand, cradling that soft, lumpy head, and the baby sighed, nuzzling into it. Jealousy spiked through me, hot and curdled, and I wanted to smack away his arm. Bite him. He hadn't done anything to make this child! Neither had I, but I'd found it, at least. I'd pulled it out of the cabinet. If it had been up to Cody he would've slept through the ruckus and the baby probably would've been gone by morning. I sucked in a breath, then adjusted my positioning just enough to get Cody to withdraw his hand.

Finally, tiredly, he asked, "Is it a boy or a girl?"

"It's a girl," I said softly, though I could just as easily have said *It's a boy* and nothing would have changed. The answer to that is not nearly so important as the question.

Nothing'll burn your heart worse than a friendship falling apart. Don't let anyone tell you otherwise. Kiara and I had smelled like fresh-from-scratch cookies baking. Warm and soft and buttery, then someone had left us in the oven too long. Fluffy on top but blackened on the bottom. Ruined, and leaving a stench that infused the next ten things cooked there.

I hadn't visited her in almost a year. I'd seen her around, but we hadn't intentionally set up any dates for months. It was no coincidence that the last time I'd been to her house had been when we'd had the closest thing to a fight we'd ever had. Children had been the subject. Birth. Babies. Motherhood and what it means to be a woman.

As I knocked on her door, my baby swaddled tightly to my torso, I could taste the charred flakes of my heart-crust, ashes in the back of my throat.

Even before Kiara answered, I could hear her inside. Little kids yelling and her telling them to clean up their toys with that false patience that thoughtful mothers use when they know someone else is listening. Then she opened the door, shoving a lose braid behind her ear.

"Jess," she said, genuinely surprised. "Hi."

"Hey. I hope this isn't a bad time."

I watched her eyes drop to my baby. "Not at all. Who's this?" she asked in that high-pitched voice you use for dogs and babies who can't talk yet.

A name. Damn, I'd forgotten about that. "Susan."

"Hi Susan," Kiara cooed. She straightened, giving me a smile clearly covering bewilderment, and stepped to the side. "Come in. It's great to see you."

"You too," I muttered, catching my toe on the entryway rug.

"Watch your step," Kiara called as she shut the door behind us.

Clutching Susan to me, I studied the house. It was exactly how it had been a year ago, but messier and covered in twice as many toys. She'd had kids then. Two, I think, but now there were at least three of them running around, maybe four; they never stayed in one place long enough for me to count them.

She hustled me efficiently into the living room, throwing two decorative pillows across the room and gesturing to the couch. I felt her eyes scanning me, studying my body for baby weight or heavy breasts. She'd seen me in the past nine months. Several times. Surely she would have noticed if I was pregnant? But I've always been small-framed and a sloppy dresser, opting for Cody's oversized sweatshirts instead of blouses from the petite section, so maybe it was possible that I'd been pregnant and she missed it. Some women don't show that much until the very end. It was possible. I sank into her lumpy gray couch with a sigh, adjusting Susan in her sling.

"Can I get you anything to drink?" Kiara asked. "No sir. Not in your father's office," she snapped, peering as if she could see through the wall.

"Sure," I said. "Some water would be great." Neutral. Clean. Unlaced with caffeine or liquor or any other questionable substance. No clues for Kiara.

"Ice?"

"No thanks."

She nodded, as if suddenly remembering that I've always hated ice, and pattered into the kitchen.

Our fight had been a quiet one. She'd been teasingly pressuring me to start having kids for two years—since she'd sloughed out her first one—and I'd been wryly dodging the topic, cracking jokes about everything from diaper rash to my tiny, nearly non-existent breasts dooming me to parental neglect, until she'd just sort of corned me one time. I'd made an off-color comment about narrow hips and a gloriously tight pussy that I'd like to hang on to, thanks, and Kiara had said, "What do you think vaginas are *for*, Jess?"

"What?" I'd realized too late that I'd unintentionally implied that she was all stretched out now, which probably hurt because it was true, or she was worried it was, and now she was going to say whatever she'd been holding back.

"If not for giving birth, what do you think vaginas are for?"

I stared at her, my mouth hanging open like a cartoon character, and then rage sizzled through me like the forerunners to orgasm: hot and building and promising violent relief. "Um, sex?" I snapped. "I think vaginas are just super great for having sex."

"Yes," she drawled, as if she'd trapped me. "And what exactly do you think *sex* is for?"

Well damn. She had trapped me. The anger seeped from me. "Fun," I said, but there was no heat left, no building release.

"Sure, fun is great. But obviously sex is for babies. Procreation is, biologically speaking, the only reason we're alive, Jess. It's what we're genetically programmed for. It's the single thing we strive for as a species. It's the whole reason we desire sex in the first place."

She'd hit something. Something tight and coiled. I had no real energy left to argue, but I said, "I don't know. I think I desire sex because it's fun. Because I'm a grown woman and the world is overpopulated already and I still want a fulfilling sex life."

"No sex life is fulfilled until there are children. I'm sorry, but it's true. The sexual life cycle of a woman includes birth. It just does. With no pregnancy, no offspring, the cycle is incomplete and the woman never reaches biological maturity."

I feel that everything she's said is true. I feel it like the coils in an oven, but my pilot light's out. Whatever biological piece that wants a baby is missing from me. Broken. Never there in the first place. That little niche in my body is hollow.

"Okay, Kiara. You're right. I'm selfish and immature for not wanting to destroy my perfectly healthy, sexually unfulfilled body."

"Jess, I didn't mean—" She never did finish. We'd both realized what we'd done. We'd spoken too clearly of fears and judgements. If this were a poem, it would dangle without punctuation. It would thrust you to the end of a strophe and shove you off the edge.

I stood up and walked

Kiara and I were no longer close enough for her to pry me for details. Instead we did a delicate waltz of her trying to gather information and me artfully side-stepping it. Finally, she landed on impersonal things I couldn't avoid.

"How old is Susan?"

Four days—straight from the cupboard. I had no idea. "Almost nine months," I said.

"Oh. Well, she's very small for nine months." Kiara tried to peer at Susan's face, which was buried against my chest as always. "Would you mind if I hold her?"

No. No, no, no. That rage. Hot and acrid like smoke off lava, cresting. But how could I decline?

"Of course," I murmured, gently working my hands between Susan's hot little body and mine, trying to pull her away.

The moment air swirled between us, she screamed. She opened her little tiny mouth with its little tiny lips and wailed—that same panicked, nerve-exploding sound she'd been making inside the cabinets. I hesitated, unsure if I should press her back to me or hand her over to Kiara anyway, but Kiara held out her hands as if the screaming didn't faze her, so I pried Susan off me, passed across the empty space how you'd pass a box of books.

Kiara flipped her over, on her back, and more rage built. That's not how you hold Susan. You barely hold Susan; she clings to you primitively, like a howler monkey. But Kiara cradled her upside down in her arms as if this were a nursery rhyme, and Susan continued to shriek, her tiny raw fists punching.

"It's okay, sweet girl," Kiara cooed. "I've got ya. It's okay."

Susan cried, working up into hiccuping gasps.

Kiara glanced at me, then quickly away, embarrassed. Good. She should be. It was my baby, not hers. Of course she didn't know how to soothe her.

"How long have you been breastfeeding?"

Oh, she wasn't embarrassed for her; she was embarrassed for me. She thought I wasn't a good mother. She thought I had done something here—hadn't done something. Some vital piece of my motherhood was missing.

I reached out my arms, and Kiara pretended not to be hurt as she handed Susan back to me. I didn't want her. As her angry, vicious little face came toward me, I suddenly didn't want her, but I took her anyway. Too late now. Susan came to me with shaky little gasps, clutching, burying her face into my skin. The crying ceased. Breastfeeding? None. I had no milk.

"All nine months," I murmured stroking the back of her soft, misshapen head.

"Jess," Kiara drawled, softening her tone. "I think she might have attachment issues. It happens all the time," she added quickly, "to all new mothers. But I know a really wonderful doctor. Have you been to see a doctor? Let me give you the number."

And then she was up looking for a notepad and Susan and I were falling off a cliff, trailing down a line of iambic pentameter that was supposed to rhyme but turned out to be enjambment, the rhyme there but buried, no punch to it.

I wasn't sure why I went to see Dr. Tresser, but I did. I told the receptionist the appointment was for "Jess and Susan," and I didn't give her a last name because generally in stories people don't really get last names. Except doctors. They don't get first names.

The receptionist looked at me over his half-moon glasses and then down at Susan, clinging to me right under my breasts, her face hidden from the world and even from me, like it was all too bright and colorful for her.

"Dr. Tresser will be with you in a few minutes," he said. "Please have a seat."

Right as I lowered myself into one of the oddly square chairs, the door to the waiting room opened and the same man called, "Jess and Susan?"

Sighing, I rose and followed him down a miniature maze of hallways until he pointed at a sign that said *1* and ushered me in. "Please put on the gown with the opening facing front," he said, gesturing to the soft square of fabric folded on the examining table. "Dr. Tresser will be with you in a moment."

Before I could tell him that this appointment was for Susan, not me, he closed the door.

Getting on the gown was difficult. Susan shrieked the whole time I set her on the table, on her back with her arms and legs up, flailing. The skin of my stomach felt cool where her hot little body usually clung. I leaned over her as close as I could while still changing clothes to try to soothe her, but she didn't stop until I picked her back up. She grabbed me fiercely, clutching, practically burrowing into the opening of my gown until all was silent and, finally, the doctor came in.

Dr. Tresser was a thin man, but strong. His face was smooth for a man of his age, his hair feather light, the color of burnt honey, his hands large but soft. He wore wireless glasses and a white lab coat over a plush brown sweater and charcoal slacks. His voice matched him perfectly.

"Hello, Jess. How are you and Susan today?"

I wrapped Susan in my arms, glancing down at the top of her pinkened head. "A little distraught, it seems."

"Well now," he soothed, coming closer, peering at Susan. "Let's take a look, shall we?"

He hadn't even asked me what the problem was. Yet he pulled her from me with sure hands, and Susan began wailing. "Yes, I know," he murmured, turning his back to me to place her on a little metal scale. "I know."

Over his shoulder he added, "Jess, go ahead and climb up onto the table if you don't mind."

I did as he asked, listening to Susan's siren going off, loud and brittle in the small, cold room. I heard him moving aside her swaddling clothes. I'd never opened them. "Let's just… Oh. Oh, I see. I do see."

Panic butterflied in my chest. What did he see?

He turned to me, his eyes gentle and kind. "You've had a rough go of it, haven't you, momma?"

Tears coated my eyes and I nodded.

He pulled open a drawer, took out an orange bottle, and shook out two pills. He gave them to me with a small paper cup of water. "This will help," he assured me.

I didn't want to, but I took them.

I woke to Susan's cries. My body felt cold and fuzzy. I tried to shift to a more comfortable position, but my arms were stuck. I lifted my head and squinted my eyes; I was strapped to the examining table. My arms were bound by leather straps. My gown was still on, thin and draped over my tented knees, my ankles bound to the stirrups. A final strap held me in place under the chest.

At the foot end of the table, which still seemed a very long distance away—I realized it was a very long distance away. I wasn't at the edge of the table like I would've been at a normal well-woman checkup. Some sort of surface extension had been pulled out to make a veritable runway of empty, paper-lined space—stood Dr. Tresser, cradling a blood-red, shrieking Susan.

"Don't worry, Jess. I've done this procedure countless times. It's always frightening for new mothers, but your body knows what to do. Little Susan here knows what to do, don't you dear?" He bounced her against him and she wailed even louder, the small drawn oval of her mouth nearly cracking at the corners.

Vinegar-sharp tears stung my eyes. Wings beat inside my chest. My limbs all strained, shaking the table but not budging my straps. My eyes roved wildly, searching the square ceiling tiles.

Dr. Tresser set Susan at the end of the table.

"No," I whispered.

Despite being scarcely strong enough to hold up her own head, she began to crawl. Or really, she began to squirm and drag herself, the paper lining crinkling.

"No," I said, louder.

I regretted opening the cabinet. I could have gone back to bed, pretended it was coming from outside. I could have drowned her, stuck her in the freezer.

Instead, I had gendered her, given her a name.

Susan's shrieking dulled into a whining little trail as she worked to pull herself closer. Dr. Tresser stayed at the end of the table, smiling. "She's a fighter, that one. Very good. Very strong for her size."

I thrashed again, tears trailing down my neck.

Susan squinted, shrinking nakedly against the cold brightness of the room, dragging and shoving her way across the rough paper, the hard table. It was supposed to be padded, but the pleather beneath the paper was pulled too tight to feel cushioned. Everything in this office was unfriendly.

As the final sound from my little Susan trailed into silence, as she approached nearer and nearer to the space between my quivering thighs, I began to scream.

I lost sight of her small head beneath my gown. I felt her tiny little breath on my skin as she crawled, determined, into my cradleadge, where everything is warm and wet and soft and dark, and how I wish this were a poem.

CHURN THE UNTURNING TIDE

Pregnancy changes everything. Every damn thing. Not just in the obvious ways, breasts and belly and hips expanding. My actual ribcage is spreading open. My face is softer. My joints are more elastic. From fuller, shinier hair all the way down to widening feet with sudden plantar warts, every part is changed in some way.

My feet ache enough that I have on orthopedic shoes even for the walk across the waterpark to set my bag on a lounge chair. I'm late on purpose, because my friend isn't coming today to grant me a protective social bubble. I squint across the broad expanse of white concrete, scanning the bright blue water of the large wave pool.

The fifty-some-odd attendees, almost exclusively over fifty years old except for me, are already scattered throughout the fan-shaped pool doing their warmup laps. The waves are on gentle, a constant roll emanating from the deep end. I shuck my maternity coverup and shoes, grab my giant sun hat, and hurry to get a noodle. We use the white foam pool toys as props that help us float or provide resistance. I get the last one and wade into the cool water, which feels blissful on a hot June morning like today. I inhale in relief as I get deeper, the water taking some of the weight of my bump, easing the pressure points on the pads of my feet.

I head in against the gentle tide, eager to focus and get a good workout from it. Before the extra thirty pounds of pregnancy, I was very fit. I never would've been welcome here back then, young and trim, but now I'm embraced into the fold like a long lost relative. Not quite one of them, but also no longer not one of them.

I come up on a hind cluster of ladies as I head deeper, and although I try to keep my head down under the shade of my hat, one of the women notices me and smiles sweetly. "When are you due, my dear?"

I suck in a breath and smile back. "Just a couple of weeks."

Her smile broadens, her yellowed teeth gleaming in the refractions of the chlorinated water. "Do you know what it is?"

I can't help it; my smile broadens too. I nod. "A girl."

"Wonderful," she says, sounding equal parts honest and disappointed. "Good for you."

"Thanks," I mutter, turning my head up to the sky for something to look at. Deep, rich, Texan blue: clouds smearing the distance like fierce omens. The air today is electric. Could be an afternoon storm setting itself up. But everyone seems to feel it. The buzz of the women chatting ahead of us is louder than normal, even, an almost startling clash of laughter and outcries and vocalized confessions forced loud under the breath.

The woman takes the hint and parts to the side, leaving me to push through the current. My shins already ache; I wonder if I'll get the famous varicose veins of late pregnancy. Each new side effect I get is one that will potentially never go away. They have that knack. Get spider veins once and they'll linger off and on for your whole life. Relentless time, steady belmishes. It occurs to me, looking at the women scattered around me, that this is how most of them came to look the way they do.

They're decked out in every color and pattern imaginable. Black, tropicals, pastels, neons, solids, and prints. Florals, stripes, polka dots, geometrics, animal prints, watercolors, and more. They, like me, have on sun protection in the form of UV shirts, glasses, dorky swim skirts, and hats of every variation. Broad-brimmed floppy numbers, ball caps, visors, and fishermen's style with the flap hanging down to cover the back of the neck. Strings tied under the chin, elastics in the hair, or gravity-defying balance at jaunty angles. Others opt for bare, over-tanned shoulders and brightly dyed hair glistening in the sun. There are wrinkled décolletages, skin browned, blued, and spotted with time and elements, neck waddles, oversized noses, large moles, and heavy arm flabs waving in the open air.

They never stop moving. When they stay in one spot, they bounce and jog in place, churning the water with their noodles arcing side to side, their knees bobbing up and down as they have loud conversations over the splash. Right now, about half of the group is to the sides of the shallower end of the wave pool, using the concrete edge to do assisted pushups.

I go deeper than most of them and do ten wide-stance pushups with my belly bump dipping in and out of the water, then ten tricep pushups for good measure. The cackling and shrieks of the group echo across the whole park. Maybe they're amped up because it's Friday? I can't imagine that it'd matter to most of them, though. Surely the majority are retired and don't much care which day of the week it is.

As I pause to stretch my arms, another woman catches my eye. "And how are you?" she asks.

"Good thanks."

"No friend today?"

I smile. "Not this time."

"How long do you have?" she asks, not needing to clarify.

"About two weeks."

"Oh my," she says. "Do you know what you're having?"

"A girl."

"Your first?"

"Yes."

She smiles, nods, turns away. "They change everything," she adds, almost not even to me.

At some unspoken signal, the women spread out, clumped in pairs and small groups as they claim their area for the bulk of the class. I use the wall to get even farther in, wanting my customary back corner. I'm tall enough to need the deeper end to keep my whole body submerged—necessary for the bouncing type of moves we tend to do there. Momma doesn't jump on land anymore.

Despite having to brush past a few ladies, no one else tries to chat with me. It isn't until I finally stand still and look up that I fully register how rowdy the girls are today. Maybe it's being all clustered in one big pool instead of spread among the length of the lazy river, which we sometimes use instead. Maybe it's Friday. Maybe it's the storm clouds in the distance lending the electricity to the bright yellow heat of the morning. They bob and churn like the bubbles in a pot, a vibrant clash of energy and gossip.

"…no it's my knee. I have to stretch it every day or it's so stiff I can't move it when I wake up."

"…he doesn't really need to keep working. She just can't stand having him home all day. On Tuesday he said…"

"…making a huge batch of cookies so I have extra to take to the party."

I jog gently in the deep, wedged between the side of the wave pool and the buoyed rope that sections off the deepest end where the waves emanate from. Beside me, on one of the flat-topped white and red buoys, I spot a tiny toad. He's no bigger than my thumbnail, balanced precariously on the foam, his bumpy back looking dry and fragile in the sun. My grandmother's voice echoes from my childhood, chastising, *Put that thing down, it'll give you warts.*

I crane my neck to look at the ledge above me, high enough to keep the waves in when they're turned up. That out of reach, there's nowhere safer for me to set the little guy. I can't imagine how he made it all the way here.

In my periphery, at the head of the pool centered above the roped off portion, I see shifting legs and sneakers. I glance up, squinting against the sun to see a new instructor. He's tall, lanky, scruffy in a charming way. He has on athletic shorts and a LIFEGUARD t-shirt, plus a blue visor that dents his poufy, curly hair. His beard and hair connect to form a dark cloud around his tan face; equally dark hair shades his wiry legs and arms, corded with muscle. He holds a bright green pool noodle and a big white megaphone that he raises to his mouth.

"Alright everybody, how we feeling?"

The women let out a raucous cheer. He grins, a brilliant flash of white teeth in his rich beard. I think I've figured out the source of the extra buzz today. Fresh blood. The other instructors we've had so far this summer have been young women, one good and two ambivalent, plus one guy who was sweet but kind of a dink. This guy is different.

I study him, and I think styles really do cycle back around. He looks like he could be straight out of the seventies or eighties, young when most of these women were young. He reminds me of pictures of my dad and his friends back when they were my age. These gals' type, I would think.

"Good to hear!" he booms through the speaker. "Everybody warmed up?"

A chorus of yeses and whoops. They love that he's playing them like a crowd. The other instructors never do that.

"Let's go then," he chants, voice carrying easily out over our heads. "What we're gonna do first is take the noodle in both hands out in front of you and push it forward and back in front of you as you do butt kicks. Heels all the way to your butt, as fast as you can. The deeper you hold your noodle, the more of a challenge it'll be."

He sets down the megaphone and mimes an out-of-water version of the exercise. I'm surprised and a little impressed by how unselfconscious he seems. He's probably my age or a bit younger, which isn't an age known for not caring. Even ten months ago I might've felt totally different if I'd been here with him instructing. I'd have thought about how dorky my long-sleeved sun shirt is, how unflattering my maternity swimsuit underneath is on my shape, the incongruity of my presence among the older group, and how generally lame it is to do water aerobics. The only reason I don't care now is that pregnancy has knocked it straight out of me. You can't be young and attractive when you're carrying a bowling ball. The bowling ball gets the youth; she happily sucks it out of you. It's a mixed blessing. Freedom from the constant pressure to look this way, act that way, yes, but also a loss of resources, a reduction in status.

So I don't care, just like all of these women, which leaves me in a bizarre and fascinating position to analyze why *he* doesn't care. Young and cute, most guys would be dragging their feet at least a little to teach this class. Just that confident, maybe. Maybe he thinks it's all a joke, but it doesn't seem like it. He seems genuinely cheerful to be here, and as he switches us to our next exercise and then our next, it becomes apparent that he's actually good at this. Far better than the other instructors so far. He doesn't stall or kill time with stupid filler moves that are too easy even for the frailest among us. He keeps us moving quickly from one thing into the next, each a decent amount of work. It's the first time my heart rate's really been up in class the whole summer.

The buzz from the ladies increases. They, too, have their heart rates up as they churn the water white with effort. They never quit talking and laughing and calling out answers to his megaphone questions. They stop shy of catcalling or flirting the way a group of younger women might. They're too old for such tactlessness. Not that they need to care. They care even less than I do what he thinks of them. Their chatter isn't overt or overtly secretive, but I sense that it's largely about him nonetheless. I wonder if he feels it, their hungry attention. Cheerful, buoyant, eager. They've been waiting for someone like him.

I notice him gesture to one of the inconspicuous lifeguards off to the side before he raises his speaker again, aims it out across the water. "Now you're going to put your noodle between your legs to float, bicycle with your feet and breaststroke with your arms. Try not to touch the bottom. All the way from one side to the other and back!"

Keenly, the women climb onto their noodles like water horses and begin paddling across. I check my tiny toad friend and make sure he's okay before I start across, the noodle bumping out far in front of me because of my belly. I hug the buoy rope, skirting only the women who don't first move to avoid me. Most of them do, though. Pregnancy trumps age when it comes to hindrance; they've had more time to get used to theirs—a more gradual decline.

As I stroke my way across the pool, I keep looking up to see what the new guard's being called over for. I can't put my finger on it, but something about the way the instructor got his attention and speaks to him in a low voice, megaphone down, makes me think it's vaguely secretive.

I'm not the only one who notices. Nothing catches attention quite like someone trying to avoid attention.

The buzz of the women turns slightly softer as they run out of breath from exertion and continue, as I do, to watch the unfolding interaction with the new guard. He's younger, blonder, tanner, more muscular, and less appealing. He looks hairless and of a new generation. He doesn't flirt with the women with smiles and dimple-winks. In fact, he avoids them altogether as he crosses back toward one of the buildings and disappears.

I touch the far side and begin paddling back, dodging grannies. I wonder if maybe our instructor dude is a head guard and the other guy got in trouble or something.

By the time I'm back to my spot—the toad is still there—the younger guard has come back out with one of those incredibly long pool nets used to scoop stuff from the water. He's trailed by three other young guards, one guy and two girls, all in red swimsuits.

The women begin to mutter and mumble, asking amongst themselves if anyone knows what's in the water or what's going on. I have the distinct feeling, as I'm sure do all of them, that we're not being told something.

"Nice job everyone!" he calls through the speaker. "Next up, we're going to do some crunches. Lean back on your noodle, and try to bring your legs up to your chest, like this. If you need support you can back against a wall."

He instructs and illustrates as the young male guard begins sweeping the net into the deep end beyond the buoys. I strain my neck, trying to see what might be there, but it's in the middle, far from my side.

One of the ladies calls out extra loudly, "What's in the water?"

The young guy looks up at our instructor, obviously afraid to answer. Whatever it is, I have a bad feeling. Their unwillingness to tell us makes me think they think we're going to panic if we know, which makes me wonder if we should be panicking.

"Now twist with your crunches," he says, angling the megaphone the other direction to repeat, "Now twist!"

We do, watching the cluster of young guards staring down at something the blond kid is trying to scoop out. Two more guards come from the building to watch.

A louder woman calls out, "What's over there?" Her voice is undeniable; she must be answered. The mood has shifted from simple curiosity to the beginnings of discontent at being ignored.

Finally, our instructor answers her, calling down not on his megaphone, but in his strong voice. "It's a tarantula."

I hear a single gasp in the very back, near the shallows, but everyone else laughs or sighs and begins chatting again.

"Is it alive?" someone asks.

A woman in the front center, who can see what's going on, answers, "Yep, it's just floating there. Got stuck, I guess. It can't get out."

"Better than that time they found a dead rat," one woman faux-mutters. She's the one who always talks too loud and pretends to lower her voice while still making sure she's heard by everyone. "Just floating by the drain in the lazy river a couple weeks back. Big old thing."

"Be careful with it," another calls up to the cluster of young guards. From where I do my careful crunches, legs wide to leave room, I can't see the tarantula in question. "They have very delicate legs!"

I nod my agreement, glancing again at the teeny toad, still

holding strong. Tarantulas can't really hurt you, and they're cool and beautiful and surprisingly fragile. I hope these young guards handle it with care. I'm afraid they won't.

I'm insulted by their assumption that we'd be scared enough to cause trouble just by its presence in the whole wide pool. They're the ones who look nervous, laughing and jumping as they ineffectually try to scoop it into the net.

Our instructor switches us to leg presses, holding the noodle underwater with just one foot, and quietly talks to the teens, getting them to be serious and make a real effort to scoop the spider carefully.

"Okay," he calls through the speaker. "Now lifts to the back. One leg at a time. If you need balance, grab a wall."

One of the young male guards tickles one of the girl's necks and she shrieks. Our instructor sets down the megaphone yet again, something of his charm leaking away as he chastises them. He takes the net from the blond guy and shoos them away. Then he silently fishes into the deep end, his movements slow and careful until the ladies in the center let out a little cheer and he raises the net out of the water.

I glimpse a dark, round spot that must be the spider clinging to the white webbing. Poor thing. I hope the chlorine won't hurt it.

"You should hold it," a disembodied voice from the opposite side of the pool calls up. "They hardly ever bite!"

Our instructor pauses, then grins as he walks his hands down the long pole extension toward the net. "Yeah right," he says without his mic. "*You* should hold it."

"You *should*," someone else calls, sounding offended. "Take it out of the net. Don't just drop it on the ground."

Several women raise their voices in agreement, croaking out commands and cheers and something perilously close to taunts.

The instructor's white smile slips back into his beard, but he does continue walking his hands toward the net end of the pole, creeping closer and closer to the dark fuzzy spot. If I can see it all the way from here, it must be a pretty big tarantula.

"Jog in place," he calls out, his voice almost lost over the growing murmur of the women. A filler exercise. Not his style so far. A little disappointing.

A woman near me echoes, "What?"

"Jog in place," another snips at her. "Just keep moving." But it's not the one hard of hearing she's annoyed with; it's him. He's leaving us hanging.

"Scoop it out," comes that voice on the far side again. Raspy and deep, maybe a smoker. "With your hand. Scoop it with your hand!"

A small chorus of consent rises. Some of the storm clouds cross the sun, sending a slight gray over the wave pool. The water is no longer white, but blue. People aren't moving much. We're all watching the young man as he carefully lets the end of the pole drop so he can hold the rim of the net instead. The spider is clinging not to the bottom, but one side.

The cluster of young lifeguards are barely visible clinging to the side of the building much like the spider, watching from around the corner like kids sent to bed early before a holiday.

I jog in place, holding my belly, pulse high.

"Jumping jacks," the instructor calls out, and we switch motions.

"Pick it up," a woman cries, like a chant, and says it again. "Pick it up!"

But instead of joining the phrase, the other women begin to call out other things. They agree, but they don't need a chant. "Scoop it out," they call.

"Hold it!"

"Let it crawl onto your fingers."

"Pick it up!"

I shrink back against the wall, still doing underwater jumping jacks, not bringing my arms overhead because I don't want the splash to disrupt my view. I feel breathless. Not unusual with my diaphragm crammed up under my ribcage, but it doesn't usually happen in this class.

The handsome young instructor carefully draws the tarantula out of the net, balancing it on the palm of his large hand.

The ladies cheer. Not the same cheer as when he asked how they were feeling or if they were ready for the next thing. A different cheer. A cheer made of smoke and moonlight and a lifetime of corrosion.

The instructor lets a small, close-lipped smile spread his beard, but he looks nervous. He begins walking toward the greenery at the edge of the concrete.

The graceful legs of the spider cling to his hand, nothing more than a blur from my corner. The clouds shift again and the intensifying sun blasts us all with fresh heat.

A small woman, the one with arms so thin they look like bones draped in skin, calls softly into a sudden silence: "Eat it."

There's a group pause, a silence broken only by the sounds of water lapping and swaying, as every single person in the wave pool waits for a reaction.

The instructor looks at us with wide eyes, hunched with his own hand far away from himself, as if he can hold the spider at bay. He says nothing.

"Yeah," a different lady calls, one of the more middle-aged ones. "They're a delicacy in some parts of the world. Good for you, even!"

"It probably won't make it after a dip in this chemical water. You might as well."

"Go ahead! We won't tell."

"Eat it!"

"Eat it!"

"Have a snack!"

High peals of laughter chime out like gleeful bells. I press my palms flat against the high wall behind me. My noodle floats in front of me, forgotten.

I can't tell if they're joking.

He can't either.

The women don't break into a chant, don't taunt him, don't jeer. They simply explode into delighted, wild conversations about the types of bugs and animals you can eat. Times they saw spiders in their houses and cars. Recipes that call for unusual things. How they're tired of cooking over a hot stove in this crazy summer heat.

But they don't take their eyes from him.

The young man reaches the bushes, begins to squat, his back partially to us, almost fully to me, so that all I can see of his arm is the very far edge of his outstretched hand—the one that holds the tarantula.

The over-loud woman, the one with the voice that carries no matter what, repeats, once, "Eat it. Do it."

I look again to the instructor, crouched over the bushes, frozen. Finally, he twitches, begins to move his arm.

My mouth parts in horrible anticipation, and I realize that I, too, want him to. Some morbid impulse, a stray feeling of revenge. I have a flash of what he'd look like, those brown, hairy legs protruding helter-skelter from his lips, almost lost in the dark bush of his beard. I can almost hear the crunch, see the waving struggle of brittle limbs.

The thought is too real, as if I'm conjuring it. If he does it now, I'll feel complicit. I can't stay to see if he'll lower his hand to the leaves or raise it to his lips.

I glance down in time to see my tiny toad slip into the water, his back legs pumping once, twice, and I scoop him out balanced in one palm, the other cupped like a lid.

He's almost weightless. I feel his quiet, frantic movements in time with my own pounding pulse as I turn without looking back and begin to wade toward the shallow.

Behind me, around me, the women boil and bubble.

In the hollow of my hand, sudden warmth as the toad releases his bladder in fear.

GREEN

I know what you are thinking.

You're imaging
that the green shadowlings
are slimy
like the slick skin
on a toad's back.

I will say…
this upsets me, dearest.

It is unfair to the green ones.

True,
they are vicious,
    brutal,
    shrewd,

but slimy? Never.

It's alright love.

I'm not mad.
You just need to know.

Stay back from the enclosures
as we walk
down this narrow
hallway—note
the rows of shadowboxes
on either side—

see the way they gesture,
    undulate,
    writhe wildly.

Observe, but do not linger.

From here on in,
it becomes difficult
to find your way out.

CILANTRO

"Come on. A little poison never hurt anyone." My elbow bites into my husband's ribs. We've realized I forgot to rinse the cilantro before adding it.

The kitchen smells like fresh, meaty garlic and watery tomato blood – sweet and earthy beneath our warm fluorescents. A tiny moth flutters and bumps along their plastic casing.

"Ha. Ha." Moments later, his comeback: "Except all the insects killed by it." A real zinger, my man.

"Well, yeah. If they didn't use *pest*icide on their *pests,* we wouldn't have anything to make our picante with."

It's a low blow. A small dose of salt in an old wound already going green around the edges. Jason is a freelance consultant to farmers and gardeners who want to make their practices more organic and environmentally buzz-word-able. He tells already-struggling growers, like my dad, that to sell their produce for twice as much they need to invest in four times the labor to yield half the product, and that unless they can switch to all indoor production there aren't any guarantees their entire crops won't be wiped out on a bad year. It's how we met – when my dad told Jason to fuck off and I felt bad for him, asking him to come inside for a decidedly non-organic cup of coffee.

It's also why most of the farmers who usually give us free food are fresh out of cilantro this year. I bought this oversized bunch at the big chain store Jason calls Volde-Mart. His cause strikes me as perfectly noble; it's his use of it to further his own personal gain at the expense of others that has worn me down over the years.

He stares into the bowl of red salsa tinged with green and white, his nose wrinkling. He knows exactly what chemical concoctions I've forgotten to rinse off.

"What kind of bugs eat cilantro anyway?" I ask. My family never grew it, and like many girls raised on a farm, I learned as little as possible about the family business and got the hell out of there when I turned eighteen. I pluck our biggest wooden spoon from the canister and stir.

"Cutworms, mostly. Other things too."

My eyes are still watery from the onion. I sniff, nudging Jason out of my way. When we were first married he'd rave over the meals I made for him. He overlooked my hodunk roots as I overlooked his hoity-toity ideals, like a farm-crossed Romeo and Juliet. Now he whines about his clients seeing me at the store, complains that I don't cook enough, and never thanks me even when I do.

What I want to say is, "If you're going to be a little bitch you can make your own dinner." What I actually say is, "If you're that worried about it, you don't have to eat it."

But he will, I know. Jason's nothing if he's not an opportunist. Animals like us can never resist a free meal.

I've always quietly resented that Jason convinced me to quit my job in advertising to help him build his business. In retrospect I wonder if that's actually why he married me – not love, but utility.

I had connections with farmers all across the state thanks to my dad, and I knew how to market.

But today it's actually lucky that I work from home, because Jason is so sick he didn't go to work. Maybe not rinsing the cilantro really was a mistake. We did put a lot in this time – too much. It's made our picante taste sweet with that soapy tang, so I add an extra jalapeño to balance the flavors, making it spicy enough to make our noses run. Could he really be that sensitive to residual pesticides? Maybe it's all in his head. But as I peek into the bedroom to check on him, it doesn't seem like it's in his head.

Our blackout curtains are closed tight against the noon sun that infuses the rest of the house with summer glow. He's stacked extra pillows over the seam to seal out that fine ray down the middle. In the forced twilight of the room all I can see of him is a pale, pupal lump under our down comforter. It's pulled all the way up over his head, probably because the room's so cold.

I hover in the doorway, leaning in while holding onto the frame, peering through the dimness, listening for breathing. I pad across the carpet and sit on the edge of the bed, picking out the dark cave of his face under the edge of the blankets. He's facing me, eyes squeezed shut with a fierceness that conveys pain. I put my hand on his forehead to feel his skin, expecting a fever.

His eyes flash open, wide and almost panicked.

"It's okay," I whisper. His skin feels cool and clammy. I raise my voice to a low murmur. "How do you feel?"

"Like shit." His voice comes out hoarse and wet at the same time. "Why is it so bright in here?"

I look at the tiny strip of light coming in over the top of the curtain rod. "Do you have a headache?"

He shakes his head.

"Maybe you're working on a migraine." He's probably about to have his first aura. I stand, wiping my hand on my sweats, and toss an extra blanket over the curtain rod. "Can I get you something? Tea? Water?"

"I'd love some more picante," he slurs.

"I don't think that's a good idea. What if it's what made you sick?"

"Then it's your fault, isn't it? God damn, you're not my mom. Besides, *you're* not sick."

My face slips blank at his words, chest twisting. It actually makes him more mad if I don't act hurt, so in a pleasant voice I ask, "What else sounds good?"

He sighs in annoyed defeat. "A salad is fine."

"Sure."

I almost skip washing the lettuce, but then I wash it twice out of guilt.

He eats the whole bowl in five minutes, huddled under the blankets, not bothering with the dressing, and goes back to sleep, pulling the bedding over his head.

The first seed of real unease blooms in my chest.

Whether out of guilt, vindictiveness, or simple curiosity, I eat two more big bowls of the picante. It's soapy-spiced but still delicious. I don't get sick. Whatever Jason has, it's not from that.

At bedtime I look in on him again. He's snoring so softly I can barely hear it, his body exposed to the cool air. I almost climb into bed next to him, but I pause. He looks… bloated. A tiny shiver fights its way up my spine, and I try to stifle it. I tell myself it is absolutely not from revulsion.

But his skin does look soft and doughy, almost creased into puffy rolls at each joint. It wouldn't hurt for him to start sleeping with a shirt on.

Jesus, I'm terrible. So he hasn't been hitting the gym as much as he used to. Neither have I. Plus, he's sick. Everyone looks terrible when they're sick.

Maybe I shouldn't disturb him. He needs the sleep.

I quietly refill the glass of water on his nightstand and leave. I'll sleep on the sofa tonight. If he's not feeling better in the morning, I'll call a doctor.

A soft sound wakes me. The box under the TV says 2:23am. The house is dark and still and silent. I wait, listening.

Something indiscernible. The faintest shuffling, followed by a muted thump.

"Jason," I breathe, folding back the throw and hurrying down the hall. I round the corner and stop in the bedroom doorway. The blankets cover him in a lumpy mass. Has he added more?

"Jason?"

He doesn't move.

I edge into the room. "Are you okay? I thought I heard something."

When he still doesn't answer, I sit on the corner of the bed. "Babe?"

I pull the top of the comforter down. Empty. He's not in the bed.

"Jason?" I stand and pace down the hall, checking the bathroom and office. He's not there. I go back through the living room and peer into the kitchen and dining room. Those, too, are empty. A strangeness slinks through me, as if I know something my mind hasn't acknowledged yet.

I ease down the hallway and into our bedroom, flicking on the lamp that sits on the small wooden desk near the door. It casts an orange glow across the tan carpet.

"Jason?"

My abs tighten involuntarily. It's the feeling I get when I know someone's about to scare me, but Jason's way too sick to jump out at me for laughs. Still, I say too loudly, "If you're in here, answer me."

There's no answer, but I know he's here.

I hem forward and toss the blankets back into place, as if he could be tucked under the fold. Then I circle the foot of the bed and look in the corner, behind the small recliner we've wedged there. With a slimy swallow, I sink to my knees and lift the bed skirt, peering into the darkness beneath. The emptiness startles me.

A sigh of relief slips through my lips at the same time as a thump emanates from the closet. I twitch, a restrained jump. Too tense to take it, I stand, march to the closet, and shove open the bi-fold doors.

Jason doesn't leap out at me. At first, I don't even see him – just the junk we have piled under the row of crammed hanging clothes.

Then the pile shifts, and I see a swollen heel sticking out from under an old cat bed. A board game slides from the pile and clatters to the floor.

Trembling, I kneel. "Jason? What are you doing in here?"

I move aside a fallen blouse to reveal his face. It's large and round and pale, jowly in a way that it never has been before, and only his wide, terrified eyes seem familiar to me. His lips are so puffed it looks like he can barely move them, but he doesn't try. He just whimpers softly, eyes roving.

I start to move some of the things off him, but he snatches at them with hands that are slow and soft, piling things back onto himself even as he tries to push his head back under the rubbish.

"Jason," I gasp, stepping back. "What the hell is going on?"

My husband tunnels further into our closet, slipping even his foot back under the pile, so that no part of him shows among our neglected possessions in the shadowed dark.

I feel as though I've had my feet knocked out from under me. I don't call anyone. An ugly part of me works hard to make excuses. What on earth would I say? Besides, I'm 'not his god damn mom.'

I shut the bedroom door, have a panic attack, and take some pills. My last emotion as I slip under sleep's blanket is small and hard, strangely anticipatory, almost starved, like an animal fed too long on spoiled feed, but still I vow to check on him in the morning.

The rest of the house is bright and chastising enough that I almost laugh at myself – until I open the door. The first thing that hits me is the darkness. He must have piled even more coverings over the cracks around the curtains; I can't see more than two feet in. I flip on the lamp, then notice an unusual odor. Woodsy, fibrous, dank, and almost fishy. Weak with nerves and hazy with medicine remnants, I take one step inside. I don't know how to explain why I don't call out his name this time. The silence seems waiting.

The sole of my foot lands on something rough and damp, like bark. I look down, raising my foot, and grasp some of it between my fingers. It feels like mushy pencil shavings. My eyes catch a pale ring around the leg of the desk, then jump to the next leg, and the next. All four of them have grooves carved out of the bottom, the wood shreds piled around them on the floor.

My pulse begins to thump harder. I glance at the bed, the covers heaped high in a strange lump, but my gut tells me they're empty.

I don't know what possesses me to look up, but I do, scanning the corners near the ceiling. Empty. Finally, my gaze settles on the open closet and the chaotic pile within. "Jason?" I mouth, but no sound escapes.

Slowly, oh so slowly, I walk toward it. The carpet brushes the remains of the wood shavings off my foot, leaving a tiny trail. My eyes never leave the open closet. The edges of the bi-fold doors, too, have grooves and gouges along the bottoms. I skim the edge of the bed as I slow, not wanting to get too close to that pile. Is it still? Can I see it moving, or is that my imagination?

Breath held, I take another step forward, squinting into the shadows.

Something grabs my ankle. I scream, jerking. Something wet and hard scrapes along my skin over the anklebone as I drag my foot away, toppling backwards into the desk. The lamp falls, the shade bouncing hard, then the metal base rolls off the edge and crashes to the carpet. The light is thrown askew, lighting the empty ceiling, but my eyes stare wildly at the bed skirt. It moves.

"Jason?" I gasp between pants.

The skirt moves again. Backing up against the desk chair, I pull my feet tightly to my legs. I grasp the lamp and shine it under the bed.

"Jason," I say flatly, but my intended command comes out a plea. "Come out of there."

The bed skirt wavers but doesn't lift.

I edge forward, gripping the lamp like a bludgeon. I peer at the small, dark crack between the carpet and cotton skirting. Finally, mouth open in a silent yawn of fear, I lift the bottom hem of the skirt and shove it under the mattress before snagging my hand away.

Something large and pale takes up the space beneath the bed. I scream, shoving myself beneath the desk. My hands skim the wood shavings and I scream again, brushing them off as if they're alive.

The thing under the bed writhes, but no hands reach for me. It's long, swollen sluggish and slimy like a pile of animal fat. I trace its creased body up from its most tapered end until I see the face. Oh, how I wish it didn't have a face. Not distinguished from its body in any way except for the gaping, gnawing mouth full of tiny, sharp teeth that gnash the air – the thing that grasped my ankle – and those eyes. Those too-small, human eyes that look painfully familiar. Those eyes that are far too aware and terrified to belong to anything that looks like that. They rove until they lock on mine, both hungry and fearful. I see regret there, but also a demand – a type of survival instinct that begs no forgiveness. A pile of wet wood chips sit on the carpet beneath that ever-moving jaw.

"Jason," I cry. "Oh, Jason."

Then I leave the room, slamming the door behind me, to go throw up.

The next time I check the bedroom I'm hollow. I remember the me who used to be in love with my husband, the me broken down by his use of me, angry at his gradual neglect, the me who found him ill and felt guilty for not caring – but I don't feel like any of them.

It's with steady hands that I open the door and walk back into the room. It smells of fetid saliva and exposed stomach acid.

The desk legs have been chewed through. The desk itself lies toppled on its side, some of the writing surface also gauged around the corners. It takes a few moments of staring to realize that the bed is about a foot and half lower than usual. The legs on it, too, have been gnawed off. The frame was metal.

I know without looking that the closet pile is unoccupied, because the only place left in the room big enough to hold him is the large, ovular mound on the bed. It's full and glossy, the color of an old penny and creased in plump segments. The mattress beneath lies bare of sheets and blankets. The closet is stripped mostly empty. The recliner sits burst open in the middle, stuffing pulled out in long, fluffy strips.

The lamp still lies askew on the carpet, light shining in a crooked pool, but this time I flip on the overheads.

Under the yellow glow, the brown surface becomes shimmery and orange. When I step closer and lean forward, I make out some letters under a hard veneer. A familiar font. "MIDIFI." Part of the box to our humidifier. Then more items become clear. The print of Jason's favorite tie. A spiral notebook. Our quilt. All buried and mixed into mush, sealed beneath the hardened exterior.

I tell myself my initial hesitation already made my decision. Too late.

Heart pounding, I back out of the room and close the door yet again.

Two days later, I stand outside it with my ear pressed to the wood door. From inside I hear shuffling and rustling, like the shifting of large, limp leaves. I picture cilantro, can almost taste our picante, now gone.

The sounds are so soft – a susurrus of feathers. The noise of wet things drying. A large, gentle, subtle, quiet hefting of wings.

I wait until nightfall to open the bedroom window from the outside. I slide it up with shaking arms. Then I part the thick curtains with a jerk, stacked pillows falling noiselessly inward. The bedroom gapes dark and silent, but as soon as the opening is cleared I run away. The night is overcast and thick with heat. Nothing comes.

In the open part of our backyard, I stack twigs. I think of how I used to love Jason for how different he was, and how he used to love me too – or at least how I thought so. Around the twigs I prop three larger logs in a triangular frame. I think of how my dad hated him for his ungrounded ideals, and how Jason secretly never thought I was good enough, coming from such stock, until he bent me to his cause as well. On top of the twigs I cross small sticks. I think of how cilantro tastes the same organic or protected by pesticides, and how the only way to ruin it is to use too much. Above the small sticks I add a layer of larger ones and finally some thick enough that I can't quite break them over my knee. I've begun to sweat.

My eyes travel to the open window and the waiting darkness.

I pull a packet of matches from my pocket and light the pile with one strike.

The growing flame draws my eyes. It's bright enough to reach inside. I think of my home farm, my family, and how I never quite believed that insects deserve to be saved.

YOU OUGHT NOT SMILE AS YOU WALK THESE WOODS

There once was a woman with a very happy grandson. Truth be told, he was simply too stupid to be sad. He was too oblivious to see others' suffering, and so he thought the world was quite wonderful.

On this particular day, once upon a time in the Piney Woods of East Texas, the grandson went to visit his grandmother, who lived in a house, cabin, or cottage in the green shadowy woods filled with creaking pines and gnarled oaks. He was to stay with her for the summer, but being a modern young man of perhaps twenty, he did not relish the stay, despite contributing nothing for her trouble.

His grandmother was a staunch woman of Czech-German descent who knew her grandson was a fool and loved him anyway, because it is actually quite difficult not to love one's only grandchild, and what's more, to dislike someone who is perpetually happy.

After a few days of sleeping in and eating far too many kolaches, the young man desired to go on a hike through the beautiful woods surrounding the home. The grandmother, however, begged him to stay. "The woods are not safe for someone like you," she told him. "You ought not smile as you walk these woods."

"Alright, Grandmother," the man said, as he spoke very formally despite being a modern young man. "I will stop smiling as I get deeper into the woods."

"I have never known you not to smile. I do not think you're able to hide your teeth, and the fairies are plentiful here. You cannot smile as you walk through these woods, Grandson."

The man smiled, nodding, and promised her that he would not show his teeth, even though he knew that the fairies of East Texas are scavengers and opportunistic carnivores. The small flying mammals posed no threat to a big strong young man such as himself.

Even still, he had grown up hearing about the creatures and their peculiar habits. They preyed mostly on dead animals, feasting on the fatty tissue of the gums, lips, cheeks, and occasionally other soft areas. They were known colloquially as teeth fairies because they loved to collect all sorts of teeth from all sorts of animals to adorn their homes.

A tooth fairy, though, is a small thing, and cowardly. The only real risk to a human from a tooth fairy is circumstantial: legends of drunks passing out snoring in the leaves, waking up with no teeth; small children left to wail outside their houses in the evening. Grandmother swore she knew a man who'd broken his leg and lost consciousness. Folklore said they had a literal sense of fairness, and that only thieves and trespassers were attacked. Others believed a pocket full of coins could protect the properly prepared. Myths, tales, stories to frighten and excite, bestowing magic and morality on a real animal. It was common for Texans to warn visitors not to smile in the Piney Woods, but it was only taken seriously by old-timers and tourists.

Truth be told, the grandson suspected that older people simply object to younger people having fun. His father often told him that smiling so much would rot his teeth, but seeing as his grandmother never smiled and had a mouth almost devoid of teeth, that didn't seem likely. (What the grandson didn't know was that his grandmother used to smile as well in her youth, and only stopped upon the death of his grandfather.)

So, smiling at her foolishness, the young man promised his worried grandmother that he would take great care once he got beneath deep trees and took off on a hardy stroll.

The woods of East Texas are tall and lovely, with shade from the large pines and constant noise from the small animals. The young man loved to be outside, and he enjoyed himself immensely as he walked farther and farther into the wild, paying no mind to trampling the delicate lichen and flora on the ground. He spotted birds and squirrels and all sorts of critters, but no fairies.

Until from the corner of his eye he saw what he at first took to be a large wreath hung on one of the live oak trees. He ventured nearer to see what it could be.

It was, he soon found, a shape created of the tree itself, having once grown around some foreign object or barrier and made an enormous ring that extended out beyond the width of the rest of the trunk. Inside this ring was a hole that he recognized from photos as a fairy knot.

The young man grinned in delight to have found one of the animal's nests at eye-level. Knot peeping was an elaborate hobby of some Texans, but the grandson had yet to enjoy it for himself.

The visitor information for the area emphasized that the fairies are endangered due to their false reputation as violent, and that under no circumstances should this fragile species be approached. But locally it was said that if you snuck a tooth from a fairy knot and did not get caught, you would have luck for the following year. However, if a fairy spotted you stealing from their home without leaving fair trade, you would be cursed. Some old folks like his grandmother even left little dishes of coins and sparkling objects out as offerings, claiming it brought them good fortune.

The grandson did not believe in luck or curses, and he failed to see how a life like his grandmother's could be called fortunate, but he did want to see a fairy knot.

Thrilled with his sneaking, he looked around for any of the animals. Seeing none, he approached the hole with care and stood on his toes to peep.

The knot was three or four feet across, and deeper than he expected into the flesh of the tree. The opening itself was lined all the way around with sharp white canines and incisors from all manner of animals, arranged to defend the dwelling. This was very effective, as the young man could not put his hands on the edge to balance as he peered inside.

The bottom of the hollow spread level but bumpy with molars worn down over time, like enamel cobblestones. Some were darkened with rotted pits, like tiny potholes.

On one side an entire jawbone sat with teeth still attached, propped up perhaps for lounging or resting against. The grandson didn't know what type of animal it was from—maybe a deer.

At other edges inside the knot, tidy piles of objects balanced like strange sculptures: fangs, claws, delicate bones, a single white shell, even a sparkling crystal.

The young man was delighted to see such treasures. He had never considered the beauty of teeth, but looking now he could see why the fairies coveted them. Come to think of it, didn't he enjoy showing his? The very constancy of his smiling was surely what angered his father so.

The day was growing late and warm and the young man was

hungry, but as he turned to leave, an object glinted in a ray of sunlight. He paused, bending to peer in and up into the knot, and he saw a chunk of gold floating near the ceiling, seemingly hovering in the air, turning slowly this way and that, glinting over and over in the sun.

A small gasp of awe escaped the grandson, as he had never seen a thing float before, much less a piece of gold, much less in a fairy knot in the Piney Woods of East Texas. There were, of course, those who swore the fairies had magic, but since the young man believed in a just and balanced world, he knew that if magic existed he himself would be deserving of having it. Since he did not, he knew magic could not be real. He wanted very much to touch the gold, to see if it would fall or continue to hover, and to figure out what it was so he could tell his grandmother about it as she baked him more kolaches.

The sharp teeth around the opening made it quite tricky, but he managed to balance with one hand against the rough trunk of the oak and reach the other carefully through the hole to poke the glistening gold.

It fell but didn't land on the cobblestone molars as he expected. It stopped just shy, and the young man gasped in glee, for it was suspended now from his own finger, as if by some invisible thread.

The grandson was too foolish to realize that it was, in fact, suspended by a fine strand of spiderweb, and instead came to believe in a single moment that magic must be true after all and that he possessed some of it, and that if that were true he had as much right as any to keep this gold. More, even. So he decided to take it.

He heard, at some unknown distance among the noises of the living woods, an unfamiliar sound, and he looked round for fairies. He saw none, although they are notoriously fast in flight and camouflaged in stillness. He began to withdraw his finger from the knot.

The spangling hunk of gold floated far enough below his finger that in lifting it over the bottom of the knot he scraped his arm against the top row of sharp teeth. A small line of wounds reddened, making it seem like the tree itself had bitten him for his trespass. But the young man smiled because he had succeeded in retrieving the gold, and placed it in the palm of his other hand to examine.

This particular young man possessed a set of teeth inside his mouth that were so strong and healthy that—despite his general neglect—he had rarely known a dentist, and so it didn't occur to him that the irregular gold object he held was a filling.

The sound came again, from the side, and the grandson looked to see what caused it.

A tooth fairy buzzed nearby, its wings so fast as to be nearly invisible, merely a blur of anger around the small rodent.

The young man smiled at the animal, having never seen one so close, realizing that the sound was not just its rapid wings but also its strange speech, something between a chipmunk and a bird, with a cricket's chirp mixed in. There are some who think teeth fairies charming, but the grandson found it quite ugly, like a bat or a possum, with its face all twisted up and strange.

He didn't want to return the gold. The fairy was just a dumb animal, protective of its knot, and he, it turned out, merited magic. Besides, it was small and alone, and he was big and strong. Clutching the gold in his fist, the grandson walked through the woods back to his grandmother's house.

At first the critter followed him, fussing and darting in and out around him. The young man laughed to see its antics, kept his fist tightly closed, and continued on.

Eventually the fairy returned to him less and less, until its wings were a distant buzz, and then lost entirely to the noises of the Piney Woods.

His grandmother's abode was a dwelling of antique quaintness, with wood walls and scalloped trim, and a chimney made of stone that puffed out aromatic smoke even in the summer months. He could hear her humming in the kitchen, and so he went inside to show her his find.

Remembering her admonition not to smile in the woods, the man tried to cover his teeth as he walked into the house, but he found it harder than he'd have thought. How could he not be happy when he had come home with gold and magic? Despite his best efforts, he grinned as he approached where she worked dough on the counter.

She turned, took him in, saw his grin, and shook her head with a tight-lipped smirk. "Boy, you probably smile in your sleep. Was your walk pleasant?"

His grin brightened even more with excitement as he held out his palm to show her the gleaming hunk of gold.

The old woman gasped, spreading flour on her weathered cheeks as she covered her mouth. "Where did you get that?" she demanded with fear and awe in her voice.

Surprised by her tone, the grandson realized she would be unhappy if he told her the truth. She was too superstitious to appreciate it if she knew it was from a fairy knot. Running his tongue over his teeth to stall, the young man swallowed and lied a very stupid lie. "I found it along a dirt trail. Just sitting on the ground. It belonged to no one." Seeing her face still clouded with concern, the grandson got an idea. Never having needed to know the value of objects or money, nor really needing this trinket, he added, "And now it belongs to you."

He gently took her shaking hand and turned it so he could place the gold in her palm.

The grandmother, too stunned and touched by his rare show of generosity to further question him, slipped it into her apron pocket to be hidden with her other savings later, and turned back to her dough. "Which filling do you want?" she asked, and the grandson grinned.

That night the old woman slipped the piece of gold beneath her mattress where she kept a few silver coins, the cash she'd saved, and her late husband's watch. Her grandson, she knew, was dull and spoiled, but she didn't think him bad. She couldn't believe he'd have stolen the gold from anyone, and so she let herself believe he'd found it as he said. Suffering and hope, as you may know, can also make a person quite foolish.

She slept the deep, hard sleep of the very old and hard of hearing, snoring loudly, dreaming of roses and copper and someone screaming in the distance.

In the morning, she woke to throbbing pain. Her whole head pounded, and she opened her eyes a slit, squinting against the horror of how she felt. Her ears and temples ached. Her jaw hung open in a stupor. A fog of confusion hazed her mind, but through it pierced a sharp fear, like cold air on an exposed nerve.

The grandmother heaved herself out of bed and looked under her mattress. The bills were still there, but before she could feel the relief, she realized that the coins, watch, and piece of gold were gone.

In their place was a pile of detritus. Bending over to get a closer look despite her aching face, she recognized them as teeth. From all manner of animals, it seemed. Teeth and a jawbone, talons, fragile bones, a seashell, and a crystal. But mostly teeth.

The woman couldn't close her mouth for the pain, nor could she bring her fingers to press against whatever made her ache so. She stumbled to her dressing mirror.

Her jaw dangled like a loose hinge, and her usual view of empty gums was obscured by white doused in gore. She leaned forward and tilted her head up to see.

Teeth, wide and white and straight, but out of order, and too big for her face. Beautiful, white teeth stained pink, lined up as if someone had forced a puzzle together incorrectly. Her head pulsed, her mind screamed, and she knew that she recognized the teeth.

Through the wall, she heard the distant whimpering of her grandson. She grimaced at her reflection, and not even the stupidest boy in the world could have called it a smile.

WHITE PAINT

He'd been painting his new apartment, so of course at first he thought it was paint. Just white. Davey liked white. Clean, neutral, fresh like this new start. The label called it "blank slate." Davey liked that. He wasn't opposed to some heavy-handed symbolism in his life. His therapist told him ascribing meaning to things was part of human nature – part of people's desire to exert control over their existence. His therapist thought exerting control over Davey's existence was a good thing. Said he needed to do that more.

So Davey painted.

It had been fun going to the home improvement store to buy the things. Expensive. He had almost no money – his new job didn't start until Monday – but that was a good way to spend the little he did have. He bought two cans of blank slate, a disposable tray, a foam roller, and one paintbrush the worker there said was great for "cutting in" along the trim and molding. Davey wasn't entirely sure what that meant, but he bought it anyway. He needed a stepstool, but instead he dug through the apartment dumpster until he found a big plastic bucket sturdy enough to stand on. Then he'd painted.

It felt good to work hard and actually be doing something. In prison the only exercise available to him was the pointless kind.

Calisthenics. Movement for movement's sake: the body lifting itself in countless variations because there was nothing else to do. But with this, he could see results, track change. The dingy grayed walls slowly became fresh. The wet shininess of progress spread around the room with the slow stroke of his brush and the long, rhythmic sweep of his roller. By the time he'd made it all the way back around to his starting point, his arms and shoulders and back screamed with aching but the walls were perfect.

So at first, naturally, he'd thought the white spot on his stubbly cheek was paint. Davey stood in front of the mirror in his empty bathroom, over-bright with too many fluorescents, and scratched at it with his finger. Instead of flaking off, it smeared, rippling up under his fingernail. It couldn't be wet paint; he'd sat in the room for half an hour or more just admiring his work, literally watching the paint dry, observing how the color changed ever so slightly as it hardened into its final form. Any spots he'd gotten on him would be dry by now.

He looked under his dirty fingernail at the white junk, then back into the mirror. He touched the spot again, switching from his nail to the pad of his finger.

It smeared in a horribly familiar way. Gelatinous and greasy. Difficult to remove.

"No," Davey said aloud, because someone needed to hear his protest, but no one did. He held up his hands, examined them, looked down, studied his clothes and his feet and then back at the mirror. No other white spots appeared that weren't the paint, flaking off easily.

But how? He'd thrown out almost everything he'd owned before.

Ah. Maybe that was how. He'd touched everything earlier that morning to throw it away. He'd had to pick it all up to toss it into the dumpster. Probably some of the stuff had been on some of his things and it'd rubbed off, that was all. That was okay. It was all in the trash now. He'd made that choice – exerted that control over his existence.

He didn't own any cold cream, though, and regular bar soap really wasn't enough.

Davey used wad after wad of toilet paper to smear as much of it off his cheek as he could, and then he used the heavy dish soap from the kitchen to clean away the rest. He washed his face three times before he felt satisfied, even though it was gone the second. Then he went to bed in the middle of the room right on the stained carpet, using his jacket as a pillow, because he'd used the last of his money to buy paint instead of a pillow and blankets. The whole efficiency smelled like chemicals but as he slipped into his first night of sleep outside the bars he thought that was good. That was symbolic too. Sharp and strong, the fumes would clean him out on the inside and freshen his lungs just as they had the walls.

There weren't many places Davey could work. Out of the jobs he was allowed to take, very few would hire him. Luckily, the inmate rehabilitation program had set him up with the warehouse gig. They'd called him "an exemplary candidate" because they believed he'd really changed. He believed it too. He was grateful for the job. And the apartment.

It was a factory that sold all kind of things. Davey didn't see what they had in common, but he guessed that didn't really matter. His job was to package each order. The training only took an hour. He took the invoice slip off the top of the stack – only that one, no digging into the middle or skipping the trickier orders – and read the items and quantities. Then he walked around the warehouse and gathered the things. Next he chose the right size packaging for it all and carefully boxed it up, making sure any fragile products were wrapped in the soft foam and then taping it all closed just around the seams – using tape over the middle was wasteful. The invoice went in a little plastic slip on the outside of the box, upside down to show the shipping label on the back, and that got taped shut too.

It wasn't fun, but it was fulfilling, like painting the apartment had been. It didn't matter to Davey that the stack of invoices never got smaller. He just liked putting the packages onto the truck backed up to the warehouse loading door, checking them off as done.

As he slid a box along the metal surface and turned around, wiping his hands on his pants, he saw a girl.

Davey froze. His eyes went wide, cut to each side, and then landed again on the bright pink ribbon tied around a perky little ponytail.

They couldn't have hired a kid. Could they? They wouldn't have let him work here if kids could too. Had someone brought their daughter to work? Hadn't his new boss sent out some kind of notice?

Davey's palms dewed up. He slipped them into his pockets. He should get another packing slip. Exert control over his existence.

Instead, he walked closer to that lovely pink ribbon, tied tight and hanging limply from the base of the ponytail. Its pointed tips hung just lower than the hair itself. No bow, just a knot.

Finally, his eyes broke free, and he took in the rest of the girl. Small, narrow, short. Dressed like him. A worker, then. They let kids work here? But no, of course not.

She turned, and Davey saw her face. Not old, but far from a kid. In her twenties, maybe. Late twenties, early thirties. Too old to wear a ribbon in her hair. She held a small taped up box in front of her, arms straight from the weight of it, elbows locked. When she saw him, she smiled absently until she noticed he was staring, and then she smiled broadly. There were only the faintest hints of wrinkles starting around the corners of her eyes.

"Hi," she said, walking past Davey and toward the back of the truck. "You new?" She was the first person who'd spoken to him besides the supervisor and man who trained him.

When her back was to him, she was a girl again, her ponytail swinging with each step.

"Mm," Davey grunted, fleeing to the invoice stack for his next box.

That night when he got home from work and looked in the mirror under the terribly clear light of his bathroom fluorescents, more white covered his cheek. A bigger spot, this time. It stretched almost from his ear to the corner of his mouth. More toilet paper. More dish soap. As he scrubbed, tired, confused tears added to the wetness of his face.

He had already thrown it all away. Last night's explanation didn't work today, and all the walls were dry, the purifying smell already fading.

Her name was Molly. Davey didn't want to know that, but Molly was nice to him. She always wore the ribbon in her hair. She wasn't really a kid. Davey kept telling himself that. She was old.

Nevertheless, he liked her. He found himself slowly coming out of his self-imposed shell to make her smile. Make her laugh. He'd pull faces or pretend to drop things or fold little shapes out of scrap cardboard and Molly would light up. It felt good, which hurt him, made him feel bad.

Every day when he got home the white spread further across his face. Nose, chin, even the forehead now. It was too much to keep using dish soap. On the way home one day, Davey stopped at the big box store. He wasn't really supposed to go in there, but it was the only place he knew to buy cold cream.

Davey stood in the makeup aisle and held his breath, hands shoved deeply into his pockets, staring at the little white jar with the green lid. He could imagine how it would feel. That rush of slick coolness, the tingling sensation, the gunky swipes as he cleaned it away, now mixed with heavier things and a blur of colors gone brown in their blending.

He wasn't supposed to buy anything like that. No makeup. None of the old gear. If his parole officer came by and found a single thing, Davey would be back in prison before he could blink. That had been part of the deal.

But cold cream was different, wasn't it? Some people just used it to wash their face. They couldn't accuse him of anything even if they found it. He didn't have anything in his apartment. Only the white, greasy smears on his face every night, slowly spreading, covering more and more of his skin.

He needed it to get that off. He couldn't let it stay – let it cover more. He needed to exert control over his existence.

Davey picked up the jar and carried it straight to the checkout line, trying not to notice how heavy and smooth it felt in his palm – familiar. He didn't stop in the toy aisle. He didn't stop in the party aisle. He didn't look at anything but his well-fitting shoes and the floor right in front of him.

He heard voices, though. Young kids crying. Begging their moms for junk. Skipping into his periphery, darting out like silverfish.

When he got home, he used the cold cream to remove all the white and the small, almost indiscernible spot of red on his nose.

The worst part of everything, the lowest moment of Davey's whole life, was when he finally believed them that he'd done harm. Over and over people had accused him of terrible things. Said he'd broken those children. Said he'd victimized them. Hurt them. But it had never really bothered Davey because he knew, down in his heart, that what he did was make kids happy. He brought them joy. And what they did was natural and beautiful and he loved them. He would never hurt them.

Until his therapist had punched through. Until the moment when, somehow, he'd said it in just the right way that Davey believed him.

He'd cried and cried and cried. He'd tried to kill himself.

His therapist had stopped him. He'd told him it was time to exert control over his existence. He said now that Davey understood, he could do better. He could make the right choice. Over and over, he'd have to make the right choice.

"Doc, you don't know what it's like," Davey had sobbed, curled in the hard-backed chair of the prison psych room. "You don't know what it's like to want something that bad."

"Yes I do, Davey."

Davey had looked up then, looked into the therapist's eyes, and seen hatred, burning hotter than coals, and had known that it was true, but not like for Davey. The doc wanted to hurt Davey. Kill him. He hated people like him – hated his patients – but even that wasn't the same thing. Even that wasn't what Davey felt. Because now he felt the same but he also hated himself.

"God forgive me. God forgive me." Davey'd sobbed. "Help me change."

The therapist had told him he would.

Molly became his friend. That was okay. They were adults and they could be friends.

Davey made a routine for her. He used the smallest size boxes and balanced them on his shoulders, letting them fall but catching them, pretending to trip, finding one on his head, a second one under it. Molly laughed and smiled but it sounded so old – just polite. They were friends and that was okay but it wasn't enough.

When Davey got home, all his insides were knotted up tight like rope. He didn't eat enough because food was expensive and hard to buy at the places he could go without giving him the bad thoughts. So he let his stomach stay empty most of the time and it grumbled and chewed on its own.

The paint smell had long since faded, but the walls were still clean. He never touched them, never put any furniture up against them or hung art. He left them wide and empty and kind of dim in the small apartment. He only had the one window.

Davey took off his shoes at the door, closed it, locked it, and walked to his sleeping spot. He had one blanket now. He sat down on it before he even went to the bathroom, thinking maybe he'd just go to bed. Maybe he could just spend his whole life sleeping or working. It wasn't quite dark outside yet.

A distant tune reached him. Davey cocked his head, thinking of that pink ribbon, like the rainbow ones that flow behind bike handles, like the soft ones that bow above presents. The tune was electric and bouncy and tinkling, bubbling through the evening heat. Sticky-sweet and happy.

Davey didn't look out the window – he left the blinds closed – but he could hear the truck winding closer. Its song stayed the same volume for stretches at a time, as it paused and continued its path. Closer, closer, closer.

He got up from his blanket in the middle of the floor and went into the bathroom. He shut the door and locked it. The hollow core wood muffled the ice cream song but didn't make it go away. Davey could still hear it outside like a little jack-in-the-box muffled by its lid.

His hand gripped the countertop, his torso leaning over the sink, and slowly, slowly, Davey lifted his eyes and looked in the mirror.

White grease paint covered his entire face, down his neck into his collar and up over his ears, which was more than most people bothered with, but he'd always been so thorough. It had mattered to him. The art of it had mattered. The paint was applied thickly and evenly, none of that patchy sheerness showing through. His stubble dotted it slightly, which normally wouldn't happen. He'd always shaved, back then. Back before prison. Back before he'd thrown away the costume and the paints.

His nose was in the midst of a perfectly red circle, his lips in the center of an oversized smile. A blue diamond speared one eye, a yellow the other. Large black eyebrows arched jauntily above his own, which were gunked in white. Davey continued to grip the counter until his knuckles ached and the truck with its noble song had faded away.

Then he opened the cold cream and set about removing the paint.

YELLOW

Do you hear that?

Ah, yes:
it is the song
of the yellows.

Isn't it lovely?

They sound like
    sunshine in the breeze,
    the hum of golden thread, spinning,
    a wordless whisper as a lemon flower
            drops its final petal.

But do not stay
too long, love.

Love?
Plug your pretty ears,
if you have to.

We must move quickly.

I have watched
others stand before
these innocent-sounding sirens
until their sweet songs
became

    shriveled straw in the bite of winter,
    the leather amber of a crow's foot, scratching,
    a scream of despair as the bloated corpse fills
            with sickly sallow pus

and nothing's left.

THE PELT

The dogs hadn't barked.

Debra knew because she'd been up all night fuming about the fight she'd had with Mike. Even if she had caught a few minutes of sleep here and there, she still would've woken up. A little whining or whimpering would've done it, but the dogs hadn't made a sniff. As she stared at the strange animal shape on the electric fence, she wondered why.

When she came out to the porch in the predawn dim with a mug of coffee so hot she had to hold it by the handle, she thought at first that a calf had gotten stuck on the fence somehow. It wasn't surprising that the fence's charge was down. They were constantly behind on something, and the fence was as finicky as a housecat in the barn. Truth be told, the place was too big for the two of them. A hundred and thirty acres for two people with no kids was ludicrous, but when the love of your life tells you this is his dream, you make it work.

And so they'd bought a gorgeous house on some land in Anderson, Texas—a town so tiny Debra instead called it by the nearest small town's name: Navasota, ten miles southwest and still in the boonies. It was the type of property people called "land," not a ranch or a farm. It was the lifestyle of those wealthy enough to be nostalgic for the good old days they'd never experienced.

They'd stocked it with cattle, a chicken coop, a few horses, two dogs, innumerable cats, and even some fish for the little pond. With two people to maintain everything, and Mike still working as a vet, it was no wonder the fence was dead as often as it was charged.

The dark shape against the fence didn't move. Debra stared, trying to force it into a recognizable form. After a few moments, she began to think it had no head. She went back inside to grab a flashlight. She shucked her flip-flops, got a pair of socks, and shook out her boots before sliding them on.

Grasshoppers vaulted as she walked through the yard. Her flashlight beam caught their movement like the backsides of tiny fleeing ghosts. The most persistent crickets of the night creaked out their cryptograms, and the air was ripe with the scent of sulfuric water but no under-notes of manure. The cattle hadn't been up to the house in a while. So what was this thing without a head?

Her light traced it, and soon she realized it wasn't actually an animal but a pelt draped over the fence. In the off-yellow beam of her flashlight she couldn't determine a color. Something middling, probably, not black or white. It was large but not overwhelmingly so. It was the pelt only. The feet, head, and tail had been detached, so Debra couldn't pose a guess at what type of animal it had come from. Why was it here?

Debra reached out to touch the fur but hesitated. Was it drying, or curing, or whatever the process of preserving an animal hide might need? And if so, why on their property? Neither she nor Mike hunted. Was it a message of some kind? Someone had to have placed it here, which meant that someone had walked over a mile from the road and their gated drive. And she'd looked out at this portion of the property last night, from their bedroom's French doors. Wouldn't she have seen it then? Had someone hung it here in the middle of the night?

She saw the random, vivid image of the animal, whatever it might be, still out there running around without its fur or skin. An unidentifiable living hunk of muscle, fat, and veins. A sound escaped her, something she'd intended to be a word that instead came out formless. She felt suddenly worried, threatened, and lifted her light.

The fence looked whole, wooden posts of about chest height holding up the four lengths of wire. She didn't see any obvious downed spots or gaps, but that didn't mean anything. It was obviously off or the pelt would've caught fire. Beyond it the land sloped gently downward to clusters of oaks. As she moved her light to the right, she saw the dark silhouette of the pond, the pale length of the drive, more trees, and then back to the house behind her, sweeping over the concrete portion of the drive and their truck parked there, the garage and its swell into the two stories of the actual house. The kitchen light was on, but the bedroom was dark, quiet. Mike was still asleep.

Should she wake him? He had work today. With their squabble last night, Debra didn't feel like begging any favors. He'd be up soon to feed the horses before driving into town. She left the pelt where it was and went inside.

Debra stared blankly out the window over her kitchen sink. From this spot she could see the back of their yard from the vegetable garden to the dog runs, but her eyes didn't focus on any of it. She was slumped in contemplation, a swirl of thoughts that didn't connect: the pelt, the fight, the dawn breaking.

"HELLO?"

Debra gasped, whirling. She brought her hand to her chest and forced a laugh, staring at the parrot in his cage next to the dining room table. "Shakes, you scared the crap out of me."

"HELLO?" he squawked again. Then he paused. "Oh, hiiiiii."

She shook her head hard enough for the tip of her short ponytail to brush her cheek. She walked over to his large wire cage that had its own stand and bent to look at him. Shakespeare danced on his perch, little head bobbing. "I've got the spooks," she told him.

"Okay, talk to you later," he said. "Bye bye now."

"It's that damn pelt."

"What pelt?"

Again, Debra whirled. This time it was Mike standing in the doorway from the living room. He looked all sexy-sleepy with his sweats hanging low on his hips and his dark chest hair ruffled and gleaming. She had a compulsion to say something. Anything. Just enough to dissolve their argument and let them move on today without the cold shoulders. It had been a misunderstanding, that was all. A poor choice of words that had blown out of proportion and left her confused all night.

Instead, she said, "I'll show you. You'll want to put some shoes on."

It looked different in the sunlight. It seemed larger. It hung symmetrically, spine aligned with the top fence wire, and the lowest dip in its belly almost reached the third wire. The ends of the legs, cut before they would become paws or hooves, nearly reached the ground.

"What is it?" Debra asked.

Mike shook his head. He didn't seem surprised or half as concerned as she was.

"Could it be a deer pelt?"

"Nah. The fur's too long."

"A bobcat?"

"Not the right patterning."

"Coyote?"

Mike shook his head. "Too big."

"Mountain lion?"

"Not the right color. Cougars around here are tawny. This is gray, and too patchy."

Debra made a sound of dismay in her throat. He was the vet. Shouldn't he know what animal it came from? "Then what the hell is it? A horse? A buffalo calf? A bear?"

He quirked a smile at the bear option, but still he shook his head. "No, I don't think so. I don't know what it was."

Neither of them had touched it yet. The morning sun was already gaining steam, and Mike's lack of emotion over this odd intrusion bothered her. "Well who left it here? Someone had to come onto our property for this."

"It's probably a gift. I'll ask around today at work. Maybe one of my clients thought it would be nice."

Debra restrained a scoff. *Hey, I brought you part of this dead animal*, didn't seem like much of a gift to her. The anonymity of it was baffling. Why wouldn't they leave a note? Why not tell them what it was?

From the corner of her eye, she saw Mike smirk. An unexpected rush of anger spiked through her. "Did you do this? Is this some kind of a joke?" she accused.

"No."

"Really?"

"Yes."

Was he lying? The thought bothered her, especially on the tail of last night's fight. He almost seemed like a stranger, standing there in his work clothes, simpering in the sunlight. She had a strong and sudden urge to slap him into a reaction she could recognize, but the thought shocked her into guilt.

Sugar meowed at them from the corner of the house, where she rubbed against the brick. Debra shook her head, walking toward her. She'd already fed the cats this morning.

Over her shoulder she said, "I would appreciate if you moved that thing before you leave. And we need to get the fence back up and running soon."

Her only answer was Sugar's erratic little mewings—something wrong that couldn't be told.

In this part of Texas the sun sunk tiredly, slipping below the high points of their land as if relieved. Dusk found Debra pacing the kitchen, circling the large center island countless times, talking to Shakes. By the time Mike got home she had all but convinced herself the pelt came from a wild hog. They were quite the nuisance and could be shot any time as vermin.

Mike walked in from the garage through the short utility hallway that led to both the walk-in pantry and the powder room, and hung his Stetson on the hook in the kitchen. There was a crease around his sweaty forehead from the hat band.

"It's hot as balls out there," he said, grinning.

Half of Debra's anxiety slipped away. He certainly had a way with words. He used "what the crap" so much it had been the parrot's first phrase. Mike had said, "He's a regular Shakespeare, ain't he?" and from then on that had been his name.

Debra felt a return grin tugging at her lips, but she was still mad. She bit her cheek to hold it back and turned toward the island. "Did you find out who left the pelt?"

"Well hello to you too."

"Wild hog!" Shakespeare screeched. "Wild hog! Itza wild hog!"

Debra turned in time to see Mike raise an eyebrow. Had she said it aloud so often today?

"Could it be?" she asked, voice softened.

"Wildhog!"

Mike shook his head, wiping his eyebrows with the backs of his hands. "It's about the right size for some of the big bastards, but the legs're too long to be a hog."

Debra's stomach clenched. "God, Mike. What is it? Did you find out who put it there?" Why wasn't he as worried about this as she was?

"Wild!"

"If someone had left it as a gift early in the morning, they probably would of called during the day to let me know. I didn't hear from anyone. I asked around a bit, but I just can't figure out what kind of critter it was."

Debra pulled her ponytail down then put it back up.

Shakes began to do the bouncing lurch he sometimes did when he got worked up. His voice could be ear-splittingly loud in their tiled kitchen and dining room. "Wild-wild! Wild-wild!"

"All I can think," Mike continued, "is that it's something not from around here. Maybe a kind of deer or gazelle or something from a colder climate with the longer fur. Or a small moose. A feral dog? I don't know. But whatever it is, it's something boring, not exotic, or we'd recognize the coat pattern. It's probably some sort of herbivore."

"Wwwwwwwwwwi-uld!"

"But why was it left on our fence?"

"WwwwwwwwI-ULD!"

"I don't know," he said. "But it seems well cured, no gashes or anything. Whoever skinned it must have known what they were doing. Anyway, I'm gonna go hop in the shower."

Debra watched Shakes churn and bob on his perch, pausing occasionally to preen. What would he look like without his skin and feathers? She supposed that underneath, everything pretty much looked like so much meat.

"Wwwwwwww-aiy-o! Why-o!"

Mike slept. How? How could he sleep amidst this? Didn't he have dozens of questions swarming his head like she did? Didn't he care at all? It infuriated her.

It had been the same last night. Debra had stayed up in a roil of emotions and he had snored peacefully. He didn't used to snore.

The fight was stupid. She knew this, but it didn't change the reality of her feelings. Her casual, "Ready to watch the show?"—so ordinary, so habitual—had been met instead with, "I don't even *like* that show."

Debra had laughed. His response was so ridiculous that laughter was her only option. Of course he liked it. They'd been watching it almost every week for three years now.

"Come on," she urged. "I know you're tired, but it's only an hour. Forty-five minutes if we fast-forward through the commercials."

"No, I'm serious."

Her smile died, because she could see on his face that he was telling the truth. "What do you mean?"

He'd gone on a tirade about the show and all its flaws.

She was stunned by how badly it hurt her. It wasn't about the show. Debra didn't care about TV, not really. It was the dishonesty.

How could he have misled her for so many years? What was the point of sitting on the couch with her week after week to laugh and discuss it if he secretly thought it was crap? Why not just suggest a new show? And if he had some good reason for the deceit, why tell her the truth now?

Perhaps most startlingly, how could she not have known?

The sound of cattle mooing in the distance brought her back to the present. Their calls were low and urgent. Was there something wrong with the cows?

Debra climbed out of bed and padded to the French doors. The cattle weren't near enough to the house to see from here, but nothing appeared to be wrong nearby. The fence where the pelt had hung was empty. She wondered where Mike put it. What animal had it come from? Were there more of them out there, lurking in the darkness, stalking over their land? Was some mysterious beast upsetting the cattle?

Or was it whoever had brought the pelt? Some*one* on their property?

Debra turned away from the glass to see Mike on his side facing her, still snoring. In the shadows she couldn't make out his features, the familiar jaw line or the dark arches of his brows. He could be anyone, lying there. He could be a complete stranger who vaguely resembled her husband in shape and form.

Could Mike have left the pelt? She'd never known him to hunt or skin an animal, but then again for three years she hadn't known he was humoring her by doing something he detested. Maybe Mike didn't go to work some days. Maybe he went out and hunted, field dressing animals before spreading and curing their hides to keep the fur as some sort of trophy. Were his veterinary skills enough to account for that?

How hard was it?

Without looking again at Mike's silhouette, Debra left to turn on the computer in the back office. From there his snoring blurred with the distant lowing until both were indecipherable. She spent the entire night researching how to make a pelt. The whole time she pictured Mike's strong hands doing these things, but she didn't know why.

"Goooooood morning!" Shakespeare sang.

Deborah stood from behind the lower cabinets to see Mike walk into the kitchen, already dressed for work.

"Morning, buddy," he said to the bird. Shakes bobbed his head. Mike turned to her. "You making something?" He eyed the knife drawer which sat on top of the counter.

"Just time for them to be sharpened and oiled."

He moved toward his hat on the hook, so she stopped him with a question.

"Mike, have you ever been hunting?"

He cocked his head at her. "You know I don't hunt."

"But even once? Maybe as a kid?"

He shook his head. "Only quail."

"Quail!" Shakes belted. Debra and Mike both jumped. "Quail!"

"Where'd you put the pelt?"

He squinted at her. "I hung it in the stable."

The answer seemed canned, meaningless, almost anonymous. It was like he wasn't even Mike at all, just some stranger borrowing his skin.

Shakespeare started to rock back and forth.

"I made you some coffee," Debra said on a whim. She pushed

her travel mug, which she had taken earlier to check on the cattle, toward him. All of them were fine.

Mike picked up the mug. "Thanks."

"No problem," Shakes chirped. "Gotta go into town."

"I put some sugar in it this time," she said. "For a nice little change."

Mike paused. He always drank his coffee black. "Oh." How odd, the small disruptions. How unsettling. How would this stranger reply? "Well thanks, I guess."

Debra nodded. It wasn't Mike. She was sure of it.

He took the hat and left.

Shakespeare was silent.

The pelt hung from a nail in the stable the way a robe hangs from a hook on the back of a door. Debra examined it, studying it for clues, but it gave up nothing. It smelled similar to leather, but mustier and sharp enough to taste in the air.

Mysterious, maddening, ineffable. But not meaningless.

Try as she may, she couldn't picture the animal that fit this pelt, exotic or not. The fur was thick, a mixture of soft undercoat and coarse longer hair. The hide on the inside was indeed smooth and free of nicks. She ran one finger along the edge, where the blade had separated the flesh.

The horses whinnied and hooved the ground. Debra fed them, but they did not quiet.

She studied the pelt from every angle.

When he finally woke up, his eyes opened very wide. They roved to look at the restraints holding him to the bed, then stopped on her. "What is this?" he asked. "Did you… slip me something?"

"Slip me something?" she repeated. The shape of the words was strange in her mouth. "I slipped you something."

He pulled at his arms and legs, but he wouldn't be able to get loose. She'd tied him securely. "Why?"

She sat beside him, on the edge of the bed. He wore only the sweats he went to sleep in. The dark patch of fur on his chest shone dully from the moonlight streaming in the French doors. She wanted to run her fingers through it, but didn't.

"Say something Mike would say," she commanded.

"Say some—huh? Debra, what? I am Mike! What the hell is going on?"

That wasn't what Mike would have said. Mike would have said 'what the crap' or 'come on baby.' This was someone else. A stranger. Who?

Was it the person who left the pelt? Had they taken Mike's skin? Was Mike out there, hideless, wandering around?

And what in God's name had the pelt come from?

The stranger in Mike's skin continued to thrash. "Look, Debra. I know you're mad, but this isn't funny. I don't know what you're trying to prove here, but this is too far."

"This is too far," she echoed. The words didn't even mean anything. There was nothing behind them.

She pulled out the gloves and the butcher knife. It wasn't quite the right kind, but it would have to do.

The person on the bed started to cry.

When she began her process of field dressing, starting with a careful incision near the pelvis, the crying turned to screams. Blathering. Phrases, words, incoherent sentences. Complete gibberish.

Finally, when she got to the ribcage and split it open like she'd learned, the noises stopped and she was able to work in peace.

It was her first time to skin anything, but she thought she did pretty well. She didn't have to worry overmuch about tainting the muscle, since she wasn't going to eat it, nor tearing the hide, since she didn't care to keep it. All she wanted was to see inside—to see what had been wearing her husband's skin.

When she was through, the pelt, organs, head, and extremities sat in a steaming pile on the tarp on the floor. The room smelled raw and metallic. She stood, removing her gloves, and looked down at what remained on the bed.

It was acutely indistinct. Meaty. Still. Not her Mike. She'd been right.

She didn't recognize what was underneath at all.

HONEY

A letter found atop a limestone coffin in the basement of an abandoned house. Autumn, 2106:

NOVEMBER 1, 2006

To My Sweet One,

It saddens me that I will never meet you, and yet I would be dead anyway, long before you are born, regardless. It is only my sacrifice that gives my death meaning – that places choice above randomness. It is only my love for you that brings worth to my life.

Do not contact anyone. If, by some mishap of destiny you are not alone, instruct the others to leave immediately. Do not show them this letter.

You need not look around, as I suspect you may be doing. I assure you, if you are holding this letter, it was intended for you. The fates would not have it any other way, just as they will make sure that all goes according to plan and that my home is not sold for precisely 100 years.

I have great faith, for there is no other way such a thing could be acted out.

It is all for you, you know.

Today, I supped my first honey – selected from imported bee hives. You will be pleased. It was delicious, and all is well.

NOVEMBER 4, 2006

To be frank, my love, I feared that I might tire of honey. But it has been three full days, I have consumed nothing else, and still the golden-brown stickiness of it fills me with indescribable pleasure. It is thick and cool when it hits my tongue, dissolving in my mouth like it longs to fill me. Sweet, so sweet, with the slightest spicy finish.

Did you know, dear, that honey contains naturally-occurring antibacterial properties?

Are you ill? If so, partaking of my gift will mend you.

Are you sad? The sweetness of my confection will cheer you.

Are you lonely? The spirit infused within will mix with yours, and we will never be apart.

NOVEMBER 8, 2006

I do not even feel the effects of hunger. It is a lovely way to go.

As I wait, I cannot help but dream of you. I cannot help but picture your visage. Are you fair? Dark? Slender? Plump? Graceful? Athletic? I long to meet you, to know you, to kiss your soft lips. And yet I cannot.

Please know that you are beautiful. It matters not how you appear. After partaking, you will feel beautiful. Because I will be inside you, and two souls intertwined cannot be anything but. I hope you see that.

NOVEMBER 11, 2006

It's working. The honey is flushing the impurities from my body. My waste has become unpolluted – pure honey. Forgive the indelicacy of my saying so, but you should know this. I am clean and sweet, for you.

NOVEMBER 14, 2006

It feels as though my very veins are being pumped with sweet nectar. My body grows slow and sluggish. It is becoming more difficult to exert myself. I have moved all of my pertinent belongs downstairs, to the cool basement, so I won't have to travel far when the time comes.

I hope you like the coffin I chose. Individually sized stone ones like this are not so common anymore; I had it specially made and brought here.

This is where we will first meet.

NOVEMBER 17, 2006

I have begun to sweat honey, I swear it. I grow slumberful and lazy, like a bear in hibernation, and when I woke this afternoon I found a trail of ants marching up the leg of my cot. They can smell the sweetness in me, love. They are a sign that I am getting closer.

NOVEMBER 20, 2006

It becomes difficult to move. I've forced myself upstairs long enough to escape the ants. (Where do they come from? How do they get inside?)

I have much to say, but already I grow tired and warm from the exertion of writing. My arm sticks to the page where my honey-sweat beads. I must go back downstairs.

NOVEMBER 23, 2006

Today, someone knocked on my door. My heart pumped thick blood through my body, and I roused myself, brushing away the line of ants that returned shortly after I came back downstairs. I think there are more of them.

I stood, listening, willing the unwelcome visitor to leave. I felt so strange, you see, for I have no one left. I love no one but you. Who would come here? My real estate agent? He is the only person I've spoken to in the past year, and I've given him strict instructions to never visit this house.

The knock came again. I held my breath. A minute of silence passed.

A pair of legs passed by the high, narrow window in the basement.

I launched to my feet, forcing my lethargic body to take the steps two at a time. I burst out the front door, hurrying around the side of the house, calling out, "Who is it?"

It was, indeed, the wide eyes of my real estate agent that met mine.

"What are you doing here?" I asked.

"I came to check on some details for the property listing." He stepped closer.

"I gave you everything you need."

He leaned forward, sniffed. "Have you been baking?"

I admit, for a moment, that my heart softened to him. It is working. Oh, it is! But then I remembered why it was a bad thing for him to notice my sweet scent. Why it was abominable that he would ignore my so clear instructions regarding this house.

I set him straight. He will not make the mistake again.

But I fear I am spent from the encounter. I lay here on the cot, panting, writing to you with the last of my energy, forcing myself to drink honey that – yes, I admit it – has finally lost its taste. And the ants return as soon as I enter the basement. They seep from the woodwork in angry hordes, and they bite me when I sleep.

It is times like this that I remind myself why I put myself through so much. For you.

Why you?

My darling, because you are the one who found me.

NOVEMBER 24, 2006

I thought of something today, and I felt a burning need to write you.

Are you afraid, my soul? Are you hesitant at the taboo inherent in my gift?

No doubt, there are those who would call me mad. They would gasp, gag, avert their eyes at the mere mention of the consumption of human flesh, but that is because they know no better. You, oh my sweet one, you must know better.

Some will call it cannibalism – atrocious word! So full of deception and hate. It has been used for centuries to demonize those who practice it, when in fact, anthropophagy is rarely evil. Perhaps, in some extreme cases, it could be perpetuated as an unwilled crime… but that is not what is happening here, love. What I am offering to you is the most precious of gifts.

I offer you me – my life.

It is said, among those who have had the privilege to try it, that human flesh is the most delicious food imaginable. This is only logical, as the human body deems delicious that sustenance which it most desires for health. Fat, salt, and sugar are so coveted because the body needs them.

Just imagine, then, how delectable human flesh must be, as it has just exactly what our bodies crave to survive. It must taste like coming home.

Picture, then, that very delicacy of delicacies infused with weeks' worth of pure, sweet clover honey – and then you will dream a small hint of the pleasure that awaits you.

NOVEMBER 26, 2006

Today I could scarcely lift myself from my cot long enough to escape the persistent ants and relieve myself, and even then I found little respite. Ants are small, but I am grown slow. They trail me in a tiny wave of stinging black.

And my body begins to shut down; I feel it. Everything slows. Everything hurts. Today I cried, and my tears tasted thick and sweet, and I am pleased.

NOVEMBER 28, 2006

The time marches ever-near. I must leave you with instructions before I have no energy left to write them.

This letter will be in an envelope attached to the lid of the coffin. It warms me to think of your sweet hands touching the very paper I touch now.

When you finish reading, do not wait. Unfasten and lift the lid. It is heavy, but the hinges are very strong. It can be done alone.

The coffin will be filled with honey, like my body, which will lie submerged within it.

Honey is perhaps the most miraculous substance on the planet. It has amazing preservative powers. Have you ever left a jar of honey in the pantry, forgotten in a back corner for years, only to open it and find it as sweet and delicious as they day you bought it? It does not spoil. Therefore, anything stored within it does not spoil either. Perhaps the truth lies in its high acidity, hygroscopy, and antiseptic powers. Perhaps the truth lies in less scientific realms. Either way, do not fear, my heart; what lies within is pure.

I wish I could claim this idea was mine. But it wasn't. It was a treasure of which the ancients knew. Such gifts have been recorded to last for centuries.

Oh. Oh, my sweetness. You must embrace what comes next.

You will reach inside, with both arms, and your skin will be coated in the thick, heavy wonder of honey. If my coffin is not perfectly air-tight, some of it around the edges may have crystalized, but that matters not. Stretch deep. Let your heart lead your fingers until they find me.

Lift me up. Wrap me in your arms and pull me out, if you'd like, or prop me against the limestone sides of my final bed. Now look at the right corner of the front of the coffin. See the silver handle? Pull that up, and you will find a knife of extraordinary sharpness. Take care not to grow clumsy in your eagerness. Gentle, love. Gentle.

It is then time to serve yourself your first taste.

You may choose any piece you like. I will not try to guide you. Do you want to touch your lips to mine for the first time? Would you prefer to feel my finger caress the inside of your throat? Or perhaps you'll sample the sweet, meaty flesh of a thigh? Maybe more personal areas catch your interest. Do not be ashamed, love. That is your right. All of me is yours.

Your society will likely not approve of this gift. Be discreet, my darling. Do not share.

This honeyed flesh is only to touch your sweet lips, only to tease your sweet tongue, only to fill your sweet body with delight.

I am only for you.

Enjoy.

NOVEMBER 29, 2006

I have moved my cot right alongside the coffin, but the lid remains closed. I do not want the ants to get inside. Everything is the sweetest agony.

Surely I will die soon. *Surely* I will die soon!

NOVEMBER 30, 2006

I can scarcely move. Today is the day. I feel it.

I crawled to the far side of the basement and stayed there for hours, long enough to attract all of the ants away from this lovely coffin. I assure you that the surge of energy it took to get here, lower myself into the waiting pool of honey, and write these final words was my last surge of energy. It is amazing, the will that comes with a love such as ours.

But I must go.

I must finish this letter, lie down, and seal the lid. Here come the ants.

With All my Being,
Your Melliferous Love

THE FILLING

"She was a stranger in a world of strangers and they were strangers she had left behind."

— Shirley Jackson

The dentist herself leads me back to the room, which I hesitate to call the operating room, but she leads me without saying Follow me or This way, please, and after all, I am here for an operation. The smell of disinfectant is strong. I try to convince myself that's a good thing. "It's nothing," she tells me over her shoulder without turning to see if I'm listening or if I've even followed her down the cramped hall. "No big thing."

Yeah, to you, I think. You do this every day. Which is what scares me. Someone who's about to drill an honest to god hole in a permanent part of my body should never call the procedure no big thing no matter how many times she's done it. Her reassurance is almost insulting. She isn't telling me it'll be fine so much to calm me down as to remind me not to make a scene.

Another cavity. I, who floss nightly, brush morning and night, rinse daily, and abstain from most vices, have a cavity anyway. Unfortunately deep teeth grooves, a different dentist once told me. Genetics. Don't worry about it; it's not your fault. Funny how I can't seem to not worry about it. Funny how we use the word funny for things that are the opposite, too.

My blood pressure rises when we turn right instead of left. Left is where I was last week to see my hygienist for my regular cleaning. She told me that if everyone kept their teeth as clean as I do her job would be much easier. And then the dentist came in next and told me I have a small cavity right beside an old filling, and that it'd be best to fill it right away. She'll have to take out the old filling and join them, but said it's still a small spot. She said it wasn't that bad—I could tell she didn't want to look at the anxiety on my face—she said if I get one of these every twenty years, I'll be doing great. I didn't retort, but I don't get one every twenty years. My last filling was probably five years ago. How will I be at that rate?

"Right there," she gestures, my first clear instruction since entering the building. Her practice is placed in an old Victorian home that they converted into a dental office. It's beautiful but heartbreaking to see it wired up for such a use. TVs hang from the corners by the ceilings, the retrofitted wires IVing down the walls to line the thick baseboards before disappearing into a dysfunctional fireplace half covered by a dental display. I look at the chair she waved to. It's a pink shade of pleather that was probably marketed as mauve in the 1980 dental supply catalog she got it from. It sits up like its own entity, a patient person just waiting for me to slide my form alongside its own, but then we both know it will stretch its feet out and down, stretching me prone and exposed on its surface like a cowardly beast offering up the belly of another for sacrifice.

I ease into it, my legs already stiffening with tension. "Will I get laughing gas?" I ask her.

"Sure, if you want it."

"I do. I want everything you can give me."

She chuckles. "You'll be fine. Don't worry."

There's a mechanical hum and the chair is moving, raising my center and lowering my ends, spreading me out and up for easy access. The assistant comes into the room, sits on a stool, and rolls near as the dentist slips around behind me to turn on the Novocain. A surprisingly heavy mask comes over my face like the sucking creature in *Alien*, both soft and rigid where it bridges my nose. The smell of medicated air.

"Just breathe deeply and calmly."

I inhale to the depths of my lungs, like smoking a joint. I force my leg muscles to loosen, but as soon as my attention shifts they flex up again. More deep inhales.

I stare at the two-handled, plastic-covered spotlight lowered to illuminate the deepest, most intimate recesses of my mouth. For now I keep it closed, swallowing and adjusting my tongue and lips compulsively, like each is the last time. The dentist and her assistant begin chatting.

"I deserve a medal for being here today."

"Why?"

"I'm so tired. I've been waking up early to make Regan breakfast every morning. She's on that new high-protein diet. I've been cooking meat for weeks."

"Ah."

"I don't mind meat, but it's something else to handle it first thing in the morning like that. I don't really want to see meat that early, you know?"

"Is it working?"

"Yeah, she's doing great. She's sore, though."

"I bet."

"She's in great shape, but these are different muscles. Different type of motion, you know?"

"Yeah."

"She comes home every day and she says, 'Mom, I'm *so* sore!'"

They both laugh.

I feel the double-headed unreality of the laughing gas slipping over me. I continue breathing deeply, my meditation practice coming in handy and eluding me simultaneously, the deep concentrated inhales sucking the chemicals into my system but bringing me no closer to calm. I force myself to relax my legs.

"Okay, open."

I swallow and open my mouth.

"This is just a numbing agent." She tucks gauze between my gum and lip on the top right. It smells like artificial cloves. "You doing okay?"

I nod.

They continue talking, and my eyes focus on the spot where the walls meet the ceiling. They're all the same shade of white, like someone was too lazy to cut in a separate color of paint. There's crown molding, but it's about half an inch below the actual ceiling line, so it forms a tiny dust-catching shelf. I find myself zooming in, hyper-focusing on that one spot, until I realize the laughing gas is kicking in. I think I'm more sensitive to it than most people. Dentists never seem to realize how far gone I am, and I don't tell them, because they also never realize how truly terrified I am. Curse of a poised demeanor—people never know how strong your feelings are.

"No, he's living there for sure."

"How do you know?"

"I've been up here in the middle of the night. Crazy hours. Two, three in the morning, and he's always there. Sometimes I forget stuff or whatever, and he's always there. He has to live there. Probably trying to save on taxes."

"Oo-o-oh." The hygienist makes her oh sound almost musical, hitting three notes before it lifts up and gracefully away.

My body is shrouded in invisible gauze now. My mind floats slightly above it, hovering above my own thoughts. But beneath the gauze, my legs are still tense. I force them to relax from my feet up to my hips, looking down my body at my shoes.

"You doing okay?"

I nod.

"Can you feel this?" she asks, prodding my gum with something.

"No," I say around the gauze. The area has become a cold type of absent that's almost its own sensation.

"Okay, good. I'm going to numb you up now. You might feel a slight prick, but it's not too bad."

I nod again, my eyes squinting against the urge to water. Tears, or tightness from the laughing gas?

I look up and away so I don't see the needle.

I don't know if I actually feel it or imagine that I feel the cold steel of a needle slide into the high corner where my gum meets the fleshy softness of my cheek. It's not that bad. I relax a fraction.

Another, nearby. Again, not that bad. She puts the instrument down and I exhale, inhaling deep relief of the Novocain. Fuzzy little blurs strum in my periphery. The good stuff, the good stuff.

"...and he named the cow Q-tip."

Delighted laughter.

"...had to get used to the cattle guard, you know? That sound when you drive over it quickly. Brrr-ept."

"Okay, we're going to do another one now, in the roof. This spot's a little more sensitive—a lot of nerves up there. Hold on."

Sharp, miserable pain clouded by a haze. My whole body goes rigid and my eyes tear up and I look back and out, past the dentist's shoulder. This is the part. This is the part I dread, and I always forget the later shots are worse than the first.

"Alright, good job. One more," she sings softly.

More. Excruciating, body-zapping pain. Like I'm being injected with lightning too heavy to squeeze through my veins. The laughing gas doesn't dull it; only disconnects my caring.

"Goooood job. You alright?"

I nod, mouth parted in a grimace.

A voice comes from the back side of the room that I can't see. "Diane needs you to check her, if you have time."

The dentist nods, then says to me, "Okay. You can relax. We're going to let that numbing agent sink in nice and deep for a couple of minutes before we get started. You alright?"

I nod.

"Okay. We'll be right back."

They're both gone.

I hear her doing her patient check-up spiel in the room next door—the one I was in last week. It's an older woman, by the sound of her voice. They talk about a tooth that must be pulled, and a bridge being the best option. The woman doesn't want to lose the tooth, but they both speak very calmly. Too calmly for someone about to lose a part of their body made of bone, necessary for survival.

My eyes rove, tracing the IV power cords pumping new blood into this old carcass of a building. I find the water-stained ceiling tiles directly above me, visible now that the spotlight has been turned off and moved to the side. I trace the gridlines between them, my tongue thickening. I find the corner where the crown molding makes a tiny shelf, and I imagine the little creatures that might perch there to watch.

"The two on the side are both solid, so it should be an easy operation."

"...Can you write it down so I know what to tell her?"

"Of course, we'll send all the paperwork directly to her so she won't have to take new x-rays."

I've been here a very long time. The mask remains weighty and warm on my face.

On the shelf, maybe a bug, or a little pixie, or something invisible that blinks like a sleepy eye who's forgotten how to roll away. A trinket, a sprocket, a gizmo magically alive. A little tooth left perched there?

There's whirring nearby, and I can't tell if it's a machine or my ears. I concentrate on it and it grows and fades, like the droning of bees. I feel my arms suddenly out to my sides, wind-milling in hyper circles, so fast they're a blur, but I look down the length of my body and see my hands still folded neatly over my crotch, resting where I left them. Maybe my arms actually make the whir. Maybe I'll take off soon.

Too much Novocain. Oh, too much of the good stuff. Have they forgotten about me?

I hold my breath as long as I can, then exhale until my lungs ache. I trick the clasp of my breathing until I'm inhaling only through my mouth, letting the mask's rhythm fall into a background steadiness. Clean air. Wading through the gauze in my mind. Up on the shelf there, an empty perch.

How strange would it be if I called out? Asked them if they could come back? Would it cause a ruckus? And what would I say? They are only one room over. Surely they know I'm still here. Hello?

Suddenly, a deep plunging cave-in, and I bounce, take off, my arms blurring into Q-tip wings and I'm launched forward, up, out, shrinking, tiny, a sling-shot self who lands on the crown molding beneath where the ceiling meets the wall in the corner.

The hygienist comes back. "You doing okay?"

From my chair, I nod. "Feeling kind of funny."

She adjusts something behind my chair. The dentist comes back in and sits down. "All right. I'm going to put a block in here so you don't have to hold your jaw open the whole time. Feel alright?"

I nod, watching from the perch by the ceiling as she gets out the drill. I don't want to be here. I focus instead on my arms where they rest on my solemn body, hazy.

"Can you feel that?"

I can't even tell where she's poking. "Not at all," around a metal tool.

"Good." She begins to drill. It sounds a lot like my arm-propellers, or a cattle guard at high speed.

A bouncy ball, perhaps, is what should go here. Instead it's me, even smaller than I imagined. Smaller even than an eye, a bug. It's me.

Tooth dust flies everywhere, the assistant sucking it up with the air tube which she occasionally lets drift toward my cheek. The suction hiccups onto my flesh like a hickey from a tiny fish, and she adjusts it. Dry grittiness coats my mouth.

"They said they don't want a big wedding, but you know how that goes. They're up to two hundred now, and they still swear it'll be beach casual."

"He put the ring in an empty oyster shell."

"Her mom was there to film it, which is sweet. I like it when…"

Three sharp puffs of air almost reach my nerves. I feel them waiting to spark and sizzle. "You okay?" Nod.

Corner me watches her fill the hole with goo. The assistant shines an awkward brown device into my mouth, aiming the blue light over the cavity. It drifts away as she speaks.

"Maybe get a dog first, and see if you can handle that."

Will it even work right if she doesn't aim it over the filling? Every fifteen seconds or so she readjusts and aims again, but she keeps looking up. Their faces are like large, masked carnival heads bobbing above me—one pale pink and one mint green. From the shelf, the backs of their heads are split by white strips of elastic. Maybe I am the bouncy ball. More filling. More light.

Finally, "Doing okay?"

"I think I've had enough gas. I feel kind of loopy."

"Alright. We'll phase you out slowly so you can drive yourself home. The worst part's over. I'm going to smooth it down real well to make sure you can still get a piece of floss in there."

I didn't realize it, but there's a long, gooey string connecting me in the chair to the little me on the perch. It sags, dropping like a spider web stretched too far, a line of honey in slow motion, bubble gum still soft between two kissers.

It will break if they don't hurry. The Novocain is fading.

"You ever ridden on a motor trike? They're really nice. Way easier to balance."

They talk over the ear-assault of the sanding. Tiny shards of tooth-grind spray into my mouth, and the assistant half-heartedly sucks them up.

The eyeball bug pixie me blinks, just once. The honey sinks to the short-pile carpet.

A silent plea.

Water, squirted in strange nooks of my mouth, shocking after so much dryness, followed by that sucking tube applied haltingly to my tissue. It slurps, waking up me up in tiny circles at a time.

"Close."

Don't ask me to speak.

Some poking. "Right there," she mutters.

She sits back. "How's that?"

The sticky thread, it sags and breaks, the two halves swinging back upon their sources. The corner of the room, my waking body. The dissolving middle trailing on the dirty floor. The little me on the perch cries out.

I look down, watch myself tongue the new filling, looking a question at the dentist.

"Does anything feel weird?"

"Well, yeah. I mean it does feel different." No more honey. I can't feel my tongue.

"Are there any ridges or sharp edges?"

"No, I don't think so."

She works a piece of floss between my teeth. I can't feel my gums. "Perfect."

Praise for their own procedure, I did great, what to expect. My chair is raised, folding down and in, and I can't feel my limbs. I can't feel how the blood trails through my body, waking each part. I watch myself look up to the corner, but I don't see me. I feel it though. I feel myself up here, detached, watching. I cry out, try to catch my attention, but they're ushering me on—no time for lagging—and I know I'll leave.

"I'll be in New Zealand for the next ten days. If there are any problems…"

I search for my bag, spy it in the corner, hoist it over my shoulder. I feel none of it. I call out again, the honey already absorbed into the tacky carpet.

I can't leave. Look up at the perch.

Closing remarks.

Me, tiny, strange and left behind up here, watching invisibly as I walk away, failing to look back as I leave down the cramped hall.

ORANGE

Watch your head,
dearest.

See how the ceiling lowers?

Oh, don't be afraid.

Just stay close
and duck down.

It will be worth it.

Can't you smell
the enticing aroma
coming from within,

like a thin trail
of smoke in autumn,
reaching like skeletal fingers
through the empty air?

Behold, it leads us
to the orange ones—
like splendid flames,
flickering, fighting, feasting—

displayed in charred cubbies,
segmented in burned boxes,
shadowed, dancing, on the walls.

Can't you tell
how carefully
I've placed them?

They bleed like peeled pulp
in persimmon passages,
among pumpkin pathways,
behind peach partitions.

Just hunch your back, love,
and mind the slick floor,
as we go deeper still
into the darkness.

THE COTTAGE OF CURIOSITIES

Patty could never decide which way to face when she got on the tree swing.

She looked across the lawn at the house. It was small and white with a pointy roof with dipped sides and pretty green trim. The stone chimney crooked like a kindly old man, and the curtains were open to let in the evening sunlight. If she faced the house, she felt more cheerful, but then she always felt the urge to turn and look behind her at the woods.

Things lived in the woods, and most of them weren't bad, but sometimes, Patty was sure, they got hungry in there. Mama said if you walked too far in you could get turned around. Through the two ropes that held up the swing's wooden seat, Patty looked at the woods, studying the narrow limbs of saplings and the ground where the first of the dying leaves collected in puddles of burgundy and gold.

A little beyond where the yard met the forest, something shiny glinted under the last touch of the setting sun, winking at her once before it disappeared.

Patty stepped around the swing and took a few steps forward, ignoring the fretful squirrel that chattered at her from the tree. The sparkle flashed again.

Distantly, she heard the cuckoo clock go off inside the house. The little bird cried six – seven times before falling silent, which meant it was time for Patty to go back in. Mama didn't like it when Patty pretended not to hear it, and Mama hadn't been feeling well for several days now, so she wouldn't want to get out of bed to ring the big brass bell that could be heard from even farther away than the cuckoo.

But Patty wanted to know what the shiny thing was. Maybe it was something neat that would make Mama feel better! Mama loved neat things; she collected them.

With that settled, Patty mustered her courage and tromped into the brush. She kept her eyes trained on the spot where the glint came from, and even though her heart was pounding, she got there quickly and squatted to pick it up.

It was some special type of rock, about the size of her small palm. She flexed her wrist and tossed it into the air. It made a satisfying smack when she caught it. The surface was rough and angular, mostly black and gray with a little bit of brown on it, but parts of it gleamed silver. It was perfect.

The deep, full tolls of the bell rang out. Mama wanted her to come inside.

With an eager bounce in her step, Patty ran back to the house.

Mama's room was the only room where Patty didn't need to shut the curtains for the night. They were already closed, and the air was very dim. Several candles were melted almost down to their bases, and the room was smoky.

When Patty walked in she saw Mama's silhouette under the covers. She must be very tired to get back in bed after ringing the bell. Patty tried to be quiet but the old wooden floors creaked beneath her feet, even when she walked across the woven rug, as she always did, to look at the shelves.

They were full of Mama's collection. There were pale seashells – one with a pearl inside it – and tusks with carvings in them, paintings and sketches that hung from ribbons, and the skull of a critter with horns. There was a stuffed bird in a big fancy cage, and a globe in its own stand. There were bugs of all different kinds pinned to a board, but Patty didn't like to look at those. Instead she looked at the little clay pot full of brightly-colored feathers.

In the center of it all hung the dark, fancy cuckoo clock with its mysterious chains and weights dangling from it like necklaces. The center piece swung back and forth, back and forth. Its ticking filled the room with familiar, incessant rhythm. Patty stared at the door the little bird lived in, then looked away.

It had been just her and Mama for as long as Patty could remember, but sometimes people traveled through the woods to see the house. They called it the cottage of curiosities. Mama liked to show them her treasures, but she never sold them, so eventually people stopped coming.

The special rock felt heavy in Patty's hand, so she left the shelves and sat on the edge of the bed.

"How do you feel, Mama?"

Mama rolled onto her back with a soft groan, peering up at Patty. Her face almost looked like a stranger's in the gloom. "Hi baby. I'm a little cold."

Patty tilted her head to the side. The breeze outside was crisp and chilly, but inside the house it was almost too warm. She reached out and put a hand on Mama's forehead, like Mama did to her when she was sick. The gilded mirror on the nightstand on the other side of the bed reflected Mama's profile.

"You're very warm," Patty said.

"I don't feel warm," said Mama. Then she pulled the blankets in tighter around her chin and rolled back onto her side. "Will you blow out the candles when you leave, sweetheart? Mama's very tired."

Patty frowned. Mama wasn't going to scold her for making her ring the bell? Or ask her what it was she was holding in her hand? She really must be feeling bad.

Patty stood, blew out all of the candles but one, and set the chunk of silver on the tray next to the bed. Maybe it would cheer Mama up in the morning. Then she kissed Mama on the cheek, took the last candle, and left her to sleep.

Patty brought Mama breakfast, but she didn't want any. The silver rock was gone though, so she must have gotten up during the night and seen it, maybe put it on the shelves somewhere. Patty hoped it made her smile.

Patty stayed inside all morning and afternoon, just in case Mama needed her. She walked around their small home and studied every single shelf and all their curiosities. She'd seen them before, but every time she looked she noticed something new.

This time she spotted several dark, oval medallions hanging high on one wall, but she couldn't read what they said. In one cabinet she saw a whole bird's nest with four eggs in it, next to some arrowheads and a piece of strangely shaped coral. There was a section of wood that felt like stone and a stone with the skeleton of a fish in it. Then there were her old favorites, like the knight's helmet and the stuffed fox with his long whiskers and glass eyes.

As fascinating as these things were – for Patty loved to make up stories about each object and where it came from – by the time the cuckoo's cries grew short and began to grow long again, Patty was twitchy with extra energy. It was still a couple of hours until she'd have to be inside for the night, so she decided to go outside and swing.

This time she faced the woods, but for the first time, she didn't feel the need to watch them just in case something came out. She wanted to go back in. What if there was more silver in there? Or something better, like gold? Or something Patty couldn't even imagine? If she could find something really good, it would make Mama feel better for sure. Only babies were afraid of the woods.

The cries of the cuckoo came from inside – six of them. She still had an hour before Mama would ring the bell.

Patty didn't even stop swinging. She jumped forward when the ropes were stretched all the way, and she hit the ground running. She'd have to search fast.

Patty's fingers trembled as she picked it up. She could hardly even believe it.

Nestled among old brown leaves was a short stick completely covered in bright orange moss. She'd never seen moss that color before – only greens and grays – but it got better. There was a little black crow's foot still attached, grasping one side. What had happened to the rest of the crow she didn't like to wonder, but there was no doubt Mama would love this curiosity.

Patty straightened back up, gripping the stick by the end furthest away from the foot, and turned to leave. Then turned again. And again.

Which way had she come from?

A twig snapped to her side, and she whirled. Nothing moved,

but it had gotten darker beneath the leaves. What time was it? Was Mama worried about her? Had she already rung the bell?

A crunch, this time from further away.

"Hello?" Patty called softly.

There was a waiting silence.

"Who's there?" Patty asked.

For some reason, Patty thought she might get an answer, and she desperately didn't want to.

She ran.

She clutched the stick with the crow's foot to her chest and bolted, sprinting through the trees like a wild doe. Twigs scraped the soft puffs of her cheeks and once she tripped on a vine, but she never looked back. She didn't know if she was going the right way until she heard the bell ring. She adjusted her direction toward it.

She didn't hear anything chasing her, but still she ran. Finally Patty burst through the trees into the soft sunlight slanting from behind the house, and she didn't stop. She ran up to front door, twisted the knob, and skittered inside, shoving it closed behind her. She stood leaning on it, panting.

"You're such a baby," she muttered.

Just to prove how silly she'd been, she went to the window and looked outside. The grass stretched wide and green and empty beyond the flowers next to the house. The woods were still. Her tree swing swayed gently. Patty held her breath, but then she forced herself to laugh. She'd probably bumped it when she ran through the yard. She shut the curtains for the night.

Only then did she remember her prize: the moss-covered stick clutched in her hand, the little crow's foot perched on the end.

Mama was lying on her side again, and the room was still smoky and dark. Patty was surprised Mama had bothered to get up to ring the bell at all.

Patty crossed over the creaky floors and the thick rug to look at the curiosities. She scanned the shelves for where Mama might have put her silver rock, but she couldn't find it. She spent a few moments studying the pretty miniature town on the far side. There was snow on some of the roofs but not all of them. Mama said Patty could put them in her room when she got a little older.

From the cuckoo came an odd, strangled cry, and Patty stared at the wooden door the bird lived in, but it wasn't time for it to come out. The clock's tick hiccupped, then kept going. Patty turned away.

"Mama?" she said softly, walking over to the bed.

Mama groaned.

Patty put a hand on Mama's shoulder, but she wouldn't roll over onto her back. Patty peered into the mirror on the other side of the bed, but it wasn't turned at quite the right angle to see her face.

"Mama, are you okay?"

Mama mumbled something Patty couldn't hear. Patty reached over to feel her forehead, but her hand hovered. She knew Mama was sick. Really sick. Patty didn't know what to do.

She lightly brushed Mama's hair back, then set the stick on the tray next to the bed. "I'm sorry the silver didn't make you feel better," she whispered. "But you'll like this one. I can tell."

When Mama's only reply was the deep breathing of heavy sleep, Patty took the last candle and left, dragging her feet behind her.

Patty had to do something to help Mama. The stick with the crow's foot was gone in the morning, which meant Mama had gotten up at least once overnight, but she refused breakfast again.

She had to go back into the woods. She had to find something really good so Mama would get better. Maybe she'd even meet a person – a grown-up who would know what to do.

As Patty headed into the green shade, her swing hung still and silent under the tree, and the squirrel watched her, holding his tail. Patty marched with purpose, heading in as straight a line as she could.

But it was impossible to walk in a straight line with all the trees in the way, and before Patty knew it she wasn't sure which way she'd come from. The first tear had started down her cheek when she spotted something white.

Sniffling a little, Patty eased toward the small fluffy lump. She nudged it with the toe of her shoe, but it didn't move. She knelt, reaching out to touch the soft fur with her hand. It was a rabbit.

Patty gently picked it up, but it flopped limply. It had two big ears so tall she could see the veins running through the insides of them. Its eyes were open but a dull, blank black. It was dead, but Patty didn't see anything wrong with it.

"You poor thing," she said. "What happened to you?"

The rabbit didn't answer.

Then Patty got an idea. Maybe this could be a curiosity. Its fur was perfectly white and pretty and it didn't have any injuries. Mama could have it stuffed like the fox and the bird, and she could add it to her other treasures. Patty was sorry the bunny had died, but she was very happy to have found the best curiosity so far. This was *certain* to make Mama feel better!

Patty stood, but something was wrong. The woods were silent. She looked around, holding the rabbit to her torso, but nothing moved. She felt like someone was watching her. Was there someone here? Could they help?

"Hel—hello?" Patty asked softly.

There weren't any sounds. No one was there, but the hairs on Patty's arms prickled and danced.

She wouldn't be a baby like last time, though. Clenching her teeth together, Patty turned and headed in the direction she was pretty sure was home.

She forced herself to walk slowly. She felt like something was behind her, but every time she looked nothing was there. Her pace gradually increased until she was shoving her way through branches and striding with stiff legs.

Patty thought maybe she saw the yard ahead. If only the bell would ring so she could be sure. A twig snapped behind her, but she knew it must be her imagination. Or another squirrel. She refused to look. "I'm not a baby," she said.

She could see her swing. Something scraped behind her, and Patty couldn't stand it anymore.

She ran across toward the lawn as fast as she could – past the trees, past the swing, over the grass, and into the house. Even as she slammed the door shut, she couldn't bring herself to see if anything was there. She ran to the window and closed the curtains without looking outside.

Patty stood clutching the white rabbit to her chest, where her heart pounded so hard it made her skin pulse all over.

"You're a stupid baby," she told herself, but there wasn't any punch to it.

She stood there until her breathing slowed down, and then she went to check on Mama.

This time Patty set her treasure on the tray by the bed right away. She propped the pretty rabbit where the moss-covered stick had been, then went to the shelves to try to find the latter. The cuckoo ticked like an echo of her heartbeat as she searched, but Patty couldn't spot where Mama had placed the stick with the crow's foot.

The floors creaked as Patty walked over to the bed and sat down on the edge. Mama was on her side again, and for a moment she seemed so still that Patty froze too. Then she saw the covers moving with Mama's breath, and her shoulders sank with relief.

"Mama," she said. "Are you awake?"

Mama didn't answer.

"Mama?" she said a little louder.

Mama let out a strange, tiny groan.

Patty reached out a hand to rest on Mama's shoulder, but for some reason she hesitated. Her hand dropped back to her lap.

"Mama I'm scared. Are you okay?"

Heavy breathing was the only reply.

Patty shifted, leaning over to peer into the mirror on the other side of the bed and see Mama's face. But Mama had the covers pulled up all the way around her head like a cape, so her face was hidden in shadows by the blanket.

Patty lifted up the candle nearby, holding it over Mama's body so she could see into the mirror. The flame made the glass glint and wink, and the glow only dimly reached it. Patty moved her arm around until the light reflected just right, stretching barely within the shadows of Mama's covers.

Patty saw a face that only half looked like Mama's. Patty raised the candle, and eyes glinted within the blankets. They were open, staring at her. They looked solid black.

The cuckoo cried out. Patty shrieked, leaping back.

Mama didn't move. Patty whirled to face the clock, where the strange little bird burst madly in and out of the door where he lived.

Something was wrong with the chime. He made a strange gurgling sound as he thrust forward, over and over.

Patty didn't wait for him to get to seven. She ran out of the room and shut the door.

She hid in her bedroom until morning.

By the time sun came through Patty's window, she felt silly but still very worried. She had been a baby last night and let her imagination get the best of her, but she knew she had to go get help. Today a new curiosity wouldn't be enough. She'd have to go not just into the woods but through them, all the way out the other side where other people lived.

Before she left, she cracked open Mama's bedroom door and peeked inside. The rabbit on the tray was gone, and Mama looked like an unmoving lump under her blankets. Patty stood in the doorway and watched long enough to see her breathing, then shut the door again.

The woods were very dark, even though the sun hadn't gone all the way down yet. The trees overhead made a roof of jagged leaves, and all of the shadows looked long and green.

Patty had been walking all day and she still hadn't gotten out of the woods. She was tired and hungry and anxious about Mama. She passed a large tree with a misshapen knot in its belly.

Hadn't she already seen that tree?

Patty stopped, looking around.

Had she already been here?

In the distance, Patty heard the cuckoo begin its mottled cry. Her throat felt tight as she turned toward the sound. It wasn't very far away. It sounded like it came from the side of the cottage.

She'd been walking in circles.

The little bird kept crying, although the sound was slow and warbled. She counted to seven, then eight. It kept going. Nine, ten. But it wasn't dark yet, so it couldn't be that late, could it? Eleven, twelve. Patty looked around, hugging her arms tight around herself.

Thirteen. Fourteen. Fifteen.

The cuckoo kept going.

Patty bounced on her heels, hugging herself. She was supposed to help Mama, but she got lost all day. The thought of going back to the house made her start breathing heavy. "What should I do?" she whispered.

The little bird cried and cried.

Something to the side caught her eye. Patty took a few steps toward it, deeper into the woods. As she began to see around a tree trunk, she realized it was the bottom of a shoe. Above it was white fabric, over an ankle.

Patty stopped.

Her heart pounded.

"Who's there?" Patty asked.

The only answer was the cuckoo's deranged call.

Patty felt tears trail down her cheeks, warm compared to the nip in the air.

"I don't want any more curiosities," she said, but the shoe stayed.

Her chest began to shake with sobs, but Patty wouldn't let them out. She wasn't a baby, and whether or not she looked, the shoe was there.

She continued walking around the tree, bringing into sight the matching shoe and ankle. Then a long skirt, spread askew and dotted with crimson leaves. Next to it, two hands that looked familiar.

Patty's whole body shook, but she stepped the rest of the way around the tree that blocked her view.

Mama lay dead in the leaves, facing up, her pale blue eyes open and staring listlessly at the trees. Her skin was gray from being outside for days, and ants trailed into the corners of her mouth.

Patty screamed.

If Mama had been here, what was in her room?

Inside the cottage the cuckoo stopped, burbling into a silence that ticked through the woods like a clock too strange to tell time any longer. The silence tocked and dangled and swayed, waiting.

Then the bell rang.

THE DEVIL TAKE THE HINDMOST

For three nights the dream had been nothing but memory replaying itself inside Hellen's mind, restless and aware she slept but unable to wake. Helpless, she stood at the front of the crowd, refusing her father's attempts to draw her under his arm, staring instead up at her mother's stoic face with her own jaw clenched tight, shoulders stiff, arms wrapping her cloak about her. The morning smelled of wet wool and animal dung.

The magistrate intoned in a low, hollow voice, "On this day of the twenty-third of October on the year of our Lord, 1596, under the power vested in me by Fyvie court and condoned by the Royal Scottish commission, I hereby condemn Marjorie Urquhart to death by burning." He lowered his torch and lit the fagots piled around her mother's feet. They caught in a hungry billow.

The villagers had refused to mix in green wood like she asked. The younger wood smoked more, and might have sucked her mother away from misery sooner. This wood was all dry, carefully gathered.

Hellen stared into her mother's eyes – so piercing and green. When Hellen was a lass she'd asked her father to tell her the story of how those eyes had made him fall in love with her mother, over and over. *Like a living emerald*, he used to say, smiling at Marjorie over Hellen's head. *Like the grass in the highlands after the spring rain. They cast a cantrip over me, those eyes. They held me enchanted. Kind she was not. She stabbed me through the heart and I loved it.*

The wording no longer seemed romantic. Not after Giles had testified against his wife. Not after he had betrayed her, innocent, to prove his innocence.

Hellen shrugged off his arm, looking into those beautiful eyes.

"I love you," Marjorie said, panic singing the edges of her tone, but still it carried the tenderness it always carried when she spoke to her only daughter. The crowd murmured, but Marjorie said again, louder, "I love you." She could have been speaking to her husband or sons, but Hellen knew she spoke to her.

I love you too, Hellen mouthed. Her heart had never beaten so hard. Her mother was over fifty, aye, but still in good health and too young to die. She'd yearned to see Hellen married with children of her own, and with Hellen over twenty and betrothed, surely she would not have had long to bide.

The flames rose to catch the plain white robe they'd draped on her. That's when her mother started to scream.

Perhaps it was the screams that drove the crowd back. They were the worst Hellen had ever heard, and she'd witnessed her mother midwife countless births. These screams were deeper, from a place of pure abandon. In long, rapid succession her mother screamed, drawing breath as fast as she could for the next, finally breaking her gaze with Hellen to toss her head back against the stake that held her.

Or perhaps it was the smell of burning flesh that drove the crowd back. Through the amazing orange flames, her mother's skin melted and crisped and sloughed off her legs, but still she screamed.

Hellen didn't know if the beads of liquid dripping down her own face were sweat or tears. The heat grew fierce. The flames leaped higher. The fagots snapped with sharp pops. Her cloak dropped to the mud. Sobs shook her chest but she refused to let them out. She stared up at the underside of her mother's throat as the screams ripped from her.

Her father tried to pull her back and she brushed him off again. He gripped her by the arm and dragged her backwards, away from the flames now wide enough to lick her. She stumbled, a shoe sticking in the shin-high muck, but she regained her balance and kept watching.

Marjorie began thrashing. Her head whipped side to side, the scream fading in and out, her arms jerking as much as her bonds would allow, and the flames climbed higher. Higher. Higher like the pitch of her relentless screams. Living agony, those shrieking wails. Someone in the back yelled out, "Mercy!" but it was far too late.

"Mercy," another woman cried, weeping, but no one moved except her mother until, finally, she didn't. The screams stopped, and the air was infused with the overpowering smell of burning hair, thick and sharp. "Mercy," the woman sobbed.

Her father turned away, and the villagers followed. Her brothers followed. Everyone followed except Hellen, staying until the blackened skeleton collapsed in feathery pieces, until the flames died, until the wood and stake itself were but a pile of ashes and all that remained were the echoes of the screaming and the lingering taste of burning hair clinging in a bitter film at the back of her throat.

Three times, Hellen had dreamed this. Every night she'd slept since it happened exactly that way, five nights ago.

This night, it was different.

This night, when she stared into her mother's jewel-green eyes as the flames caught and billowed, dancing up her clothes and skin, her mother winked at her.

A trill of fear flipped in Hellen – not fear for her mother, but for herself – and she started, looking to see if any of the villagers had seen the gesture and what they might suppose, but she was alone. No one had come. In real life, the entirety of Fyvie, their small village north of Aberdeen, had turned out to watch the purification of Marjorie Urquhart. But now Hellen stood alone in the gray sludge.

"I'm dreaming," Hellen muttered.

When she looked up at her mother, those sharp green eyes still stared. This was where Marjorie said, *I love you.* Twice, she'd said it.

Marjorie remained silent.

"I love you," Hellen said, prompting the dream. She wanted that part.

Her mother did not scream, did not blink. Her mouth remained closed, her eyes staring into Hellen's.

"Mother?"

The fire grew, eating away the skirt, the legs, the flesh. The smell of healthy wood smoke thickened into the aroma of cooking meat, then the tang of burning hair assaulted the air.

Her mother didn't break the gaze, didn't fight the pain.

The flames lapped the air, searching for new tinder. One caught the cloak over Hellen's chest. Still she couldn't pull her eyes away from her mother's stare. Her silence was terrible. Hellen had thought nothing on this Earth could be worse than her mother's screams, but surely this silence was.

Hellen was hot. Even hotter than she had been in real life. No one pulled her back this time. She must be burning. The wool smoldered over her chest, scalding her in a sharp bite.

She shrieked, gasping, but choked.

Tears streaming from her eyes, she looked back at her mother. Marjorie's hair was on fire, the skin on her face pitting like spoiled cheese, but still her eyes remained, watching motionlessly from inside the blaze, appraising her daughter as the flames ate her alive.

The smoke crawled down Hellen's throat, rushed into her lungs and sank there. Heavy, thick, warm. So warm. Smothering.

She woke up.

Two otherworldly green eyes stared into hers from inches away, piercing her soul. They floated in the blackness of her room, and Hellen was still burning, still choking, but she couldn't move, couldn't breathe for the terror those eyes filled her with.

"Mother?" she coughed out, and before the word was finished she hated herself for saying it, for thinking it, for attaching it to the fear.

The eyes blinked over vertically slit pupils. The cat.

The eyes stared. The fear lingered.

Hellen sucked in a deep breath – possible. Harder with Mery's warm weight on her, but possible. Not the deadly suffocation of smoke.

"Mery-bell," Hellen whispered, swallowing another cough. "You frightened me."

Hellen's hand trembled as she worked it from beneath the cover to stroke Mery's silken fur. The green eyes closed in bliss, a deep purr emanating from her small body. The delicate chin rested beneath her own, balanced on her neck so the rhythmic breath coated her flesh.

Did Mery sense something was wrong? Did she know Hellen needed comfort? Or did she simply seek the warmth the nightmare brought?

Closing her eyes, Hellen floated down through the darkness back into sleep, hoping the memory was done for the night. She sought comfort in the cat's warmth. The last thing she felt was the concentrated lick of Mery's rough tongue on the soft, sensitive skin of her throat.

Hellen woke to the vague sensation of dreams fleeing, feeling a heavy weight on her chest, but when she opened her eyes, Mery was no longer on her. Nothing was on her but the cover.

The morning was cold. Mery had left her sometime during the night and her father and brothers had never started the fires before leaving for the field. As the woman of the house now, Hellen would be expected to rise the earliest and ready breakfast, but so far her father had said nothing. The men hadn't touched the cold bread sitting on the table, growing hard with blue-and-green spots. Had her father not lit the fires because he, too, could think only of the flames? Did he dream? Did it still seem better her than him?

Hellen stared at the leaking thatched roof. Her limbs felt heavy as the cauldron they boiled water in, heavier than the stones that made the walls of this low, squat house, heavy like the weight of her future holding her down.

She lifted herself wordlessly beneath the covers, sliding her bare feet onto the cool, packed dirt floor, and shuffled toward the dead coals, debating whether the warmth was worth the pain. Her foot landed on something soft and round, pressing into her arch.

Hellen cringed, closing her eyes and lifting her foot away. Mery often left her hunted treats, anything from mice to birds and once even a hare, some still struggling. At least this felt dead. Bracing herself, Hellen glanced to see what she'd stepped on.

It was small, pale gray, and doughy, slightly curved. She looked away with revulsion. A slow-worm tail. Mery often caught those snake-like, legless lizards, and they were notorious for dropping their tails as a diversion. She shuddered, hoping the rest of the creature wasn't sliming around somewhere she might step on it, too.

Why did Mery bring her such things? Was it an offering? A game, warning, or threat? An attempt at mothering? The disconnect between people and cats had always struck her when she looked into Mery's nearly featureless black face. Even her whiskers and nose were black. The only color besides her green eyes came when she yawned or hissed and Hellen caught a glimpse of her bright white teeth or long pink tongue. They bonded, aye, but they did not speak the same language. Any communication was subject to misinterpretation.

Whatever the reason, she couldn't bear to touch the tail. After slipping on her shoes, Hellen took the broom from its hook and swept the grotesque wee thing toward the open doorway at the front of the dwelling. She shoved it with the stiff bristles, trying to send it far with each swipe but not squish it. Glancing only from the corner of her eye, she got it to the threshold, but it caught on the straw layered there to stiffen the slick mud outside. The smell of the outdoor fire wafted to her, low and smoky beside the midden.

Hellen swept at the stuck appendage furiously, trying to thrust it up and over the edges of the straw, but it wedged in.

Feeling eyes on her, she looked up.

Across the street their neighbor, Euphemia Prat, who her mother had called Old Effy, watched her with a sneer, her pock-ridden nose curled in disdain.

Confused, Hellen looked down, wondering if her skirt was up, then realized she held her mother's broom. The very broom Euphemia, Jonet, and the others had claimed her mother rode to the revels. Her cheeks burned. Such lies.

Hellen lifted her chin. She would not be shamed. "Good morning, Euphemia."

"'Tis a good morning, with the village free of evil once again."

Hellen held herself still, but her body trembled with rage. "I do not believe sending an innocent woman to burn is a good deed.

I should beg the Lord for forgiveness had I been involved in such happenings."

Euphemia smiled. She had three teeth left. "Marjorie Urquhart confessed. Only the guilty confess."

The heat in Hellen's cheeks melted down her neck, spreading wide across her chest. "Anyone would confess when put to the rack long enough."

"Aye, but she confessed to more than was asked of her, didn't she? She admitted to seeing the Devil himself traipsing through the woods."

Hellen nearly burst forth a reply, but bit her tongue. Finally, she said, "She said she saw him leading others. I should hope none of it was true, for if so our village isn't free of evil yet." She hoped Euphemia thought about that. She'd been close with her mother. Marjorie had refused to list names, but should any others be accused, surely Euphemia would be amongst them.

"Is it not? The mothers and fathers of Fyvie have slept soundly since Marjorie was taken in, knowing their babes are safe. And who can see the Devil?" Euphemia asked, jaw wagging. "Who can see Old Scratch save for witches, eh? I never seen him. I never walked with him. 'Twas your mother who admitted to what she was by claiming to see others follow."

"My mother was a good woman."

Euphemia sent a pointed glance to the broom Hellen now grasped like a bludgeon. "If you like. And did you ever see him, Hellen Guthrie? Did your mother introduce you to his pact?"

It was a threat, as surely as Hellen's, but far more likely. The village was already suspicious of her, wondering how much mother passed to daughter. She couldn't afford to play these games. "Of course not," she demurred, ducking her head. "I have never seen him." *But neither did my mother.*

She leaned the broom against the wall, knelt, and grasped the dead thing between her thumb and forefinger, letting emotion override revulsion. She carried it toward the midden, the dunghill where they piled their refuse.

Euphemia gave a delighted scoff before retreating into her dwelling. Hellen turned her back, staring at the rotting waste, panting, trying to calm herself. Finally, she raised her hand to toss the thing.

She paused, drawing it closer to her face instead. She eyed it, freshly calm in her curiosity. It wasn't smooth enough to be a slow-worm tail as she'd thought. It had two puffy creases in it.

Hellen cocked her head. There were no scales either. It was smooth gray. Not a lizard part.

She set it on the flat of her other hand, turning it with a finger. At one end, tiny and delicate and shockingly familiar, she recognized it: a nail. A fingernail.

It was a finger. Small.

A baby's.

Swallowing a gasp, Hellen studied the opposite end, where it had been detached. Indeed, there was a bone in the center. Her stomach heaved a great lurch. It was an infant's finger, drained entirely of blood and going gray.

She hurled it into the fire beside the midden. The flames continued on unhurried, growing slightly at the new tinder. With a glance to be sure Euphemia hadn't seen, Hellen darted back inside.

Over and over she punched the dough's firm, tacky mass into the use-smoothed wood of the family table, folding it onto itself. Her mind turned endless revolutions with the kneading.

A baby's finger. From whence had it come? If anyone but her should have seen it, they'd have thought it damning evidence. But it hadn't been in their house. Mery had brought it from elsewhere.

Hellen had no doubt there were those who practiced witchcraft, but not in Fyvie. Theirs was a small village of good people. Maybe in Aberdeen where the market was large and the officials corrupt, but not here. Not her mother.

Her mother. Those burned at the stake never received proper death rites. Where did her mother's soul go then?

"'Twas only because they were babies," Hellen whispered. As soon as the words left her she felt spied upon. She looked up, searching the dimness. A twitching motion caught her eye. Mery perched in an open window, sitting on the wall. Her tail swayed back and forth, brushing against the stone. With her dark fur and the gray of the day outside only slightly brighter than the gray inside, she was but a silhouette.

"Oh, Mery-bell," Hellen sighed, kneading in a gentler rhythm. "I thought someone was here."

The cat stayed motionless but for her tail, and though Hellen couldn't see them, she felt those green eyes on her.

"You brought the… thing to me." Hellen always spoke to the cat when she was alone. She had since she was a lass; it eased her loneliness. "You left it for me where you always leave your treats. Where did you find it?"

Mery turned her head, showing Hellen her delicate feline profile.

Hellen shifted the dough to spread more flour beneath it. "You ken that's why they burned her? They accused her of using them in her flying ointment. The midwife is simply the easiest to blame when babies go missing."

Mery jumped from the sill in a graceful fall, onyx fur gleaming as she prowled past Hellen's feet to sprawl between the table and the ashes of the cooking fire. It was unheard of for the Guthrie family to let it go out, but Hellen thought it right. Something should change. It wasn't right for life to go on as usual, and the quiet coldness of the house seemed better suited than any other change.

"And those babies didn't go missing." Hellen continued, keeping her voice low. "They died. Their parents killed them through neglect or meagerness or bad luck and they felt guilty, grew feart, and they hid them. Buried the bodies so no one would—"

Hellen stopped, fingers sunk into the dough. That was it! Mery had dug up one of the bodies that could prove her mother's innocence. If the child were buried in the dirt, it couldn't have been used in an evil concoction. Hellen turned to the cat. Mery was sitting up, her tail wrapped neatly around her two front paws, and staring at her with those wide green eyes, her head cocked ever so slightly to the side, as if listening. The look on her pointed, alien face was so alert, so alive, so seemingly intelligent that Hellen froze.

Mery dipped her head and began cleaning the fur on her chest with great, limber licks of her tongue. Hellen let out a breathless chuckle. She placed the dough in the pan, covering it with a cloth and setting it to rise.

"That is it, though," she said. Mery continued her bath. "Maybe I can gain my mother's death rites and set her soul to rest. Will you lead me to the bodies?"

Mery's ear twitched to the side. Goose bumps rose on Hellen's arms.

"Tonight when you go out to find your dinner, I will follow you," Hellen whispered, bending to scratch Mery between her velvety ears. "And see if we can prove them wrong." A gentle purr rose in the air.

Hellen leaned over the cat to gather fresh peat blocks to set in the ashes.

Mery let forth a vicious hiss.

Hellen jerked back, shocked. "Mery-bell," she exclaimed. "I didn't mean to startle you. I just need to start the fire."

Mery stood, arching her back, and hissed again, flashing fangs.

Hellen was so surprised that her feelings were hurt. "What's gotten into you, lass?"

When she stepped forward again, Mery swatted at her ankle. This time Hellen brushed past her, letting her skirts force the cat out of the way. Mery meowed, fluffed her fur, and ran out the door, tail standing.

Hellen piled the peat blocks with a deep sigh. There went her company for the rest of the day. She grabbed the molded bread off the table and tossed it to the far edge of the midden where the goats could pick it off. 'Twas every man, woman, child, and beast for himself in this world. Hellen was learning that faster than any, but even goats had to eat.

Hellen sat at the table with her father and two brothers. She had made a large batch of stew with boiling fowl, leeks, rice, and prunes, seasoned with sugar, pepper, bay leaf, and thyme. The remains still steamed in the bronze cauldron, but the portions in their wooden bowls had already begun to cool. The men dipped bread into the stew and slurped. Behind them, the cooking fire smoldered, the smoke rising in a ghostly column to drift out the hole in the ceiling.

Her father drank the bottom of his stew and leaned back, the old wooden bench creaking with his shifted weight. "The Meldrum lad has called off the betrothal," Giles said.

Hellen dropped her bread into her bowl, pulse quickening. "Richard? Why?" She needed the engagement. She was twenty-five, of the age to marry, and it was the only way she could leave her father's house.

Stew glistened on her father's reddish beard. He sighed. "He's changed his mind."

"You can hardly blame him," Norman muttered.

Hellen looked at the elder of her two younger brothers sharply. The beard he'd been trying to grow was patchy and thin. "What does that mean?"

"It means," Norman dragged out, "that now the lads are feart you'll do to them what Mother did to Da." Giles had testified that his wife had cast a cantrip to render him impotent.

Her father sighed. "Norman, stay out of this. Hellen, the villagers are nervous. Give them time. I'm sure Richard will come around."

But Richard wouldn't come around. He'd only set to marry her because she was pretty and apprenticed to make money as a midwife. There was no love there. What would she do now? Hellen pushed her bowl away and Norman slid it toward himself, sopping up the remains.

"Father," she said, already regretting what the anger would make her say, "did you ever consider it was your age that stole your manhood, rather than my mother?"

Giles's face went from weary to grim. "Watch your tongue, lass. I ken my own wife."

Norman chimed in, "The Guthrie men have never faced that struggle. We are a virile line. Only witchcraft could weave such a curse."

"Yeah," Duncan added. "We are a virile line."

"Duncan," Hellen snapped. "You aren't even old enough to ken what that means."

"Mother was a witch," he hissed. She drew back, struck. His big brown eyes gleamed as he added, "And you might be a witch too!"

Giles stood, putting a hand on his youngest son's shoulder. "Now lads, don't say such things in anger. Hellen is a good lass, a righteous lass, and you mustn't throw such words about. Especially not now, when the villagers are hot. Do you understand me?"

Duncan lowered his head. "Aye, Da."

Norman echoed, "Aye, Da," but he smirked.

"I'm sorry, Father," Hellen said, standing to clear the table. "In my grief I've let my tongue run away with me. Forgive me."

"Of course, lassie. 'Tis a hard time for us all, but it is well that the Meldrum lad has broken the betrothal. With your mother gone, we will need you more than ever, here, to tend the home."

Hellen stayed awake after her brothers and father had gone to bed, slowly adding peat blocks to the fire as she waited for Mery to return. She was drowsing with her head on the table when she heard a soft shift. The cat sat in the window, tail swishing. She stood, stretching, and circled herself on the sill, turning as if to lead Hellen away.

"Finally," Hellen whispered. She stood and pulled on her cloak, moving toward the door.

"Hellen," came a deep voice.

She whirled, swallowing a gasp. Her father stood in the shadows.

"What are you doing awake? I thought I heard your mother sneaking late-night bread as she used to."

The casualness with which he spoke of the memory pierced Hellen, and she could not breathe, much less answer.

Then Giles took in her cloak and shoes and stepped closer. "Why are you dressed to go out? Where are you going at this hour?"

"I… needed some fresh air. I felt stifled. I was going to walk for a bit in the cool."

"Tonight? Are you mad?"

She shook her head, unable to gather what he meant.

"Have you lost track of the days? The beginning of Allhallowtide is nearly upon us. The morn marks Hallowmass Eve."

She'd forgotten. She hadn't been out of the house in days, hadn't seen any of the villagers' traditional preparations. Aye, it was the thirtieth of October tonight. But Mery…

She looked for the cat, but she was nowhere to be seen.

"You cannot wander about, Hellen," he said, taking her by the arm and leading her toward her bed. "If anyone should see you, at a time like this…"

He didn't have to finish. All Hallows' was the time of witches, when they ventured out to dance with the Devil, and it was true she couldn't risk being seen out, not now.

"Aye, of course, Father."

"Good lass. Get some sleep now," he said, pulling back her covers for her as if she were a small child.

She wanted to find where Mery had dug up that thing – see what it might mean for mother, for herself – but now her father would be too watchful, and besides, he was right. It was good of him to look after her.

But as he pulled the covers and tucked them tightly under her chin, she wondered if that was actually the reason. Was he protecting her, or suspicious?

Had he been waiting up, keeping his eye on her?

Lying awake in the dark, listening to him make his way to his bed and climb inside, Hellen imagined this was how her mother had felt, turned upon by her own family, accused under the guise of salvation.

The nightmare came again. It began as the memory. When it reached the part where the magistrate lit the fagots and her mother was to say, *I love you*, Hellen was relieved the villagers were there. At least it wouldn't be the isolated, twisted version of last night. They crowded behind her in the mud as they really had, and her mother said it.

"I love you." The broken, fearful tone. She looked into Hellen's eyes with that brilliant green gaze. Murmurs from the crowd. "I love you," she repeated.

I love you too, Hellen mouthed, as she had.

"What's the matter?" Marjorie said.

Hellen looked around. Everyone stared.

"Aren't you going to say it back?" Marjorie asked, angry. "Aren't you going to tell your mother you love her before she burns to death?"

The crowd's murmuring grew into concerned discussion. If she said it, would they accuse Hellen of being a witch too? Would they call her loyalty allegiance?

The flames reached her mother's robe and she began to scream. Hellen felt sickly relieved at the return to the actual order of things. At least it wasn't that silence, that horrible silence of the night before.

When the screams grew frantic and ragged, just before her mother had tossed back her head and begun to thrash, the nature of the screaming changed. It was gradual at first. The screams slowed, grew false, and then Marjorie was pretending to scream, the way you would mock someone else who was screaming.

The crowd was silent now. The flames leapt towards Hellen's cloak. Her father didn't try to pull her back.

Marjorie's cruelly mocking screams morphed and bubbled into

laughter. Rich, boisterous, atrocious laughter. She tossed back her head and laughed, her breasts jiggling with the motion, and the flames continued to climb, to eat her, and she laughed.

She laughed and laughed as her hair caught fire and the flames bit Hellen's cloak and the smoke slipped down her throat and smothered her, so heavy she couldn't breathe.

She woke with a start, hot, sweating and shivering, Mery's weight balled on her chest. It was well before dawn, pitch black, and the cat's eyes must have been closed for Hellen could see nothing, only feel the pressure of her, only taste bitter fear on her tongue, only hear the echoes inside her mind of mother's maniacal laughter as she burned.

Hellen rose with the dawn, cold and tired and heavy again, the men gone already to the fields. The harvest was largely over. Now they gathered the waste for burning in great heaped piles spread around the village. The air was distinctly colder and sharper, bordering on November.

She remembered to put on her shoes, so she didn't step on the pale gray thing left for her on the floor, but it still startled her. She bent, gripping it in the bottom of her skirt.

This time it was a foot.

It was larger but still tiny, chubby, with nails at the ends of the toes. It stopped cleanly below the ankle, cold and drained of blood. Hellen hurried to the outdoor fire, imagining the babe it'd come from. Had she been able to follow Mery last night, she might've found where the poor thing was buried. Probably behind the house of his or her wretched parents.

She tossed it into the flames, covering it with scraps.

As she turned to go inside, a wail rose from down the path between rows of dwellings. People clustered outside, a woman on her knees in the center of them. Who? Young Agnes, perhaps, with the newborn.

Hellen's stomach sank. Not again. Not another.

"Aye," came a scratchy voice from the side. Hellen jumped, peering into the shadows under Old Effy's front covering. The woman watched her with sharp gray eyes. "Another babe gone missing."

Jonet stood beside her, an unusually pretty woman of about her mother's age: one of those who had testified against her. She, too, watched Hellen rather than the small crowd gathering around Agnes.

Hellen's heart pounded. Maybe she wouldn't need to follow Mery to the bodies. "'Tis the first child since my mother was taken in. This proves her innocence! It cannot be her, for she is gone."

Euphemia laughed, the skin under her chin waddling. "Gone? Gone. Who's to say? There are those who will think someone else has taken up her wicked quest."

Blame. Aye, of course they would blame her. Unless she blamed someone else first. She imagined accusing Euphemia. *'Twas her*, she would shout out, righteous, *'twas Old Effy all along!* But she wouldn't do it. She couldn't do it. She could not stand the woman, but she did not believe she would kill babies. Probably Agnes's baby caught the cough like so many did now, and helpless, afraid of being accused herself, Agnes had buried the child.

Was that whose foot Mery had brought her? She had to stop her cat from continuing this. Should someone see Hellen with such a thing she'd be found guilty without explanation.

She looked into the women's eyes. "I was home all night," she whispered, voice cracking. "I never left the house. My father can attest to it."

Jonet spoke for the first time, her voice melodious and soft. "He can, aye, but will he?"

"I…"

"Have you been sleeping, child?" Jonet asked, crossing the straw-coated mud. In the gray light of dawn, her smooth skin looked radiant.

"Not well. I have this dream…"

"Poor thing. Have you tried valerian root? A tad in your stew will ease your slumber."

"I haven't any."

Jonet reached a wrinkled hand – so much older-looking than her face – into the apron tied over her dress. She pulled out a large, knotted mass of tubes that for a moment reminded Hellen of the baby's finger or a slow-worm tail, but then she saw the nest of them tangled over and upon each other and they looked exactly like the knotted veins pressing against the skin of Jonet's hand. The bunch was fibrous and earthy, the bottoms of the roots diminishing into thread-thin wisps.

Hellen did not want to touch it, but Jonet proffered it between them with the expectation that Hellen would accept it, so she did. They felt smoother than they looked, slick. Downhill, Agnes's cries had calmed to a muted sobbing.

"You need but a small bit of it," Jonet said. "'Tis effective in any brew. Just a pinch will ease your sleep, lass."

Then why did you give me so much? Hellen wanted to ask, but she kept her mouth shut and drew the tangle of roots toward her skirts.

"Aye," called Euphemia, still huddled in the shadows. "And don't mix it with ale, mind you, unless you wish to sleep like the dead."

Hellen stared at the hag. She never drank ale. What was such a caution? Through the dimness under the covering, Euphemia's wide, gray gaze caught hers, and she winked.

Shock ran through Hellen's tired body. She remembered her mother's green eyes in the dream, her wink, her stalwart, silent gaze as she burned. Hellen's hands trembled.

"Head inside now, lass," Jonet urged her. "I will come for a visit first thing tomorrow morn. Perhaps you miss a mother's ministrations." Fresh fear filled Hellen. What if Jonet found one of Mery-bell's leavings?

Euphemia's taunting call came next, following over Hellen's shoulder as she hurried toward the doorway to her family's small, squat hut. "Aye. Head inside now, Hellen Guthrie. Stay inside tonight, if'n you're a good lass, for Allhallowtide approaches, and the Devil's dues are due on Hallowe'en night!"

During dinner only a few lads came to the door begging firewood, and they stopped well before nightfall. Giles gave them each a bundle lest they bring any mischief on the house, but he cautioned them to go home and stay inside, and would not allow young Duncan to join in the old games. Fyvie was somber this year. If anyone told fortunes or tales of fairies, they did it quietly.

Hellen went to the window at dusk, where Mery sat flicking her tail against the stone. She stroked her, watching the neighbors light their bonfires before turning away. Mery jumped from the window and lay in the corner.

"No one is to leave this house tonight," their father said, closing the shutters. He looked at Hellen. "No one. Understood?"

All three of them nodded. Hellen bowed her head. "Aye, Da."

Giles and Norman both drank heavily at dinner, Giles even allowing young Duncan some ale. Hellen quietly refilled their wooden mugs before the bottom was dry. She kept the fire burning hot so the room would be warm, and she served them large portions of hearty stew, and by a couple hours after dark, Giles snored in his bed. Norman slept quietly, and Duncan fell asleep sitting at the table. Hellen carried him to bed and tucked him in.

If they'd tasted the valerian root, they showed no sign of it.

She changed into her darkest frock and took out her cloak. Mery twined in and out of her legs.

"Are you ready to take me on your hunt, wee one?"

A rich, hearty purr rose.

"Lead me to the same place you've gone the past two nights, alright? Let's dig up the proof my mother was no witch." Even if the villagers wouldn't believe, she could at least prevent Mery from bringing back the pieces and putting Hellen in danger. It would be safer on any other night, but Jonet had promised to pay her a visit first thing in the morning. Hellen couldn't chance the nosy woman finding Mery-bell's next gift. It must be tonight.

With the bouncing, hurried walk only a cat can make graceful, Mery darted out the front door, leaving Hellen no time to question her rightness of mind or the risk she was taking, and she was glad of it. Drawing her cloak over her hair, she followed.

When she was a lass, some of the braver villagers would take candles out onto the hills on Hallowmass Eve to leet the witches. Should the candle burn brightly the hour through, the village was said to be safe from evil, but should the flame go out it was taken as an omen of great woe. As she hurried now, hunched and silent, through the darkest space between two bonfires, beyond the village's bounds, Hellen wondered what it meant to have no candle at all.

Indeed, she longed for a light, but she couldn't risk it. Most people would be asleep by now, locked safely inside their homes, but a few may be out to keep the bonfires burning, and some may watch in dread of fetches approaching their home.

She was amazed by how quickly wee Mery-bell could run. She didn't get the impression her cat was trying to lose her, though, for she occasionally looked back as if to check Hellen followed. As they burst into the open hills, the air was cold and crisp.

Mery darted across the long grass, tail high, and Hellen followed. It wasn't until the bonfires were small behind them that she paused. The cat continued. Hellen whisper-called, "Mery-bell, where are you going?"

Two flashes of green as she looked at Hellen, but she did not stop.

Hellen pulled her cloak tighter. Surely the cat wouldn't lead her into the woods? She'd been so worried lest villagers think she was something to fear that she hadn't stopped to wonder if she should fear others. She was reminded of the jeer she and the other children used to yell at each other fleeing the bonfires on All Hallows' Night: "Every one for himself and the Devil take the hindmost!"

She glanced over her shoulder.

Swallowing, she quickened her pace, and Mery led her uncannily, relentlessly, into the dark, heavy shadows of the woods above the village.

Hellen had always known Mery prowled at night. She was the best mouser in the area, which was perhaps the only reason the villagers had not demanded her burned as a familiar, but had Hellen known how far and wide the cat traveled, she'd have marveled that she made it home alive.

They were deep into the woods, and although the air was less cold, Hellen kept her cloak wrapped tightly, for the very trees moved and shadows shifted and Mery led her through it – always quick enough that Hellen couldn't stop to rest, but never so fast she lost sight of her.

At first Hellen thought she heard her own panting, heavy and airy, underscored by the pounding of her heart, but as she continued deeper and deeper into the woods, the sounds separated and made themselves clear: chanting. Did she hear drums?

Her skin prickled. "Mery-bell," she whispered vehemently, "Stifle your pace, lass. Someone is afoot." Her throat was tight, mouth dry, eyes wide enough to burn in their attempt to see through the trees, but Mery did not stop. Hellen followed as quietly as she could.

The chanting grew louder, the distinct rhythm almost detectable as words, and Hellen grew less afraid of being heard over the din and more afraid of being seen. Ahead, striped by the ever-shifting trunks of trees, a fire burned. Shadows moved around it.

Mery headed directly toward it. Hellen was too frightened to call out to stop her.

Were there drums? Hellen couldn't tell. Perhaps it was the relentless chanting that gave the impression of drums. Perhaps it was her heart, pulsing in her ears, making her whole body feel warm. Or perhaps *that* was the nearness of the fire.

Hellen stopped, having come upon the outskirts of the gathering before she meant to. A single tree stood between her and the flames, and the mad figures that cavorted around them.

The words were clear now. Women's voices chanted:

Power, money, beauty, and prestige:
The Devil gives his gifts on Hallowmass Eve.
Murder, mayhem, sacrifice, and fright:
The Devil's dues are due on Hallowe'en Night!

Rich, gleeful laughter rose at will. Hellen stared, recognizing a face. The long, wavy white hair and the shriveled nose belonged to Euphemia Prat.

Hellen swallowed a gasp, searching the others. There was Jonet with her pretty face and old hands, and Mavis who was missing an ear, and even young Katherine, Hellen's childhood friend, large with child.

Mery-bell walked calmly into the middle of the revel.

I should have picked her up! In the center of the ring, hung over the fire, was a large bronze cauldron. Large enough to hold a cat. For a moment, Hellen felt certain the wild women would throw Mery into whatever foul concoction simmered there, and she should lose her only remaining tender companion on this Earth.

Mery stopped, sniffing low to the ground, and only then did Hellen spot the baby.

An infant child was bundled tightly, perched against one of the rocks that ringed the fire. Mery sat on her haunches beside it and licked the delicate hair on the top of its head, mothering it with long, efficient strokes of her pink tongue.

Hellen was so enraptured by this strange kindness, this unexpected familiarity, that it took her a moment to realize all movement had stopped except for the flames and Mery's tongue. The women stood still. When Hellen lifted her gaze, she gasped.

All four women stared at her.

"Hellen Guthrie," said Old Effy. "I warned you about this night."

Katherine, cradling her stomach, asked, "Do you come to join our Sabbat?"

"I—I didn't mean to—I'll go. I followed Mery…"

Jonet looked at the cat, who was still vigorously cleaning the baby, and said, "That isn't her name."

"Mery?" For a moment, confusion dulled Hellen's fear. "Aye, it is." She tilted her head to study her cat. The gesture she'd at first thought was tender now made her cringe. Mery's tongue was so rough, with its barbs, and a baby's skin so soft. She must be hurting the child.

"Perhaps when she was but a cat," Jonet said patiently, as if speaking to a child. "But you don't think a cat could find her way here, do you?"

The cat's furious licking did not cease. The baby's face scrunched in frustration. Still that black face hovered over the bundle, licking, licking… tasting?

Hellen shook herself, appalled. "That is my cat," she snapped, darting forward to shoo her from the babe. Then she realized she stood in the circle, beside the women. Her mouth dried.

Euphemia tilted back her head and cackled gleefully. "Aye, and what's more, your mother!"

A log on the fire broke in two, collapsing in a fresh shower of sparks. Hellen jumped, backing up, damp shoes shuffling through the dead leaves. "What?"

"Your mother's soul, anyway. For now," she added. "But not for long if she doesn't pay her dues before the dawn!"

Hellen's heel bumped the base of a tree and she stopped, pressing her hands into its rough bark. She stared at her wee black cat who now undulated sinuously in the air as if she were rubbing against the legs of someone who wasn't there, as if her spine were being stroked by invisible fingers. Around and around she circled, turning her head as if to better press it against something, but nothing was there.

"Mother?" Hellen asked, her voice small and high. She felt faint, but she could not pass out now.

The cat looked up, locking onto her with wide, piercing green eyes. They stared at each other for a long minute, and Hellen knew. Her mother's soul resided in this cat. Tears tightened her throat, threatened her eyes. "Mother." Her whisper cracked on the word. Then the cat blinked and continued sinewing back and forth as if about invisible legs.

The baby fussed, kicking in helpless lumps beneath its swaddling. Was it Agnes's child? Hellen's face felt painfully pale, drained of blood.

"You can't blame Marjorie, Hellen," Katherine said. "She had no way of knowing they would burn her before she paid."

"Before she paid?" Hellen echoed, looking at her old friend.

"Aye, before she paid the Devil his dues."

"The Devil," Hellen gasped, breathless.

Euphemia's jaw wobbled. "Marjorie owes Old Scratch a soul. If she doesn't pay up tonight, he'll take hers with him straight back to Hell." She tossed back her head and laughed.

Jonet eyed the cat, still rubbing itself against the air, and added, "No matter how much she tries to sweet-talk him. The Devil's dues are due."

All four of the women repeated it, chanting: "The Devil's dues are due on Hallowe'en Night!"

"My mother really is a witch?" Hellen whispered. Why had she brought her here? Her head spun with dizziness.

Katherine set a hand on Hellen's arm. She twitched. Katherine said, "Aye, but you can hardly blame her. What choice do we have, those of us with nothing?" She stroked her belly again. "We will do anything to protect what we hold dear."

"Did she—do you…?" Her balance wavered, fingers gripping the bark. "The babies?"

They turned to look at the infant propped by the fire, crying now in earnest.

Euphemia grinned, showing off her few remaining teeth. "The Devil deals in souls, lassie. 'Tis a small price to pay for all he can bring you."

Hellen's whole body trembled, but she raised her chin. "If she pays?"

"Then she'll keep her soul, as promised."

Jonet's smooth, pretty face folded in sympathy. "There are worse things, Hellen. At least you'd still have your mother."

The cat's black fur gleamed in the firelight. She paused to look at Hellen. Hellen's tears spilled over.

"It's up to you, lass," Jonet said. "There are three souls here tonight, and the Devil only needs one."

"Three?" She looked at the baby, at her mother. Revelation shocked her. "Me," she muttered. "I am a soul. I can give myself to save my mother?"

"If you wish."

Who'd spoken that? The voice sounded deeper than the women here.

Goose bumps rippled on her skin. "Will giving my soul to the Devil make me a witch?"

"No, not a pure soul. You have to sign the pact to gain the power of witchcraft."

"But won't the villagers think me a witch if they see the Devil's mark upon me?"

"If they see it, aye."

As if they wouldn't look. It was inevitable. The next person to be accused would accuse her in turn to save themselves.

Hellen pushed away from the tree, clenching her fists by her side. "I want assurance that the villagers won't turn against me." She pictured her mother screaming in the flames. "That my father won't betray me. I need out of his house." She thought of Richard breaking their betrothal so casually. "And not by marriage. I don't want to marry. I want to bide on my own."

Euphemia drew close, her neck skin waddling. "You'll need to pay something for all that, lass. You get no protection unless you sign a pact."

Jonet stepped forward as well, drawing a scroll from her apron. "Kneel, child. You can give yourself to save your mother, but you must pay to save yourself." *With what?* She placed the scroll on the dirt and Hellen unrolled it with shaky fingers. If she had to pay to save herself anyway, she could pay to save her mother instead, and then run, but that still left her powerless against the villagers. She lived in dread, every day. She knew how it would end.

Her mother wove through her arms, purring. "Mother," Hellen whispered, "how did you get yourself into this?" She closed her eyes as the soft top of the cat's head stroked the bottom of Hellen's neck. "I will save you. I will save your soul."

Eyes clenched, Hellen signed with the tip of her finger.

When she opened them, her name appeared in blood. For a moment her mother's tail wrapped her neck like a noose. Panic tightened her stomach, then her mother moved away in a silken caress, rubbing in and out again, but now it wasn't empty air she stroked herself against. No, it was strong, muscled calves balanced strangely atop two large, bird-like feet. Their thick, putrid claws dug into the leafy ground for balance. Hellen held her breath, gazing up. Bulging thighs, and, oh – her cheeks hollowed, burning – an atrocious manhood, grotesque in its prominence. An eerily luxurious torso, ruddy, dark skin, beastly shoulders, a thick neck, and… Hellen almost fainted.

A face so handsome and so horrid, topped by vicious, curved

horns. He crossed his arms over his chest and two large wings shifted and flexed behind him, leathery as a bat.

"My child," he said, deep voice vibrating through the air like thunder.

She could see him. Hellen could see him.

Witch.

The other women began dancing, laughing and chanting as they circled the fire. Their comfort so near him told her more than she wanted to know. What had she let herself be backed into?

Hellen reached shaking arms to scoop her mother away from him, cradling her, the warm purrs vibrating against her chest. *Mother, what have I done?*

He knelt to look into her eyes, and Hellen's very spirit shrank, cringing away from him. His smile was profane, teeth thick and yellow as a horse, but his eyes fiercely human. The worst part was that he looked almost… familiar. Not someone she had met, but someone she should know, maybe. Like finally tasting a food she'd long smelled cooking from afar. Was this the presence she'd often felt when she was alone in the dark, hurrying through the village at night or afraid, as a child, to check for when she heard sounds across the room? How long had he been watching her?

"You owe me a soul," he said. His voice echoed with an almost bird-like chorus, like a flock of rooks taking flight, like the cries of the damned cawing up from Hell.

Her body shook, but it would not be her mother's soul. It would not be her own.

Hellen nodded, swallowing, and turned to the baby now screaming beside the fire.

REDLESS

It's the stop sign that finally does it. As I stand at a crosswalk, grimacing at the brilliantly green grass and the softly blue sky and the obnoxiously yellow sun, I look up at the octagon standing above my shoulder, and it's brown.

Brown.

Not faded, either. Not that dull orange or dusty maroon that some stop signs eventually slip into after years of faithful service. No, this sign is distinctly, shiningly brown, as if printed that way.

I cross the street, hurrying toward the next stop sign. It, too, is off-colored. I jog to the next: orange. I sprint to the next: burgundy. I look around, my eye twitching, head aching, and I suddenly see it. The utter lack of my lady. The missing.

How have I failed to notice? For how long?

It's always been my favorite color. It's the boldest, so you can't just douse everything with it. My lady, she's an accent, not a base. She's special. She's the star.

Most people seem to get that, more or less. Sometimes you'll see some color-dumb dope paint a whole living room or go overboard with matching shirt and accessories, but by and large, people know instinctively to use her sparingly. Her matching game is strong, too, so she can't be part of a "motif" or you end up with that overly-styled look. Just a hint – a pop. Let her breathe.

That's almost certainly why it's taken me so long to realize she's missing. I don't know how long, exactly, but I sense it's been weeks – maybe even months.

So many other things were subconsciously explainable. Apples come in green and yellow. The strawberries were under-ripe. My sister got a new phone case. The flowers in the office were white, blush, and lavender. Bookshelves were still an odd assortment of neutral and bright. Blue jays and sparrows still flitted outside. Emergency exits have always erred toward that faded, orangish hue.

Perhaps her absence explains my growing sense of malaise. We never realize how important color is to us until it's gone. I haven't been able to put my finger on why I've had trouble waking up in the mornings, why I feel my patience shortening with every person I talk to – my gaze roaming their outfits – or why the headache behind my left eye has grown from a dull ache to a constant throb that makes my skull pound and my skin twitch. Until now, I couldn't put my finger on what's changed, why I feel bland and angry, why everything seems pointless. I've broken up with my boyfriend, stopped calling back my mom (which hurt) and my sister (which didn't), and started showing up late to work.

I run to the candy store downtown. Every brand of sweets the store sells is quietly missing one shade. The rainbow cacophony of the store is still present, still sharp, even, with neon pink, yellow, and orange, but there's no raspberry to be found. No strawberry. I ask the clerk for cherry gumdrops and he scoops out white. "No, cherry," I correct, and he tells me they're white cherry.

I go home, search my house. I've used her sparingly, but I have always used her. The pillow in the entry chair is faded coral by the sun. The only condiments in my fridge are mustard and ranch. My favorite scarf is nowhere to be found.

It's not right, this world. It's not right without her. If she's no longer here, I don't want to be either.

I go to sleep under my gray comforter, in a cocoon of colorlessness, eyes leaking, head throbbing, and don't come out for days.

Vaguely, I become aware that my cell phone's been ringing for a long time. It blinks with messages. There's also pounding at my door, nearly synchronized with my head. My sisters's hollering through the window. Typical. When I finally drag myself into the living room, I see her peering through the door window, phone pressed to her ear even as she knocks. With a heavy sigh, I unbolt the lock and let her in.

"Are you okay? Where the hell have you been? Why did you lock the door? I've been worried sick. Damn, you look awful. Are you okay?"

I shut the door behind her, shuffling to the center of the room. I lift my hands in a lackluster gesture. "Notice anything?"

She falls silent, looking around. "No?"

"You don't notice anything missing?"

She looks again, searching, but her eyes keep sliding back to me, wary and concerned. I shake my head, stumbling into the kitchen. I stick my face under the faucet and gulp water.

"You don't notice anything at all?"

Suddenly, I know that she knows. I see that she sees it but doesn't care. I glance at her shoes, an uncharacteristic shade of noxious pink. Her nails, mauve. Her lipstick, a gross blueish purple. Boysenberry or some shit – the color of the season – and I know she chose this. Maybe even caused it.

"No," she lies. "What the hell is going on? Your boss said you've missed a whole week."

The knife block sits half a foot from my hand. I imagine all the tomatoes they've sliced. Ripe watermelon and fresh strawberries and raw steaks. I see their black handles and I gently withdraw the largest one. When my sister finally starts screaming, she screams until her wind is gone.

The first spurt eases my headache. The second ceases the twitching of my eye. The third splashes the floor. The fourth the cabinets. On the fifth, I begin dragging my sister through the house, into the main room, where my lady coats the floor, accents the sofa, paints the walls. I aim her at the ceiling, make sure she covers. On and on she goes, and only now do I finally realize that I was wrong about using her sparingly. She's an accent, she's a base, she's the world.

My living room has never looked better.

RED

Of all the colors,
there are more red
than any other—
each one
    exquisite,
    unique,
    covetable,
like you.

Right or left?
It is your choosing, love.

Please,
lead the way.

See the shadowlings?
Boxes of burgundy,
walls of crimson,
roomfuls of ruby.

No, just forge ahead.

You must make
your own path
through the maze.

It's like wandering through
a network of veins, isn't it?

Lovely.
Oh, lovely, dear;
you've reached the end.

No, there is no way out.

You've chosen this path,
after all,
and it is perfect.

See the empty space?
How flawlessly it fits your form?

Step in, darling,

and let me close the glass.

ZANDERS THE MAGNIFICENT

"My handsome, darling boys," Mrs. Zander said, placing a hand on each of their shoulders. "Which one of you wants to be alive today?"

Robby and Bobby turned their heads inward at the same time, staring at each other with identical dark eyes. Bobby blinked, followed shortly by Robby's blink, and they both said, "Bobby. Robby was alive yesterday."

Mrs. Zander nodded approvingly, clapping her hands against their shoulder blades. "Good, yes. I like it when you agree," she said. "Now both of you go get Bobby ready for school."

The boys lurched into a sprint together, their narrow shoulders brushing past the door frame at the same time, their synched footsteps thumping down the hall.

When they were safely within their bedroom, Bobby shut the door. Robby went and flopped on the left bed – indistinguishable from the right bed in everything but placement in the room – and sighed. "I wish it was Saturday so we could both live," he said, covering his face with his arms.

"I know," Bobby agreed.

They weren't supposed to be talking like this, and Robby was supposed to be getting ready at the same time as Bobby, but their mother probably wouldn't check in on them so soon.

"You'll tell me everything?" Robby prompted.

Bobby pulled on a red and white striped shirt. Once his messy hair poked through, he shook his head like a duck ruffling its feathers. Robby never noticed that before. He tucked it into memory to practice later.

Bobby grabbed the matching red and white striped shirt out of Robby's drawer and tossed it to him on the bed, his silent urge to get up and get ready. "Of course," he said. "I always tell you everything."

Finally, Robby stood, pulling the shirt over his head and settling his hair like a duck.

The door opened, and Mrs. Zander's eyes raked over them. "What are you doing?" she snapped. Robby's eyes dropped to his pajama pants. Bobby already had his jeans on.

"Sorry Mama," they said simultaneously. There was a scramble as Robby rushed to change pants and Bobby tried to decide whether to take his back off to mimic Robby or wait for him to catch up.

"This will take more dedication than that," Mrs. Zander scolded them. "Didn't you learn anything from your father?"

The boys looked down at the ground, and Mrs. Zander huffed and walked out, leaving the door open behind her.

Robby put his hands over his face. Bobby mirrored him.

Mrs. Zander sat in the rocker as Robby watched out the blinds. Bobby walked down the sidewalk to the bus stop. Robby's feet stepped in place with his twin's; his hands rose to adjust an invisible backpack when Bobby adjusted his.

Mrs. Zander let out a strangled sob, and Robby turned. "Don't cry, Mama."

She sniffed and held out her arms, and Robby climbed into her lap. She wrapped him in a tight hug. "I'm just so sorry that you can't both be alive today," she said into his hair.

Robby's hand patted her arm as his ear pressed to her chest for her heartbeat. Unlike when he could hear Bobby's, he did not try to match his heart to hers.

"So sorry that both of my boys can't yet stun the world with their splendor."

Robby heard her crying quiet, and then she was chuckling.

"But it will be the most magnificent trick," she said. "It will be the most magnificent trick, my darling. It will all be worth it."

She began humming, deep within her chest, and the chair rocked back and forth, back and forth.

"So you will stay home with your mother today. You will be dead, and we'll have a marvelous time."

Robby, Bobby, and Mrs. Zander were all in the practice room. Robby and Bobby stood on either side of the stage, and Mrs. Zander lounged in a seat at the back of the room, the knitting forgotten on her lap. The boys were practicing the mouse trick, although now they were just using golf balls.

Robby lifted his cape with one hand, raising the wand in the other. A fraction of a moment later, Bobby's flowed out as well, but Mrs. Zander interrupted.

"Timing, boys. Timing. Bobby, you must start precisely when Robby does. And both of you must use more drama in your movements. Remember your father's stage presence, and work toward his proficiency. You must master that before we can learn the truly show-stopping tricks. To impress today's audiences it must be something new. Something edgy."

Robby scratched his cheek. Bobby scratched his cheek.

Mrs. Zander frowned. "Again."

This time, both capes swept out simultaneously, like black wings lined in blood.

"I am Zanders the Magnificent," they declared as one. Their capes stayed extended on one side as the support arms snapped into place, making it appear as if they were still holding them up.

"Welcome to the show!"

Each reached down on cue to retrieve the golf ball "mouse" from the clear plexiglass box. Bobby's fingers snuck in as quickly and furtively as a mouse itself, as did Robby's. But on the way out, Robby messed up. The lid to the box snapped shut on the tip of his fingers with a violent crack.

Robby howled in pain. He jerked his hand out, and as he did so he screamed louder, dropping his wand to hold the brilliantly red fingers up in front of him. His mouth formed a perfect oval bordered by his small teeth.

Bobby looked anxiously at Mrs. Zander.

"Bobby," she said sternly.

His face flushed. "But Mama."

"Robert Zander, don't make me come up there."

Bobby gritted his teeth together, sliding his trembling hand back into the box. A loud crack, and Bobby began wailing as well. He dropped his wand and held up his own red fingers, forming his mouth into a perfect oval.

Mrs. Zander stood and set her knitting on the seat before she walked up to the stage. She swatted Bobby firmly on the butt. "That's for hesitating," she said.

Then she swatted Robby, too, because she would never spank one and not the other.

"You must both be more disciplined," she scolded. "Think of your father, and how disciplined he was, and even that was not enough. You must never forget what he went through. You must always remember that it is life and death on the stage. You must give the people what they want."

Their yelling began to simmer into hiccupping sobs, each casting looks out the corner of his eyes to get the timing right.

"Now come on, my sweet boys," Mrs. Zander said. "Let's tend to those slow little fingers." She drew them both to her and led them out of the room. "Let's make sure those hands are fixed up good."

In the empty practice stage glowing under the lights, the two white practice mice sat in the identical corners of their identical clear boxes, dead as golf balls.

As Mrs. Zander sat in her rocker and did her knitting, she imagined what the boys would look like at their first public show, when they were all grown up, even more famous than their father. With no paper record to prove their dual existence, their tricks would fool even other master magicians. They would become a worldwide sensation.

As Robby walked down the sidewalk to the bus, he longed to have his brother at his side. He imagined how many other people on the planet might be dead.

As Bobby watched him from the window, walking in place, he longed to be at his brother's side. He imagined what it might be like to be alive every single day.

"Ladies and gentleman, you're in for a treat! Tonight is the debut performance of the son of legendary escape artist

Robert Zander, who, as some of you remember, met his tragic end over two decades ago during the stunt that is now known as the Chamber of Death. But thankfully for the world of magic, he has left a son to carry on his great name. May I introduce to you the one, the only… Zanders the Magnificent!"

Applause exploded through the room.

Bobby – all grown up – dashed onto the stage, tall and lean with his black cape billowing behind him. When he stepped into the spotlight, the red and white sequins on his shirt sparkled and winked at the dark, packed audience. In the front row sat Mrs. Zander, her hands clasped tightly in her lap, her eyes alight with a strange glow.

Backstage, Robby watched, hidden in the black curtains, his lips ghosting the shapes of Bobby's words, his arms sketching phantom movements.

"Welcome," he intoned in a deep voice, "to the most magnificent show you will ever see." The crowd grew hushed, and he sent his words out like sleek promises through the shadows of the room.

"Tonight, I bring you wonder!" He took a deep bow, extending his cape out behind him with both arms, and when he stood back up, he held a long-stemmed red rose between his teeth. The crowd hummed.

"Danger!" He tossed it out over the seating, and in mid-air the rose changed to a cluster of scarlet streamers, falling like fireworks over the audience. The crowd ooed.

"And possibly even death!" He swept his arms in and back out, and the lining of his cape had changed from black to glistening red. The crowd gasped.

"But one thing is for certain: by the end of the evening, you will feel more alive than you've ever felt." Thunderous applause.

"Let the show begin!"

With a billow of smoke, Bobby disappeared into a trap door. Instantaneously, Robby appeared on a balcony over the stage, and the crowd went wild.

They looked so much like their father had at their age.

Mrs. Zander's eyes filled with tears as she watched her boys – no, boy. Tonight they were indistinguishable. With the heavy black eyeliner covering the single tiny freckle under Robby's eye that allowed her to tell them apart, she could not even follow which was which. They were that identical. In their first public performance, they had truly become one.

They had truly become magnificent.

The young man on stage sent the audience into delighted giggles as the white mouse disappeared from the small clear box, only to reappear in the pocket on the front of his glittering shirt.

Mrs. Zander knew that there were truly two white mice, identical in every way, one hidden from the eyes of others at all times so it appeared to the world that only one existed. It was the oldest trick in the book – one that took grave dedication to execute so seamlessly.

Robert would have been proud of them all, she knew.

The tears in her eyes spilled over.

"And for my last trick," pronounced Robby, "I will need a volunteer."

His words brought a deep silence to the room, followed by a rush of movement as arms all over the theatre shot into the air. He looked against the stage lights into the darkness, scanning the front row for his mother's surprised face.

"You there," he said, sweeping one arm in the direction of her seat. "Yes, you. Come on up. Ladies and gentleman, can we give her a hand?"

Grudging applause sounded as Mrs. Zander made her way onstage. Robby could see the confusion in her eyes; this was not part of the act they'd planned. He caught a cordless mic tossed to him by a stagehand.

"What is your name, ma'am?"

Mrs. Zander blinked at him.

"Ladies and gentleman, it would seem we have a shy volunteer! Can we give her another round of applause?"

The crowd cheered loudly, and under the roar Robby said, "Play along, Mama. It's all for the sake of the show."

When they quieted down, Robby put the mic to her mouth and she said, "My name is Marie."

"Well hello, Marie. Thank you for volunteering! For the assurance of our audience, please tell us: do you have any knowledge of the trick we are about to perform?"

"No," she said honestly.

"All the better," Robby said, shooting the crowd a conspiratorial grin. They all chuckled with anticipation. "You have lovely legs," he told her, and Mrs. Zander gave him a baffled look, shifting nervously on her feet. Then an assistant wheeled out a large box roughly the shape of a casket. Robby centered it on the stage and pulled out an enormous saw with ragged teeth, lifting it to glint in the stage lights. "I hope you aren't overly *attached* to them."

The crowd laughed.

Unseen backstage, Bobby mouthed the line with him, timing perfect.

Robby set down the saw and lifted the top of the box upward so the audience could see inside. Their surprise was palpable. They could clearly see that there was no divider inside the box – no second woman curled up in the lower half to put her legs out the opening.

"Marie?" Robby asked, lifting out a hand for support. "If you would be so kind?"

Mrs. Zander eyed the restraints visible on the bottom of the box.

"Don't get cold feet now," Robby said. Again, a chuckle from the crowd.

Mrs. Zander stepped up and stretched out in the box. Robby went about fastening the restraints tightly around her shoulders, wrists, waist, and thighs. The silence in the auditorium grew so full that even the back row could hear the rubbing sound of the straps being pulled tight.

When Robby shut the lid, all that stuck out were Mrs. Zander's head and her feet.

"Tonight," Robby declared, "you will see a woman sawed in half." Backstage, Bobby's lips traced the sounds.

In the booming applause, Mrs. Zander turned her face toward her son, away from the audience. "I don't know how this works," she whispered. "How do I undo the straps to pull my legs up?"

"You must give the people what they want," he told her, smiling. "Something new. Something… edgy."

Mrs. Zander's eyes grew wide as golf balls.

"Which half of you wants to be alive today, Mama?"

Robby picked the saw back up and grinned at the crowd. "On three," he told them.

"One!" He raised it dramatically over his head.

Mrs. Zander looked at the audience with terrified, roving eyes.

"Two!" He lowered it to the notch in the middle of the box.

Mrs. Zander thrashed her feet and head about, trying to break free of her restraints.

"Don't worry, Mama," he whispered. "You will be dead, and we'll have a marvelous time."

In the wings, Bobby's arm had already begun a sawing motion.

"Three!"

GLOVE BOX

There was no one in the store, save the two of them. The air was still nippy from the brief opening of the door when she entered several minutes ago. The lady had already picked up a bag of crackers—the air-baked kind—and was now pacing slowly back and forth in front of the drink fridge, either looking for something specific they almost certainly didn't have, or surveying the options quite thoroughly. Rose added prices in her head, accounted for tax. It would be over the three dollar credit card minimum for sure. That was a relief. It was always the small totalers who wanted to use change.

Her boss, Dipti, had refused to stop accepting cash like most everyone else in the state. She said assuming everyone nowadays had smart phones with pay apps was privileged nonsense. She said there were still poor people who couldn't get approved for credit cards, and immigrants who couldn't even get the necessary IDs to apply for credit cards. She said they as a business couldn't afford to turn away their two-dollar sales. She said they as a society couldn't afford to turn away their most desperate members. Rose thought Dipti was right, but she also thought Dipti wasn't the one who had to work night shifts alone, and wasn't the one who had to reach out to accept that change.

The lady had paused in front of a particular glass door, her line of sight trained low, her head dipped to the side to study the label without bending, without even lowering her neck, and something about that refusal of her spine to bow made Rose think she was wealthy. The woman wore jogger sweatpants, ugly boots, and an oversized sweater, but Rose couldn't shake the impression she had on stilettos and a fur stole. She was the type of woman who could pull off linen pants. Rose thought if the woman turned, she would have artfully smudged eyeliner, large pearl studs, and hair glossy enough to refuse an up-do. The woman didn't turn, though, not yet. She opened the door and squatted, and Rose pictured heels that weren't there, a mini dress she would know how to bend in without risk of flashing, and she reached out one hand to take a bottle of iced tea mixed with lemonade.

$3.49, then, and of a class to pay with a credit card, surely. The only risk would be if she were so wealthy that she'd try to hand the credit card to Rose instead of swiping it herself. Rich people did that, sometimes. Like they were so accustomed to others doing for them that they couldn't be bothered to learn for themselves. Rose had literally reached around customers before to swipe their card for them, and still had the customers watch—not go, *Oh, goodness, I didn't see that there. I could've done that!* Not a drop of embarrassment, simply a glazed look of long-suffering patience.

Of course, that was before. Rose had always been one to politely accommodate customers. She'd swipe their card for them if that was what they wanted. But not now. Now she would say, *Please swipe your card right there, ma'am*, nodding with her head, and her arms would remain straight by her sides. She would lift one only to type in the prices—not even scan the products—and the receipt would hang uncut from the printer until the customer walked out the door, unless they specifically asked for it, in which case she would tear it quickly and shoot it across the counter like a paper dart.

The lady turned, the crackers in one hand and the tea in the other, and Rose immediately wondered how much money she spent on skincare. Not under-eye cream or wrinkle reducers, either. Real heavy-duty stuff. Office appointments and lasers and practitioners with medical degrees rather than licenses. Monthly maintenance appointments. Middle-aged, but flawless. Exquisitely beautiful.

She smiled at Rose. Caught off guard, Rose smiled back. "How are you tonight?" she asked out of habit. She was going to say it either way, but she'd expected the lady to mutter *Fine thanks* and avoid eye contact. Not this—not this solid look and authentic smile. No stiffness to the cheeks, either. Either she was naturally gorgeous or her doctor was even better than Rose had thought.

The woman set her products down in the middle of the counter, halfway between them. Her nails were surprisingly free of polish. "I'm well, thank you. How are you?"

Always fascinating to hear the replies, when there was one. The forcedly cheerful. The blatant ignoring. The surprisingly honest answers of the worn-down. The life stories that poured out and continued out the door, as if the person didn't really mind who they were talking to so long as they were talking. But the reciprocated question was a rare one. Not unheard of, but definitely on the unexpected end of the scale.

"I'm good. Thanks for asking. Did you find everything you need?"

Rose typed in the price of the crackers and drink, hit the total button. Tax popped up and $3.49 appeared on the credit card scanner.

"I did."

Rose nodded, smiling. "Good deal. Your total is $3.49." She

indicated the scanner with her head, hands feeling the fabric of her pants where the seam ran down the sides of her legs.

The woman smiled again, looking sympathetic. Rose almost heard the word *Dear* before she spoke, but it was left invisible, hanging. "Do you mind if I pay you in cash?" She opened her large purse and parted its leather pocket, pulling out an antique coin pouch hand-painted with a floral design.

Rose couldn't say no. Her pulse surged, finally waking from the caffeine drop. "No ma'am," she said, her words stumbling into each other like toddlers. "We still accept all forms of payment." She tried to hide the pleading from her eyes.

The woman opened the pouch, her perfectly rounded fingernails flicking open the metal clasp with a muted click. Maybe she had exact change.

She pulled out a small rectangle of tightly folded bills. They were ones, though, not twenties. She could still pick out some coins and set them on the counter. And if she couldn't, maybe she'd set down four and leave the change. That's what most people were doing now, even the desperately poor. They wouldn't ask you to give them money back. Two quarters and a penny, it would be. Just leave it.

She unfolded the rectangle slowly, precisely, and counted out four ones. She held them delicately in her left hand between the ring and middle fingers, using her right hand and the remaining fingers and thumb to fold the rectangle back up, tuck it into the coin pouch—click—and slip it into her purse. Then she took the bills in her right hand and stretched her arm toward Rose.

High. Her arm was too high: up in the air instead of reaching to set the bills flat. She was handing them to her, not putting them down.

She expected Rose to take them.

Rose's throat spasmed, trying to swallow, but her mouth was too dry. An ordinary gesture, before. A thing she'd done thoughtlessly a thousand times. Surely this woman knew what she was asking of her. Rose could stare, silently refuse, outwait the woman until she set the money down and pushed it forward, where Rose could snake up a quick hand, grab, and tuck it furtively into the near-empty register.

But the woman carried such quiet authority—that posture like she was used to the weight of diamonds draped across her collarbones. It couldn't be her, could it? Everyone seemed to think it was a man, and for whatever reason the victims weren't talking. Despite what had been done to them, they weren't willing to talk.

Too long. The moment was stretching near to breaking. She could refuse, but Rose hated this world, this feeling of intentional aloofness, this tired, required slackening of care.

Her hand trembled when she stretched it out, cupped. She stopped halfway, beneath the woman's hand, breath held.

When the papery fabric of the dollars touched her palm, Rose tensed. The woman's skin grazed hers for just a moment—a fraction of a second—and an electric current jumped between them. The hyperawareness of cells on a single part of the body.

Rose withdrew her hand, with the dollars, letting out a shaky breath as she put it into the register and waited. She was still hoping the woman would say, "Please, keep the coins," but the woman smiled at her softly, expectantly, her hand still hovering there, cupped now.

Two quarters, one penny. The dirty smell of old money. A metallic taste in Rose's mouth, like she'd accidentally swallowed one when she wasn't looking.

Her motions weren't slow, but her racing thoughts contrasted them so as she reached out again, her fist clenching the textured sides of the quarters, her hand still trembling, positioning it above the woman's outstretched palm, they seemed slow by comparison.

Right as she opened her fist to drop them, the woman spoke. "What beautiful nails you have," she said softly, and Rose startled so hard the coins jumped.

A quarter and a penny landed in her hand, but the second quarter went rolling off the counter, racing for the edge.

Instinctively, Rose smacked it, flattening it to the counter with a sharp slap. Her heart pounded. They both froze. Rose remembered they'd been talking.

"Sorry," she said. "Thank you." Her arm was locked, her upper body leaning forward, her hand very near the woman, whose hand was still cupped in the air.

"Do you paint them yourself?"

Rose dragged the quarter toward her across the plastic surface, scraping it along. When it was near enough that she didn't have to lean forward, she lifted her palm and gripped the edges of the coin with two fingers. "I do," she answered, picking it up.

"That's lovely," the woman went on, palm still waiting.

It was fine. She was fine. She'd handed Rose the money with no problem. She hadn't moved for her when Rose had dropped the coin. It wasn't her. She wasn't the one. Slowly, moving through air thick as chewing gum, Rose lifted the final quarter and placed it gently atop the other two coins in the woman's hand, so that metal touched metal but no skin.

The woman watched Rose's eyes, not her fingers. "I wish I could add more color that way—I love the red you chose—but about this time of year I start wearing gloves, and it's a shame to cover up such pretty work."

Panic iced through Rose. She froze. "Gloves?"

The woman deftly dropped the coins into her left hand. Rose almost sighed in relief, but before she could withdraw, the woman's right hand gripped Rose's, across the knuckles, then twisted them side to side, like she was examining the polish. "Yes, gloves."

Rose's eyes locked onto hers, breath lumped in her throat. She tried to pull back.

The woman's grip viced down. She tucked the coins away and reached her left hand out too. She traced her fingers up Rose's arm, stopping just before the elbow, just to where the victims' skin had been removed. "Beautiful soft gloves that go all the way up to here."

She traced a line circling Rose's forearm, her smooth unpolished nail digging in just enough to leave a red pressure mark.

"Don't scream," the woman whispered, a voice used to giving gentle commands that were followed.

Rose didn't scream.

THAT WHICH NEVER COMES

At fourteen, Daniel was much too old to be afraid at night. That made it worse. No one close to him had ever really said anything overt or teased him – he had nice parents and good friends – but he still felt their silent assessment and the less-silent assessment of kids who weren't his friends. He was generally a wuss. Adding in a fear of the dark would ruin him.

It was in the closet, whatever it was. It was alive, but not breathing. Unspeaking, but audible. Invisible in the darkness of his bedroom, but absolutely present. Daniel couldn't help but wonder if there was some seed of truth to all the monster-in-the-closet stories. Was it coincidence, or had people's lizard brains been on to something from long since before he was born? It didn't matter. It was in his closet now.

It hadn't woken him. He hadn't been asleep. He'd been lying in bed thinking about Todd Okiro at gym. The utter lack of light in his room usually helped him sleep, but when he couldn't sleep, it helped him dream.

It had started as a faint click, like the sound of two plastic coat hangers tapping together. *Click, click, click*. The air conditioning wasn't on, though. It was still spring enough to feel cool at nights. So how had the hangers clicked? The slow slide of gravity finally shifting a shirt, maybe, or a fly hitting a wrinkle just so on its path through the air, or maybe even a distant vibration snaking imperceptibly through the house, up the wall, and through the wooden rod the hangers rested on, moving them ever so slightly from beneath.

Daniel's eyes were open wide, staring into the darkness above his face, imagining the fine crack in the ceiling though he couldn't see it – couldn't even see the color white floating there above him.

Click, click, click.

Or a long fingernail tapping the painted shell of his hollow closet door.

Silly. Kid stuff. Still, his blind gaze slid to where he knew the door to be, shut tight in its jamb. There *was* room in his closet for a man to hide. Or something else.

Silence then, as if it knew he'd heard it – as if it knew exactly when to bide its time.

Daniel stared so hard into the darkness where his door should be that shapes began to shift inside it, his eyes projecting motion he couldn't possibly see, even if it were there. Was it possible that some other sense picked up movement and told his eyes to make up impressions to match it? Could he hear something? Would he hear anything at all if the doorknob should turn ever so slowly, slower even than five deep breaths, until the metal tongue was fully out of the way and the door could be pushed forward from the inside, easy, the gap below it just tall enough to keep the bottom of the wood from brushing the carpet fibers, the hinges just well-oiled enough to withhold all protest, and would he hear it if the knob was gently released, again slowly, so slowly that he would almost fall back asleep before it was done, so that the knob was still and the door fully ajar so whatever waited inside it could come out?

And did Daniel sense these things, or did he imagine them?

His pulse jerked through his body in constant, violent cycles, trying to convince him to pant, but Daniel forced his breaths to be slow and low and deep. Even so, he could barely hear beyond his own body – or maybe his own body was the only sound left in the room.

If the closet door were open, would it come out? Had it?

The muscles where his jaw met his temples ached from straining his ears, as if they were exterior muscles he could flex to listen better.

Something shifted. Low, against the carpet.

Not a step, exactly. Certainly not a man walking, but not a shuffle, either. Not a drag. What then?

Almost imperceptible, but distinct. Definitely real. Not his imagination.

Again. Longer, even softer. So quiet that Daniel began to question the distinctness of the original sound, but no, it was still there. It was approaching.

It was very near.

Daniel held his breath completely, but blood still beat through his head, forced between his skull and skin, thick panic in a thin space. His eyes were wide, unblinking. He stared straight up, because he suddenly couldn't bear to stare toward the closet – toward the still-creeping sound.

What was it? What would it do to him?

The sound of motion on the carpet stopped directly beside him. If it were a person, it would be standing over him, looking down, arms straight and fingertips almost brushing the blanket where it collapsed over the corner of his mattress. If it were a slick, rolling thing, it would be puddled beneath him, reaching up one long, sinuous appendage to feel along the corners first, working inward, sensing like a snake's tongue or an anteater's snout. If it were a bunched, muscled thing, it would be crouched beside him, limbs bent and tight, face frozen, leaning forward until its forehead touched his.

If it was any of those things, did any of those things, Daniel didn't know. Instead he stared through blackness and tried to remember white, only feet above, and begged his imagination to sense the space between as empty, but it couldn't, because it wasn't imagination; it was senses. Something was near Daniel, silent but alive, waiting. Waiting, waiting, waiting. For what?

Unable to stand the thought of finally seeing something – of finally seeing whatever would eventually happen even in this darkness – Daniel closed his eyes.

When the insides of his eyelids began to lighten, he knew it was morning, but still he kept them closed. He tried to convince himself that he would see a shadow through them if something stood above him, but what if something stood beside him, or below? Or what if it was aware of where its shadow cast, and stood in a position to cast it out of the way? No, even with sun warming his face and brightening the backs of his eyelids, he kept them closed. Whatever it was, perhaps it waited only for him to look.

Finally, footsteps came down the hall, swift and distinct. His mom. Daniel almost cried out, almost told her to stay away, but he couldn't bring himself to do it. Instead, he clenched his jaw and waited, listening here and there, trying to hear if the thing was leaving, but he heard nothing, and his mom opened the door.

He held his breath. What did his mom see? She stood still, silent. Was she looking at him, or the thing? Would it attack her?

"Daniel," she said. "Time to get up."

He opened his eyes. Nothing stood between him and the ceiling with its thin crack. He turned his head. Nothing sat or crouched or puddled beside his bed. He sat up. Nothing waited at the foot of it, nor between him and the open closet door.

But it was open.

"Mom," he said, as she turned to go. His mind raced for a reason to get her to stay. "I can't find my plaid shirt. The red one."

She frowned at him. "It's hanging in your closet."

Daniel shook his head, swallowing a thick lump. "I can't find it."

She sighed, hand falling from the doorknob, and marched to the closet. She pushed the door all the way back to the wall and rummaged through the hanging clothes. While she looked, Daniel sprung from bed and walked quickly around the room, checking corners, behind the curtains, even under the bed.

"Daniel, it's right here. For heaven's sake, did you even look?"

When she turned, holding it up to him, he looked not at the shirt but behind it, behind her, into the empty corners and spaces of his closet. Nothing there.

"Sorry."

She smiled at him, laid the shirt on his bed, and left, shutting the door behind her. "You have fifteen minutes," she called back.

He was ready for school in five.

The worst part about it was that it didn't happen again.

He took the little square nightlight from the bathroom and put it by his bed the next night. It was tucked behind the nightstand so if his friends came over they'd be unlikely to see it unless they were in his room at night, and when people slept over his mom insisted everyone use sleeping bags in the living room, so he was relatively safe from humiliation. Even though he knew he'd likely never use it even if it came to that, he also put his dad's crowbar beside the nightstand, propped between the wood and his mattress, leaning against the wall.

Daniel stayed awake for hours, listening, looking. No sounds, no impressions of movement, no sense of something just beyond him. All night he stayed awake, vigilant, smothering slowly in a thick, ugly fog of impending horror, but nothing ever came.

At school he lived in a bubble of falsity – his efforts to seem ordinary feeling disjointed and over-bright. He moved about in a cocoon of his own dread, but no one seemed to notice. At night, he stayed awake as long as he could, waiting for it, but eventually he had to sleep. Night after night, sleep came earlier and earlier, until after weeks he was sleeping almost normally again, save for the way his brain kept one light on, waking him at the slightest sound, but even so, no sound was ever again as sinister and terrible as the clicking had been. They were all explainable. Mundane.

As time went on, it was enough to make Daniel question what had happened – to doubt his own senses and memory of the event. Had he forgotten to close the closet door the night before? (No; he always closed the closet door before bed.) Had he imagined he heard the sounds? (No; they'd been quiet, yes, but real.) Was there a reasonable explanation? (Not that he could find.)

Daniel lived in silent dread of the thing returning, but he wanted nothing more than for it to return so he could verify that it had really happened. He never spoke a word of it to anyone.

Over the next several years, Daniel's mind got better at holding that part of itself separate. He pretended to be normal so long that eventually he almost felt it. He certainly seemed it. Life went on.

When he graduated from high school, he considering going to college somewhere far away. He didn't know why, exactly, but it probably had something subconscious to do with putting distance between that night, that room, that closet, and where he was now. Instead, he found himself touring the local university because it was cheap and close to home. He was moving out to live with his friend Tessa in an apartment, but his mom quietly encouraged him to stay in town, and since she was the closest person in his life, he did.

He went alone to the campus, parking in a lot he'd driven past his whole life but never stopped at, and walked inside the beautiful building with its ornate façade, four stories, and straight rows of tiny windows. Somewhere inside was the division of student affairs, where an undergraduate volunteer would walk him around and tell him how great his life would be here.

Daniel entered through what he thought was the main door, due to its double-width and central location, but when he stepped inside he was met not with a front desk or kiosk telling him which direction to go, but with a small stairway platform, empty and unlabeled, that branched in four directions. He leaned to peer down and saw that the right and left stairs both led to the same hallway; they opened out only yards from each other. The top two did the same, perhaps for up and down traffic, although it was hard to picture this building ever being that busy. It was so empty Daniel wondered if he was in the right place at all. Most of the lights were off, too, the halls lit only from the sun coming in the doors' windows.

Well, it was a Saturday. He could see that both up and down led to hallways lined with classrooms – clearly not the office of student affairs. Should he go down one of them in hopes that a professor or someone was here for office hours? Surely they'd be able to tell him where to go, but the space seemed too quiet. So quiet Daniel could almost hear the echo of his own breathing. He didn't believe anyone was here.

He turned, thinking he'd go out the way he came and walk around the outside of the building to find a door that opened directly to the office. To his side, he saw a narrow door to a stairwell. Ah, this was what he wanted. An actual stairwell that went straight up and down like the spine of the building. It probably had a marquis inside listing what was on each floor. Since he could see much of the second and third floors, he gambled that the office of student affairs was either down one in the basement or up two on the fourth. And at least if he took this way someone would be less likely to see a dumb fish wandering around lost.

He turned the metal knob and went inside. If the building and hallways were quiet, the stairwell was desolate. It was yellow and dim. There were no windows and no overheads, so Daniel imagined the only light must be at the very top of the fourth floor, and its multi-story filtering was all that lit the lower levels. He looked up the ascending row to his right and saw the air grow faintly… not brighter, but more yellow, as if color saturated the air without lightening it. He peered down the descending steps, to his left, and saw them wrap the sharp turn into what looked like pure darkness.

Up it was, then. Who puts an admin office in the basement anyway?

Daniel moved forward, wincing faintly at the loudness of his own motion and how it filled the space, rebounding off concrete steps and painted cinderblock walls. He took the first few steps, grasping the metal railing to his left, but it felt cold and vaguely sticky, so he wiped his palm on his pants and centered himself on the stairs as he climbed, as if buffering his shoulders from touching the dingy walls on either side.

Six steps in, there was a faint sound from below.

Click, click, click.

Daniel froze. No other sound came. It had been soft, but he recognized it instantly. It was the exact same click that had come from his closet four years ago, on the most terrifying night of his life. How could he recognize a click? As if the materials here were the same as whatever had tapped together in his closet at his parents' house. That made no sense. He knew it didn't, but it was still true.

His limbs grew heavy with extra blood. His breath ticked up a notch, shallowing. Such foolishness. Maybe someone else was in the stairwell. Maybe the door down a level had snapped shut. Maybe a switch in the tube-covered wiring lining the ceilings had flipped over, doing its ordinary job in an ordinary way, automated.

Oh but his leg was heavy as he lifted it to climb the next step.

When the sole of his shoe met the surface, another noise came from below. Not a click, exactly. More like a creak.

Daniel froze again. The sound halted.

He lifted his other foot. Silence, waiting. His shoe touched down.

Another creak.

He stepped quickly three stairs in a row.

The creaking came, rebounding up to him, and Daniel listened through the pounding in his ears. The creaking was rhythmic, almost mechanical in its pattern but the sound was organic – that of joints and sinew, not metal.

He stilled. It waited.

Another step. Another creak. He almost thought he could hear a sticky resistance to its first motion, as if lifting something fibrous off a tacky surface. Then that creak, soft and measured – perhaps exactly the length of rising one step – and the crouched, waiting silence of stillness.

Whatever it was, it listened to him as surely as he listened to it. But he wasn't fourteen anymore, damn it.

Daniel demanded, "Who's there?"

He cringed at his voice. It was too loud. The sounds bounced back to him and raced overhead. There was no reply, but he thought he could hear an almost imperceptible shift, like tissue on tissue, like a grimace or a smile.

He wasn't a kid anymore. He paid rent now. He had a job. He was about to start college. He couldn't let the silent dread of years ago chase him into the next four years. This was ridiculous.

Finally, without moving his feet, which stayed one on each step, Daniel turned and looked over his left shoulder.

He was halfway up the first flight, so he could see to about halfway down the one below before the angle was blocked by the sloped bottom of the one above. All he could see was empty. Of course.

Yet just beyond that angle, something waited. He could chastise himself as much as he wanted, but he knew below his outraged disdain that it was really there. It probably crouched splitting the stairs like he did, balanced, still, just out of his line of sight.

Keeping his gaze trained down where the angle blocked his view, Daniel felt his foot up another step, slowly, feeling through the air like a spider sensing a drop with its front legs. The toe of his shoe touched the rise. His sole pressed down. If he weren't listening for it, he might not have heard it at all, but there it was:

Creeeeeak.

His line of sight moved, keeping the source of the sound blocked. The hair on his neck and arms rushed to standing.

What if he charged down?

He would die.

The answer came so swift and sure that Daniel almost laughed, almost barked out a release of his growing panic, but he couldn't. If he'd been with someone, going down to investigate would be the thing to do – like proving to a partner during the night that the noise in the living room was just the cats so they could both laugh at it and fall asleep easier – but he wasn't with someone, and looking wouldn't bring him peace of mind. It would end in something horrible. This was real, and this he knew. Whatever it was, what it would do to him was worse than anything he could imagine.

Out. He had to get out.

The door to the second floor he'd come in on was behind him, below, and now it was almost equidistant from him to the noise. If he made a run for it, would it spring? Would it scramble to meet him? Would it reach for his ankle just when he thought he'd made it through? He looked up, where the stale air got yellower, and decided the third floor was better.

Sucking in a deep breath, Daniel forced himself to calmly walk to the midway platform.

Creak, creak, creak, creak, creak, creak.

Past the platform and up two more steps.

Creak, creak.

It moved when he moved. He would be able to get to the next door before it got to him.

Unless. Oh. Unless it was taking two stairs at a time.

Daniel's skin rippled up and down his spine. His palms felt slick and heavy. He couldn't bring himself to look. What would happen if he saw it? Is that what it was waiting for? Did it want him to see it before it got him? He wasn't lying in bed; he couldn't close his eyes. He had to see to climb or he might trip, and surely that was the worst thing of all. Falling now. It making its mad dash for him while he was down, hovering directly over him so he'd have to look to get up.

His mouth was dry, his lips parted on silent pants, and the back of his throat tasted like acidic copper. Slowly, Daniel raised his hands to his face, cupping his palms to the sides like blinders so he could only see the floor directly in front of him.

Step. *Creak*. Step. *Creak*. Step, *creak*, step, *creak*, step-*creak*, step-*creak*.

Each step drew Daniel's shoulders tighter. Was it taking two at a time? Was it gaining? He could see the door. Should he run for it? Would the extra speed give it the momentum it needed to catch up?

Step-step-step-step.

Creeeeeeak.

A small sound of panic wheezed from Daniel. He narrowed his eyes to thin slits, trying to see less, trying not to feel the air shifting behind him, beside him.

As he waited, panting, forcing himself to be still, another creak came. Unprompted. Directly behind him.

Daniel bolted.

He leapt up the last four stairs in one bound. He dropped one hand to stretch for the door handle, shutting that eye, squinting the other so tightly he could barely see the silver handle through the blur of his eyelashes.

His hand met cold metal. He yelped, twisting it, pulling it toward him. It smacked him in the knee because he refused to step backward to give it space. It was directly behind him, and if he moved into it, he was done.

The opening grew. Daniel thrust through it.

The hallway was like the one below, dim, open, and empty.

The door smacked shut behind him, but he didn't turn to look at it. He dropped his hands from his face, but he kept his face forward.

He stood on a platform identical to the one he'd first come in on.

Screw the tour. Keeping his eyes trained only on the ground directly in front of him, Daniel hurried down the large open stairs and shoved through the double doors, back into the sunlight of the parking lot. He didn't look around as he got into his car. He didn't even look in his rearview mirror as he drove back to his new apartment. He didn't look behind him until he'd gotten inside and locked the door.

Tessa was in their tiny kitchenette, pouring pancake mix into a lime green pan. It struck him then that she knew as little about him as his mom did. Their friendship was authentic but superficial. "Hey roomie," she said. "Perfect timing."

It took Daniel longer to slip into something resembling normalcy than it had when he was younger. He was more deeply ashamed. He was more deeply afraid. And although he had once quietly wished for confirmation that he hadn't been delusional or over-imaginative, that confirmation turned out to be far worse than the small comfort it brought him. He wasn't crazy, he hadn't been "just a kid," and it would come for him again.

Yet, it was amazing how things just kept going. Time, life, those around him. Daniel was swept into it and when he couldn't experience it deeply, he just pretended. He never told anyone. No one ever seemed to suspect that there was something wrong, something deeply, stealthily wrong.

He did end up going to that college, because he couldn't work up the nerve to uproot his life, but he only took the open stairways, never the closed stairwells, and he tried not to be in the buildings unless classes were going on. He threw himself into his studies as a way to avoid thinking of other, darker things. He allowed his teachers to decide his degree and his path for him, simply going where they pointed: he graduated pre-law with university honors, and went on to become an attorney, hired out of school at the firm five minutes away.

No matter the years that passed, no matter how he tried to convince himself otherwise, always, always, the closet in Daniel's mind was dark and waiting, the door cracked open like a sleepy, watchful eye.

He was thirty-eight when he made partner, amazed at his success at something he cared so little about. They stayed at the office after-hours to celebrate, which struck Daniel as more of an excuse for them to get drunk and hook up with each other than to actually congratulate him. He was the youngest person at his firm to make it. Hard-working, dedicated, and disciplined, is what his boss said, over and over like a mantra. Hard-working, dedicated, and disciplined. Maybe that was why he was the last one left, cleaning up the mess from his own "party." Still, if his coworkers hadn't thrown one for him, no one else in his life would have.

Don't worry about it, Gigi, the secretary, had said, waving a hand at him. *I'll get it in the morning*, and then she'd smiled because she knew Daniel would get it tonight.

He tied off the big black trash bag and propped it against the wall by the door. They could at least do that much. No need for him to take it down to the dumpster.

After turning off all the lights in the back, Daniel made his way to the door, the trash bag taunting him. He ignored it, leaning into the copy room to flip the light, but Brett and Maria were wedged between the scanner and the plastic ficus, sucking on each other's faces. Maria's short, curvy body blocked most of Brett's broad frame. Daniel sighed. "Goodnight, you two."

Brett raised a hand to wave without lifting his head.

Daniel left the light on, left the trash there, and took the elevator down to the parking garage. When he stepped out, he paused, looking around the shadowy, sloping floor trying to remember where he'd parked that morning, already tired at the thought of going home to an empty house. Behind him, the elevator doors closed and the car rose quickly away, leaving a soft hush in its wake. Ah, there was his sedan over there, by the large concrete pole. He remembered now.

Click, click, click.

It had been twenty years, but Daniel knew. His brainstem knew. His spine muscles knew. His body hair knew.

He'd spent two decades quietly trying to convince himself it wasn't real, and he'd spent two decades quietly preparing for this moment. His plan had been to charge straight at it, to expose it, to prove or disprove, to bravely meet his fate.

Now, listening to utter silence for the next hint of a sound, Daniel knew he couldn't do it. As a soft, soft susurrus slithered in the deepest shadows, Daniel ran.

Daniel was two years from retirement when his older brother got his first grandbaby. A little girl. Somehow, it hurt even worse than when Eric had had his three kids – or maybe it was just fresher. Daniel loved his nieces and nephews, of course, just as he would love their children, but he couldn't pretend it didn't ache when Eric and Denise invited him to parties and showers and weddings.

No time to settle down, that was the line. Too busy at the firm. Business was good.

Then suddenly, Daniel was sixty and his hair had gone full white. Not gray, not silver: white. Pure colorless, and no one told him it suited him. Eric and Denise did ask him to play Santa Claus once their granddaughter was old enough, though.

Daniel was holding her – Braxley, they'd named her – when it happened again. Outside, in Eric's backyard, everyone lounged around the pool and grill. The whole space smelled like lighter fluid and chlorine. When Braxley started to cry, Daniel offered to go change her. He'd always been good with kids, and frankly, his nephew's friends gave him a headache.

It was on his way out of the nursery that he knew it was there.

There was no click, or if there was, Daniel's hearing was too far gone to have heard it. Maybe some other part of his mind heard it. Or maybe he just knew. Sensed it. Felt his arm hairs rise against Braxley's onesie where he cradled her against his chest. He clutched her tighter, turning, to look down the hallway at the back of the house that led to the master bedroom and guest room. The lights were all off, dim but not dark. Afternoon sun still came in the windows, petering before it could reach entirely across the carpet.

"Is anyone else in here?" Daniel asked. Perhaps someone had come in from outside to get out of the noise.

Silence answered, and again, Daniel was struck with a certainty he couldn't justify or argue with.

This was the first time he wasn't alone. Braxley made a small sound of annoyance or curiosity, and Daniel forced himself to loosen his grip slightly. He had always known it was after him, but what would it do to her?

He thought about screaming out, calling for Eric. He could pretend to fall. But even through his rising panic, he knew that'd mean the end of him holding Braxley and his other great-nieces and -nephews. He'd be the old man who had to be watched when he was with the kids.

Of course he couldn't charge it, even if he'd been brave enough this time. Braxley changed everything.

So he backed away, careful not to trip, his eyes darting back and forth to the two open doorways, not knowing which it would come from.

Until he felt something shift right beside him, over his shoulder. The bathroom doorway. He was right in front of it.

Daniel bolted forward, running into the guest room and shutting the door. Braxley began to hiccup like she was working her way into a cry. He rocked her back and forth, bouncing on his heels, even as he backed away from the door, heart pounding. It actually hurt inside his chest; he was too old for this much excitement. He sat on the edge of the bed because he was rocking her too hard; she could feel panic in his motions. He forced himself to be still and let Braxley grab his finger, her tiny hand clenching it as she decided not to cry.

Daniel lay down on the bed, putting Braxley between him and a pillow so she couldn't go anywhere, and stared at the doorknob, waiting for it to turn.

The baby was breathing sleep bubbles like an innocent mockery of Daniel's terror by the time footsteps vibrated softly down the hall. He wouldn't have heard them; he felt them through the floor because the house had a hollow crawlspace beneath it. They had the rhythm of regular walking, but still Daniel's anxiety built, winding him tighter. Was it finally coming? He drew Braxley even closer to his chest, cradling her with one arm. The vibrations grew closer. The muscles around his spine contracted tighter, tighter. Tighter.

His eyes watered as he kept them open wide, staring at the knob, willing it not to turn.

Still, it turned. Slowly, quietly. Should he look?

At the last moment, breath held, Daniel closed his eyes.

"Uncle Dan?" Sara called softly. His nephew's wife.

He hesitated. What if it was standing right behind her?

"Uncle Dan," she said louder.

Daniel opened his eyes.

The space behind her was empty, as was the room between them.

What did she think? Her expression was gentle. Was she touched that he'd lain down with Braxley or annoyed that he'd taken her from the party? How long had they been gone? Could she see the fear on his face? Did she think he was a crazy old man? He wasn't crazy. Decades it had been, since the last time. Decades of unbearable waiting.

"We just laid down to rest our eyes for a bit," Daniel said, rubbing the round bulb of Braxley's tummy.

Sara smiled. "Okay, well a few people are starting to leave, and they want to say goodbye to Braxley."

"Alright," he said, hearing the age in his own voice as he sat up, drawing Braxley into his arms. "Back into the sunlight, little lady."

As he trailed Sara down the hall, he saw nothing, he heard nothing, but he still felt it, lurking, hiding, waiting.

"No tubes," Daniel had said, and he was ninety-three, so they obliged. Weight sat on his chest like an invisible rock, making each upward expansion of his ribs more difficult than the last, air wheezing past his lips in a thin trickle and rushing out in a heavy puff.

He had no one, really. He'd never settled down or connected deeply with friends. His brother had died twelve years before and since then he'd slowly lost contact with his nieces and nephews and their children. Braxley had a baby of her own now, and Daniel quietly set about dying in his nursing home bed. It wasn't so bad, he told himself. He didn't have a cumbersome roommate like many of the patients here. Aside from a bone-deep fatigue and the weight on his lungs, he wasn't in pain. And he had an extra-large-print book to read, propped on a pillow. A yellow lamp attached to his headboard shone over his shoulder, illuminating the text in the otherwise gray room.

Daniel had always enjoyed reading. Of all the ways to go, this wasn't the worst. He wished he wasn't quite so alone, that the room wasn't quite so empty, that there was at least someone in his life to sit by the side of the bed and cry, but still. There was always the call button.

The sound came from so near that Daniel could hear it even with his hearing aid out.

Click, click, click, it went, right on the metal frame of his bed, and he flashed back to his childhood bedroom and the mental image of a fingernail tapping on his closet door, almost politely begging exit, and how it had appeared again years apart at a time, always waiting, always hunting, always chasing, and now here he was and here it was, right under his bed.

Daniel's hands shook all the time – that came with age no matter how he fought it – but now they trembled beneath their shaking, moving the text of his book around so much that he couldn't read it even with the bottom propped on his stomach.

He had been a coward. So many years, he had failed to look.

Now it was directly beneath him. Was it long and slender, with human hands and a sly smile? Was it tiny, insectoid, and creeping? Or was it impossibly large, crammed in a space with bunched muscles and razor-sharp teeth?

All Daniel had to do was force himself out of bed one final time. Even if he fell and broke his hip, what did it matter now? Maybe he didn't even have to do that much. Maybe all he had to do was turn his head and look.

The words in front of him shivered and shook. He tried to tell himself that this was the end. It didn't matter if it finally got him now. What difference did it make? He tried to convince himself of it, but he couldn't drain his weak body of the heavy, leaden dread that suffused him. It would be terrible. He couldn't.

Daniel carefully moved the dustjacket of his book to save his place, shut it, and laid it atop the blanket. He looked only directly at the closed book. He resisted the urge to shift his gaze even to his periphery, where another series of clicks came. Instead, he looked up at the cork ceiling tiles, panting in weak, shallow gasps.

Click, click, click.

Something dim moved beyond the side of his eyelashes, and Daniel shut his eyes. The shuddering of his tired heart worsened the ineptitude of his lungs. Heavy, so heavy was the air, thick with the unseen, thick with malice, thick with waiting.

It might have crept from under the bed. It might have climbed the side, or slithered beneath the foot of his blanket, or hovered bent over his eyes squeezed tight, but Daniel didn't know. He died waiting.

SO SINGS THE SIREN

You can hold yourself back from the sufferings of the world, that is something you are free to do and it accords with your nature, but perhaps this very holding back is the one suffering you could avoid. — Franz Kafka

When the woman moved forward to order, the girl stepped within her shadow. "A vodka Sprite, please, and a bag of peanut M&Ms."

The girl tugged on her mother's brushed satin dress. "Mom, I'm thirsty too."

The woman glanced over her shoulder. "There's a water fountain by the bathroom, sweetie. I'm not paying six dollars for a bottle of water."

The girl returned her hand to her own dress of royal blue velvet, a fabric both heavy and soft. She liked to rub a fold of it between her fingers, feeling the nubby pile slip back and forth under her thumb. The dress's straps kept slipping from her shoulders beneath her sweater. Her mother bought it one size too big so she could wear it again next year. The girl didn't mind. It was the most beautiful dress she'd ever had.

The woman sat on an upholstered bench in the hallway, sipping her drink, but the girl couldn't sit still. She twirled to make her skirt flare, dancing back and forth across the hall as she crunched her candy.

"Hurry up, sweetie. We can't take those in with us."

The girl poured more M&Ms into her mouth, then spoke around them. "Mom?"

"Hm?"

"Will the siren have wings?"

"Yes, she should. I think they always have wings."

"What color will they be?"

"Whatever color her skin is, probably."

The girl twirled. "Will she have bird feet? And a beak?"

The woman smiled. "No. That's a myth. Stay here for a minute. Finish your candy." The woman walked down the hall and around the corner to throw away her empty plastic glass.

The girl rubbed her skirt between her fingers, tipped back the bag, and spun and spun and spun. She bumped into a man.

"Sorry," she muttered, glancing up at him. He was tall and crooked.

"That's all right," he said. "So much energy – best to get it out now. You'll be sitting still for a long time."

The girl glanced down the hall to where her mother had gone, then eyed the man warily. "How long?"

"That depends on the musician. The best ones can draw it out for hours."

"Hours?"

He wiggled his eyebrows. "Hours. Is this the first time you've come to hear a siren sing?"

She nodded, crushing velvet between her fingers.

"Is that your mom you're with?"

Another nod.

"Did you get seats on the floor or up in the mezzanine?" he asked.

She glanced to the corner. "We have a box."

"Oh, I see. Does it face the stage or the audience?"

Velvet specks stuck to the dew on her fingertips. "The audience."

"Ah." The man straightened himself. "That's a shame. You won't be able to see the siren's face that way."

"What does it look like?"

The man wobbled his jaw. "Her face is contorted in beautiful agony. Her pain is what draws the beauty of her voice in contrast. The better the musician, the more beautiful her song."

The mother hurried toward them. The girl asked the man, "What does he do to her?"

"Surely your mother told you that he tortures her."

"Yes, but how?"

"If you faced the stage, you would see for yourself. You would see the tools and methods he uses to play his instrument. He is a master, this man. A true artist."

Her mother took the girl by the hand and pulled her several steps away. "I have no desire to see his vulgar artistry, nor for my daughter's mind to be filled with such things."

The man raised his eyebrows. "The siren is willing. You don't respect the musician's work?"

The lights dimmed off and on. Crowds of murmuring people moved toward the auditorium.

"I respect the song itself, and the siren for sacrificing herself to give it. I respect the musician for drawing it from her, as is her wish." She raised her chin. "But I do not respect those who would watch the musician do his work rather than listen to the song. The musician is always a sick man. A mad man."

The man said, "Yes. He must have an exquisite sort of madness, to do what he does without breaking. Playing the song of a siren is not for the weak of will, nor the weak of heart."

The woman dipped her head in strained acknowledgement and turned to leave.

The man added, "What with the prying up of fingernails, the spindling of intestines, the flaying of skin. God forbid we see where the beauty is coming from."

The woman gasped, dragging the girl by the arm into the crowd. When the girl looked back, the man was shaking his head softly to himself. Then the cool, muted cave of the performance hall enveloped them. The brightest part of the room was the dim spotlight on the stage, where a beautiful but ordinary-looking woman sat on an empty stool in front of closed curtains.

"Where are her wings?" the girl whispered. Everyone whispered here. When her mother didn't answer, the girl tugged on her dress. "Where are the siren's wings?"

"Oh. They're down right now, sweetie. Closed like a bird, not out like a butterfly. They won't show until the musician spreads her arms."

"Mom, can I watch the stage when they start? Just for a little bit?"

Her mother didn't stop her path toward their box. "Not until you're older."

The lights flickered on and off several times, and the entire room sunk into silence at once, seated but fidgeting. From her seat, the girl watched them in the darkness. An announcer introduced the musician, then the siren, who said in a soft voice that she was honored to be here sharing her art, that she could imagine no better cause for a life. Clinks and shifting from the stage punctuated long moments of silence.

Finally, the audience members grew still, the air grew thick, and a collective gasp charged the room. The siren began to sing.

It was unlike any music the girl had ever heard. There were no instruments, no lyrics, not even a melody to carry the voice along, but the girl knew at once that, somehow, it was still a song. She rubbed the nap of her skirt, leaning forward. The audience members' faces grew taut and full of emotions the girl couldn't name. The siren's voice grew and grew, filling the space with perfect clarity, slipping between notes in a way wholly unpredictable, yet perfect.

Some women fainted. A few couples got up and left. One man vomited into a bag even as he wept. Eventually, the girl closed her eyes and listened, crushing velvet between her fingers, and let the song fill her up with something she would someday learn was worth suffering for.

So felt the girl, that night. So sang the siren.

CALL OF THE SHADOWLINGS

I have collected
so many shadowlings.
They spot the darkness
of my home
with brilliant shades
of color.
I am never truly alone
anymore.

Sometimes at night
when I lie awake,
I hear them shifting
in my shadowboxes
behind panes of glass
that scarcely contain them.

They click and slither,
mutter and rumble;
they call to me
in thirsty silence—

ask me with their many
glowing eyes

why I have not yet
taken my place
among them.

ACKNOWLEDGMENTS

The only thing I've ever done alone as a writer is write. Everything else has come with the help of others.

There are nineteen stories in this book, and all but one of them were first published elsewhere. Each was made possible by countless people: my parents who raised me to love reading (mom) and horror (dad), loved ones who listened to my oddball passions and strange ideas, my writer friends who encouraged them and me, my critique partners who helped make the stories stronger, the editors who pulled them from the slush pile and often improved them even more, the publishers who put out the magazines and anthologies they were accepted to, and the people who then backed and shared them.

I owe so much to my husband Kyle who has supported me in this dream for nearly two decades now. It's because of him that I've been able to write and submit and hustle as much as I have. He is my biggest believer, my patron, my partner. I love you, Kyle.

Special thanks to Dan Hammond Jr. for writing a gracious and beautiful foreword. It's no small thing to have someone of his talent value my work. Dan, I'm grateful to call you a critique partner and a friend.

To the Denton Writers' Critique Group, morphing and moving

over the years. Most of these stories passed through that crew and are the better for it. I am the better for it. I'll never forget bringing y'all "Honey." Love you nuts.

Eternal gratitude to editor Doug Murano for picking up first "The Pelt" and then this collection. Your belief in my work means so much, and you are a fierce champion of it. I'm so lucky to have landed with you for this book. You really can do a lot with a bad hand.

Finally, thank you to my readers. To the readers who read these stories one by one over years of following me. To the readers who talked about them and taught them and nominated them and reviewed them and reached out to tell me how you love them. You all have kept me going. Truly. And to the readers who've just found me. All I've ever wanted is what you've given me: to have my work read. Thank you.

ABOUT THE AUTHOR

ANNIE NEUGEBAUER is a novelist, blogger, nationally award-winning poet, and two-time Bram Stoker Award®-nominated short story author. She writes horror, literary fiction, thriller, science fiction, fantasy, weird fiction, poetry, and anything sharp, dark, and beautiful that might linger in the mind. She has a penchant for high concept ideas and making readers question her mental health.

Annie is also the author of *The Outsiders Sequence,* a series of novellas (*The Extra, The Other,* and *The Spare*) through Shortwave Publishing. Visit her at AnnieNeugebauer.com, in most places under @AnnieNeugebauer, or frolicking through the abyss.

PUBLICATION ACKNOWLEDGMENTS

Hide, *Black Static Magazine #43: Transmissions from Beyond*, TTA Press November 7, 2014

Hide, *PseudoPod 511: Flash on The Borderlands XXXIII: Corpus*, Escape Artists October 8, 2016

What Throat, *PseudoPod 640: Artemis Rising 5*, Escape Artists March 24, 2019

The Little Drawer Full of Chaos, *Nox Pareidolia*, Nightscape Press, LLP November 7, 2019

The Call of the House of Usher, *Killing It Softly: A Digital Horror Fiction Anthology of Short Stories* The Best by Women in Horror Book 1, Digital Horror Fiction, an imprint of Digital Fiction Publishing Corp. October 12, 2016

The Call of the House of Usher, *The Spirit of Poe: A Charitable Anthology*, Literary Landmark Publishing July 28, 2012

The Call of the House of Usher, *Haunted are These Houses*, Unnerving September 14, 2018

Churn the Unturning Tide, *Other Terrors: an Inclusive Anthology*, William Morrow Paperbacks July 19, 2022

Cilantro, *Fire: Demons, Dragons, and Djinns* Elemental Anthology Book 1, Tyche Books Ltd. August 14, 2018

Cilantro, *Year's Best Hardcore Horror Volume 4*, Red Room Press April 16, 2019

You Ought Not Smile As You Walk These Woods, *Shadow Atlas: Dark Landscapes of the Americas*, Hex Publishers LLC November 30, 2021

White Paint, *Cemetery Dance Magazine #78*, Cemetery Dance Publications April 1, 2023

The Pelt, *The Hideous Book of Hidden Horrors*, Bad Hand Books June 28, 2022

The Pelt, *Fears: Tales of Psychological Horror*, Tachyon Publications September 10, 2024

Honey, *Blurring the Line*, Cohesion Press November 26, 2015

The Filling, *Vastarien: A Literary Journal, Vol. 2, Issue 3*, Grimscribe Press December 1, 2019

The Cottage of Curiosities, *Memento Mori: A Digital Horror Fiction Anthology of Short Stories*, Digital Horror Fiction, an imprint of Digital Fiction Publishing Corp. January 23, 2017

The Cottage of Curiosities, *Strange Little Girls*, Belladonna Publishing March 14, 2016

The Devil Take the Hindmost, *Dark Hallows II: Tales from the Witching Hour*, Scarlet Galleon Publications, LLC October 25, 2016

Redless, *The Binge-Watching Cure II: An Anthology of Horror Stories*, Claren Books December 25, 2019

Redless, *Year's Best Hardcore Horror Volume 5*, Red Room Press May 1, 2020

That Which Never Comes, *The Shadow Booth: Vol. 1*, Dan Coxon December 8, 2017

Glove Box, *The Dark City Mystery Magazine* July 2018 Issue, Dark City Books July 2018

Glove Box, *Tales to Terrify Episode 389*, Tales to Terrify Podcast July 12, 2019

Zanders the Magnificent, *Fireside Magazine Issue 21*, Fireside Fiction Co March 2015

Zanders the Magnificent, *Pseudopod Episode 669*, Escape Artists October 11, 2019

So Sings the Siren, *Apex Magazine Issue 101*, Apex Publications October 12, 2017

So Sings the Siren, *Year's Best Hardcore Horror Volume 3*, Red Room Press May 4, 2018